ESCAPE FROM OBLIVIA

*One Man's Midlife Crisis
Gone Primal*

Brian Kindall

DBB

Other titles by Brian Kindall

Adult Fiction:

SIDESHOW, A novelette introducing Didier Rain of
The Epic of Didier Rain
DELIVERING VIRTUE, Book One of *The Epic of
Didier Rain*
FORTUNA AND THE SCAPEGRACE, Book Two of
The Epic of Didier Rain

Middle-grade fiction:

BLUE SKY
PEARL

ESCAPE FROM OBLIVIA

"A man's truest life is a fiction." – Dick Zag

I

IT begins with her voice – a little island of sound arising from this vast sea of silence in which I am drowning.

"Pardon?" she says.

I clear my throat, flounder a few strokes in her direction, and rephrase my request. "I said I would like to see the notebooks of Richard Henry Banal, please." I smile and hold out a slip of paper with Banal's name printed on it. "Can you help me?"

She takes my note.

I watch her eyes – forget-me-not blue. Her damp lips move ever so slightly as she reads. A tendril of black hair falls along her cheek and she absentmindedly tucks it back behind her ear with a middle finger. The gesture, inexplicably, takes my breath, causes my heart to pick up its pace. I feel I have asked for something forbidden.

She hands back my paper and then, without looking at me directly, says, "I am new at the library. I am unsure where are these notebooks."

The trace of an accent. That charming lapse of syntax. French, I think.

"Oh, well, I can show you! I know right where they are." I sound a little too courageous. It surprises me. I wonder if the tops of my ears are turning red in that way they did when I was a boy. "If you just want to come with me, to make it official."

She considers this, nods indifferently, and pushes away from her desk.

And so, like some wannabe hero, I guide her through the labyrinth of bookshelves – these hallowed chambers where are locked away the secrets of the dead and mostly forgotten. Our heels clack on the polished parquet. Astral motes of dust drift on the rare winter sunlight slanting down through the high windows. This place – this realm – has alternately struck me, over the last months of my project, as both a sanctuary and a morgue.

"Here we are." I pull out the cold metal drawer in which are kept Banal's seven spiral-bound notebooks. Ghosts. Cadavers. They wait to be exhumed, to be brought back to life. I am Dr. Frankenstein; I am God. These thoughts always sort of freak me out.

I extract the third notebook in the series, demonstrating a reverent gentleness and care, and then hold it flat on my palms. "Now I show you my card and sign for it."

"*Oui*," she says. She knows that part. I have exceeded my helpfulness.

I fumble with my library card and sign my name on her clipboard, declaring it out loud, as if to introduce myself, as if in invitation for her to do the same. "Will Kirby." I think that since she's a librarian she might possibly have heard of me. She says nothing.

"I should be about three hours."

She doesn't care.

She leaves me alone with my fat, yellowed archive.

I sit at one of the humongous tables, open my computer, open Banal's dog-eared notebook, and struggle to open my mind. I have a profound sense of some long dormant part of me being stirred awake. It's distracting. I need to get at task. I need to accomplish great things.

"Okay, Kirby," I whisper. "Concentrate."

The faint suggestion of her lemon-scented soap lingers on the air.

The girl is quite possibly half my age.

Although I cannot see her over the many rows of shelves, I sense her there. I am completely baffled as to why this gives me a thrill.

2

THAT evening, after washing the supper dishes, helping my daughter Ava with her homework and reading her another chapter from *Ivan's Island* – the story of a marooned, anthropomorphized mouse – I take a long shower and then stand before the mirror, a battered gladiator assessing himself for another fight. This is what I see – a man who has navigated life for nearly half a century. Post prime. Post full head of hair. Post – let us be frank – post instantaneous erection at every smile from a pretty girl.

I used to live in a little mountain town, skiing and hiking daily, drawing my power from the sun and wind. I was a whitewater raft guide in my college days and did some rock climbing. I was one of those rugged young bucks you see in outdoor magazines. But that was years ago, and we have since moved to the city where I am relegated to three two-hour workouts per week at the gym. Treadmills. Rowing machines. Elliptical trainers. It's not the same as pitting oneself against Nature. It's too civilized and calculated. It lacks that primal element of danger. City life feels like a long, slow slide away from what is essential. Somewhere along the line, life's current carried me away from the wilds to this urban outpost – a place from which I long to escape.

A framed photo sits on the table beside the bed, an icon – an image of me as a young man in my glorious days as a river guide. In said photo, I stand shirtless and tanned, an oar in one hand and a raging river in the background. My physique is ridiculous in its perfection. The look on my face is one of a self-assuredness verging on arrogance. There is nothing I can't do, I seem to be saying. I am indomitable. It is the standard represented in this photo by which I now gauge where I am on the sliding scale of physical adequacy.

I turn to the side and admire the bulge of muscle on my hip. A little bit of sag, kind of thick around the middle, but I still have that core strength. I'd like to think if I were dropped into the wilderness – say, abducted by aliens, or trapped in some post-apocalyptic predicament – I could survive. I could swim across an ocean full of mutant sea beasts. I could live in a bamboo hut and hunt game with a spear. A man clings to his boyish fantasies.

"How are you holding up, Tarzan?"

My wife Jane comes into the bedroom and catches me flexing.

"Goooood," I say, and do a little jungle jig, wagging my wares at her. "I'm one hell of a man."

She laugh-snorts and rolls her eyes, indicating that she thinks I look less like a buff Tarzan and more like George Jetson in the buff.

I am struck with a sudden inspiration. "Are you going to take a shower, too?"

(This is code for – do you want to make the two-backed beast with me? I have no idea when it became necessary to be clean for sex.)

"I wasn't planning on it."

(This is counter-code for – No, I have absolutely zero desire to copulate with you.)

I stand there naked and suddenly without purpose. Even after twenty-three years of marriage, Jane can make me feel instantly laughable in the bedroom. This, I understand on a rational level, is not her fault. It's a male ego thing. Nevertheless, it irks me, even though I try not to show it. The air in the room seems to have abruptly changed; it is both warmer and more frigid at once.

Jane sits on the edge of the bed in her nightgown, shoulders slumped. "Would you like me to take a shower?" (It is her duty to ask, even though she lacks conviction. This is code for – marriage to you can be such a drag, but if you really want me to, I will purify myself at the fount so you can satisfy your pathetically juvenile desires.)

"Not if you don't want to," I say, selflessly. (I am every woman's sensitive guy.) "After all, ... (I can't stop myself.) ... it's already December. Why don't we just wait until spring?"

(This means, sarcastically – who needs to get laid more than once a year anyway?)

"Don't be a jerk," she says. "I had a big day."

"Fine. Sorry."

I clomp to the window and crack it open to let in some fresh air, then I turn out the lights and jump into bed.

Jane sighs, and slides into bed too. We lie in the dark, not touching. She is on her back; I am on my side, turned away from her.

"Aren't you going to put on some shorts or something?" she asks.

"No."

"I swear, Will," she laughs. "Sometimes you're like a little kid."

"Oh yeah, meanie?"

She reaches over and pinches my butt. "Yeah!"

I slap her hand away. "You better watch it, sister, if you know what's good for you."

Jane snuggles up next to me and squeezes me in her arms. "Tough guy." She presses up close. "Nice ass," she whispers, and yawns.

I haven't given up hope for getting some sex. This little tit-for-tat mating ritual seems to be working its magic. It feels like things are taking a positive turn between us. I bide my time, allowing Jane's own unbearable feminine cravings to take her over. But then, almost immediately, almost comically, she begins to snore. Her arm dream-twitches against my side. Unbelievable.

Now, resigned, I try not to wake her. When I'm sure she's fast asleep, I disentangle myself from her tentacles. She rolls away from me, mumbling.

I lie there for a long time in the darkness. It is raining outside. A siren wails somewhere across town. I miss the mountains. That hush of snowflakes tumbling down through the pines and rarified air. In the strangeness of this restless night, I miss things I have never even known.

"'I am unsure where are these notebooks.'"

I whisper to the dark ceiling in my best French accent, imagining the fragrance of lemons.

But then, like a burst from a tommy gun, Jane breaks wind beneath the covers.

"Un-friggin'-believable!"

A man's daydreams never quite prepare him for the pedestrian details of his life.

3

NEXT morning, I'm back at the library, early. I'm disappointed when I see Roxanne behind the desk. This is unfair of me. She's very nice. An adoring fan. But still...

"Good morning, Will."

She's like my only groupie.

"Hi, Roxanne."

Hair in a pageboy, dyed red. Horn-rimmed glasses, retro-style. A fuzzy sweater snugly holding her ample and perky breasts in place like a pair of strategically placed warheads. She's a geeky bookworm. Her wrists are white as paper. One suspects no ray of sunlight has ever warmed her subterranean persona.

"I missed you yesterday," I lie. "There was someone new."

"Oh," she scowls. "That was Martine, the new recruit." Roxanne leans forward in confidence. "Between you and me," she whispers, "that imposter knows absolutely zilch about library science."

"Really?"

"Yeah." She huffs. "I wonder who she had to blow to get this job?"

And then Roxanne's green eyes go large behind her glasses. Horrified. Her cheeks burn pink.

"Oh, gosh," she says. "I didn't mean that any of us ever..." Profoundly flustered. "I mean, um, Martine's nice."

I wink. "Between friends."

She forces a smile and flips her fingers open in the air like little explosions beside her face. "Sometimes I forget where I am."

"You're spontaneous," I say. "It's refreshing. If you ask me, people are too guarded."

"Heck, yeah!" She is pleased with this bit of wisdom. "I think so too."

"But the new girl... What was her name?"

"Martine."

"Yes. She was very helpful. She seems nice."

"Sure. I'm sure she's great. We'll doubtless become bosom buddies in no time."

"Will she be working here a lot?"

"Who knows? The schedule's a mockery of time slots. Admin in the Head Office is messing with we underlings, moving us around like Gestapo to suit some devious plot."

"Well, I hope I'll get to see you at least."

"Oh, I'll be here to help you with anything you need, Will. *Anything*." Her cheeks burn pink again. Her eyelashes become the powdery wings of agitated moths. "I read your book again last weekend."

"Really?" It seems she has told me that at least a dozen times since we first met.

"Yes. It gives with each reading. You've hidden so much stuff between the lines."

"Sure," I say, but I honestly don't remember hiding any stuff at all. "Only a close reader would see that."

"Oh, I *am* a close reader."

This is loaded with a meaning that makes me uneasy.

"Do cowboys really talk like that?" she asks.

"Well, it is fiction, you know. I made it up, mostly. But yes, I suppose they do talk like that. Or at least they did in the old days."

9

Roxanne nods, pondering this. "It must have been a lonesome life." Her voice grows wistful.

I nod.

"But at least they had the stars and moon to keep them company. And they could find themselves comforted by the mournful serenade of the ubiquitous coyotes."

"Sure." Now I'm getting embarrassed. She's bastardizing my novel's more sentimental lines in paraphrase. "I'm sure there were good things about that solitary life in the open spaces. Otherwise, those cowpokes would have moved to town, gotten a desk job, and maybe raised a family, or something."

"Or maybe you could open a book shop full of nothing but your favorite books, and then the lonesome cowboys could come by sometimes and browse and talk to you and..." She trails off with a shrug.

Roxanne has just offered me an open portal into her deepest, most secret soul, one I'm inclined to close and back away from.

We stare at each other for an awkward eternity. My mind goes blank. Finally, I glance past her to the clipboard. "Well, shall I go ahead and sign in now?"

"Oh. We better follow protocol. You never know if the Head Office has spies."

"Of course."

She leads me through the rows, describing a fan page she has started for me and my book. "What you need is a gimmick," she tells me. "Something that makes your readers feel like they're part of your process and work, sort of an insider's attachment and pledge of allegiance to you, their favorite author."

"Oh. Hmm." I really have no idea what she's talking about, but I guess I'm flattered she cares enough to be thinking about it.

Then Roxanne switches tracks and begins nonsensically telling me about a novel she is writing herself – something about a seemingly naïve and mild-mannered librarian who lives an alternative life when the sun goes down. "Sort of a female Jekyll and Hyde, only way more self-empowered and primordial." She would draw on her own experiences. She blushes again. She wants my opinion. "Do you think it would be good? I mean, can you see that as an e-book, or even maybe as a paperback?"

"Sure. Why not? It's just a matter of plumbing your deepest secrets, wrestling with your demons, and unabashedly pouring out your naked soul for all the world to see in some masochistically honest and entertaining way."

"Really?" She's intimidated. She never thought of it like that. So is that what writer's actually do, she wonders? She looks at me with a new respect, almost fear.

"Here we are." I have moved on to volume four of Banal's notebooks. I deftly pluck it from the drawer and go sit at my usual spot at the far table. Roxanne follows, lays her clipboard on the table, and I sign my name on the designated line.

"I better note the condition," she says, "just to make it official."

I lean to the side as she bends to examine the journal. Still, I am unable to completely get out of the way and her left breast presses squarely into my right triceps, smashing against the flesh of my upper arm like a warm, partially deflated water balloon. I am trapped. If I move farther to the side, it will be obvious that I have noticed and am trying to avoid this awkward position, possibly embarrassing her. I've never had breasts myself; maybe Roxanne doesn't even realize. But if I don't move, it might seem I am sending her a signal, maybe even a reciprocal invitation to become familiar. True, it is far from unpleasant. I had a chemistry teacher in high school who did the same thing once when she leaned over my shoulder to explain a formula for heat transfer. I have fond memories of those mammaries. I decide not to move, to wait patiently for Roxanne to do her duty as a conscientious practitioner of library science.

Her breath blows a warm breeze along my face.

Is that her nipple poking like a fingertip into the back of my deltoid?

Could I ever in a million years take Roxanne as my mistress, run away to the island of Stromboli, settle into the simple life of a sponge diver, and bathe with her in the passionate sea every evening at sundown?

An errant thought.

"Oh," she says. "That's odd."

"What?"

"Page 69 is missing." She flips the pages back and forth. "Someone has removed it."

I lean forward. "Really?"

"No problem," she assures me. "I'll just make a note in the records. You won't be held accountable."

That I might possibly be "held accountable" is slightly exciting to me, but I am more intrigued that someone would lift a page from Banal's notebook. It appears to have been ripped out. The ragged fringe of perforated paper is still caught in the tube of the spiral binding. I wonder if it was Banal himself, or some snoop with more devious intentions. Could someone have gotten here before me, extracted the page, and snuck it out of the building? It seems suspicious. And what sort of secrets might that page have held to make it valuable enough to risk being reprimanded by the library's Head Office, possibly even leading to the revocation of one's library card? I shudder to think.

"There we go," says Roxanne. She finishes her note about the journal. "Okay, Will, enjoy your secondhand adventures. And don't hesitate to ask for my help."

"Of course. Thank you."

Reluctantly, Roxanne walks away.

I watch her out of the corner of my eye.

I am the only one in the room besides an old man who has fallen asleep, face down, on a table. He looks dead.

I rub the back of my arm, and then open the notebook to page one.

Richard Henry Banal.

Penname – Dick Zag.

He has become my hero. I feel a near-unhealthy affinity for

the guy. A real man's man. No nonsense. Larger than life. A man of action. An inspiration. But one, honestly, who intimidates me. He was such an ardent overachiever. When I read his notebooks, I am astounded that one person could ever pack so much into a single lifetime. It's like watching a hundred action movies end-on-end. His life imitated his art to the nth. Or vice versa. It's hard to know for sure where the fiction stops and his life begins. And it's foggy how he finally came to his own ending. The details are simply absent. He just sort of vanished, was sucked into a black hole and ceased to exist. It's one of the many mysteries about the man that I'd love to solve. Of course, scenarios too far-fetched for lesser men seem quite feasible for the extraordinary Mr. Banal. Was he abducted by Martians? Was he knifed by Soviet she-thugs while doing espionage work for the CIA? Was he devoured by a giant squid while scuba diving into the Mariana Trench? Whatever the truth, he managed to make his enigmatic exit at roughly the same age I am now. Comparing myself to Banal, which I cannot help but do, makes me feel severely under-accomplished. I've quite obviously been striving in the wrong direction all these years. I've clearly been squandering my lot.

Admittedly, Banal was not what one might think of as a *great writer*. His genius – his masterpiece – was in his earthly existence. He only wrote novels to pay the way to his next adventure. His books were nothing that the highbrow literary establishment would look upon with anything but scorn. Pulps. Sweats, as they were called by the men's publishing industry. He wrote stories for cheesy magazines with names like *TRUE RISK* and *BOLD* and *MAN HAZARD* and *CONQUEST*. Adventures packed with relentless action. None of that namby-pamby introspective crap. These were raucous tales loaded with hit-'em-over-the-head machismo. A consumable, ironic fiction printed on cheap paper of which little has survived. His books were guilty pleasures for men who wanted to escape the tedium of their lives. His was an anti-literature for men who appreciated a writer daring to thumb his nose at conformity and pretention.

After all, he was writing in the Cold War era of the 1950s and 60s. Post World War II America. Post Korean Conflict. Men were reeling from all those years of being called upon to fight for the sake of the Free World, and now, as their reward for victory, they were held prisoner in a sunny, Tupperware-laden hell of suburban peace and false security. Banal knew it was a sham. As did the men for whom he penned his tales. His readers were hungry for the truth, an outlet for their pent-up masculinity, a placebo to help them endure the near-to-insane world in which they lived. Dick Zag provided them with exotic, vicarious adventures of heroes saving damsels in distress from the hideous threats pervading modern society – mutated creatures let loose after H-bomb tests gone horribly wrong, Commie spies and pinko assassins, aliens from other planets hell bent on enslaving our innocent women for their bizarre bordellos. All based on Banal's own myriad experiences around the globe. Granted, at times it verged on porn, but of that almost quaint variety offered up pre-internet. Lots of creative descriptions of breasts. In book after book, the ever-grateful women repaid their champions in the only way that truly mattered to a real man – spiritual salvation by way of sexual release.

These stories were relentlessly incorrect by today's standards. The bulk of them were embarrassingly sexist, leaning toward misogynistic, appealing to a repressed animalism in men that has ostensibly evolved from our species since the women's movement. We men have learned to give, and not just take. We are now more sensitive and caring. Besides, a fella would be castrated and hung out for the vultures if he tried to write anything like that these days.

Which is what I find so intriguing about Banal. He was different from the other pulp writers. Ahead of his time, while still being *of* his time. He somehow managed to respect women and still get from them what he needed. How can that be? It's hard to explain. I don't exactly understand it myself. But when I read Banal's notebooks, I find a man who did not force himself on his many mates, did not slap them around, but rather allowed them to gratify their feminine, animal hungers by way of his own. His fictional heroes were the same way – merely extensions of the writer. He understood women like no other man. Banal had a certain class and je ne sais quoi, a certain earthy, but transcendent, charisma that obviously appealed to womenfolk and set him apart from other guys. It wasn't uncommon, according to his notebooks, for Banal to bed and fulfill "two or three dolls at once." They were glad to be part of his virile sexplorations, even grateful to have found a gentleman stud so willing and able to escort them to the throes of unbridled ecstasy. He tells of one lady friend in particular – one "Lovely Indira" – whom he met in Sri Lanka – "... who traveled with me through all the pages and postures of the *Kama Sutra*." Banal elaborates freely in his journal in a muscular handwriting indicative of his own robust libido – that kind of penmanship from the past, before technology and its keypads had sapped and homogenized humanity – back when a man stood proudly behind his inkish marks on paper. Banal writes unabashedly in his notebooks of engaging with Indira in that copulatively enlightening position known as the *Congress of the Cow*.

I read my first Dick Zag classic as a thirteen-year-old kid. A buddy and I had gotten a job cleaning out a neighbor's garage and we found a couple of Zag novels in a dusty corner. We spent all afternoon in our tree fort plowing through the pages, our hearts thumping during the fight scenes, our adolescent groins mysteriously tingling during the sex. Reading Zag was a wholly visceral experience. One that felt directly wired into one's soul. That first novel I read was an autobiographical account based loosely on Banal's own wartime experiences in the South Pacific. He had been a well-decorated Marine Corp pilot. After downing two Jap Zeros in a dogfight, his F4U Corsair was taken out by a lucky shot from an anti-aircraft gun on an enemy destroyer. Banal parachuted into the ocean, and after swimming all day and through the night, found himself washed onto the sunny shores of a tropical atoll – a place he called Oblivia.

Oblivia. A weird world. A mix of pleasure and torment. A magical land where time stands still, and sex doesn't inevitably lead to offspring. So far, Banal's journals have been extremely vague about this strange island. But I've gleaned a few details. Supposedly it concurrently existed/exists in an almost-other dimension, a separate plane from the one in which the rest of our world goes ignorantly about its business. It had/has the ability to erase the memories of any visitor daring to stay there too long. Banal teetered dangerously close to lingering too long himself, losing all recollection of his life elsewhere, and thus finding himself in peril of Oblivia's brain-erasing powers. Somehow – he doesn't tell us just how – he made his escape. He occasionally alludes to his irrational longing to return there permanently, before he gets too old to enjoy it. One suspects that he might have. He is hesitant to divulge too much information about Oblivia. He won't give away the exact coordinates of this lost world, or how to find the portal into it that he claims to have discovered much closer to home. He wants to protect those of us who might not possess the survivalist talent to escape. It's like a clandestine domain locked away inside of his now inaccessible mind. Anyway, it isn't anywhere on Google Maps. I've scanned virtually every inch of the Pacific Ocean trying to find it. I'm hoping Banal's notebooks might eventually tell me secrets that will at least help me to pinpoint it on a map.

I feel extremely lucky to have stumbled across Banal's notebooks in the very city where I live. It feels like destiny. That no one has ever written about the man seems ludicrous. In this age when every other Joe is the subject of a biography or YouTube documentary, how did Banal and his alter ego Zag slip through unnoticed? Maybe it's because no photos or films have survived. That's unfortunate. Still, I see the man in my mind. Fighter-pilot height of six-foot nil. Grinning, muscled, a pack of Lucky Strike cigarettes rolled up in the sleeve of his white t-shirt. An effervescent sparkle in his eye. An air of knowing about things a man should know. It makes me anxious. I need to get my project finished before someone else discovers him. Is that a real danger? Am I just kidding myself that anyone in this media-saturated age would ever care enough to actually read a book about this ghost from the past? This fear has stopped up my own pen. I'm a writer made impotent by the magnitude of my subject. I've been contemplating this project for years, but as of yet, I've not been able to write a single coherent paragraph. Just phrases. Gleanings from Banal's notebooks. Snippets from his few surviving novels. I am undoubtedly out of my comfort zone here. I've never written such a research-dependent book. I ate up two whole weeks just reading about Japanese war planes. Maybe I should just chuck the whole project and learn woodworking, or become a racecar driver. But some over-watching angel has blessed me with this treasure. I need to take advantage of it. In my imagination, I see a tome as brilliant and intriguing as Banal himself. In my wildest dreams, I see myself formulating a book that will reinstate Manliness as a relevant force to contend with. A real society-changer. If I can only pull it all together. If I can just bring the pieces of this puzzle together into some sort of tantalizing whole. If...

My phone dings in my pocket, shooting me down from my flights of grandeur.

It's a text from Jane.

Can you get A from dance this afternoon? I'm too busy.

I sigh, and with my less than dexterous thumbs peck out a reply – *I'll get Ava, but you owe me a b j.*

I reread my message, imagining how my harried wife will take the joke, lose my nerve, and decide to delete the part about the blowjob. I replace it with a sweetheart emoji. Then I hit send.

My phone makes that whooshing sound, indicating that my dispatch is off and on its way through the ether.

Banal – that lucky devil – he lived in a time before the omnipresence of cell phones. If someone wanted him to pick up his daughter from ballet class, they would have had to send out a search team to find the man, or maybe launch a message by Morse code.

"But then," I whisper. "Zag didn't *have* any kids." Or a wife, for that matter. At least I've not found any mention of a family in his journals.

"He was free as a bird."

What must that be like?

4

A throng of beaming mothers surrounds me. They come in every shape and color. We are all crowded before the inadequately sized observation window placed in the wall between the dance studio and the foyer. A blur of pink ruffles twirls and pirouettes and stumbles en masse to Tchaikovsky on the other side of the Plexiglas. On this side, a maternal cooing, as of delighted doves.

I am older than most of these women. It wouldn't surprise me if they thought I was here to pick up my granddaughter. For many years Jane and I avoided – no, dodged like a heat-seeking torpedo – the perils of parenthood. But then, through some trick of biology that still has me confounded, the gods sealed our fate.

Occasionally, amidst the flurry of tutus, I catch a glimpse of Ava's face. A concentration that belies her eight years of age. A determination to stick that *grand jeté* like a prima ballerina. Her brow is damp with sweat. It's impossible not to be proud of her. My heart always feels a little surge. She is mini-magnificent.

However, the overwhelming aroma of so many mothers in a heated room is making me swoon. Plus, I'm taking up too much space.

Someone more deserving should have my place at the window – this is understood – someone who has actually carried a child to term in her womb. I work my way through the soft crush of moms – "Sorry. Excuse me." – and step across the room to lean against the wall.

From behind, the trained eye cannot mistake the appearance of bulk maternity. Even the most athletic and determined of the lot has taken on that slightly spread mien. Female infrastructure just settles out that way after the harrowing, cell re-ordering rigors of giving birth. Their subcutaneous under-layer swells. This is not as sexist as it might sound. At least, I try not to think of myself as an old-school chauvinist. I place my hand on the padding of my own lower belly. The same thing, mysteriously, happens to dads. It's a vicarious phenomenon. Like it or not, parenthood spares none of its victims.

Right then, the outside door bursts open with a blast of cold air and a man blusters into the room, dripping wet. "Christ!" he grunts and shakes his arms so that raindrops flip from the sleeves of his trench coat and splat on the tile floor.

The moms turn as one, shooting him through with a barrage of disapproving glowers. Some inadvertently shake their heads, as if silently reprimanding a poorly behaved child.

The man smirks. He doesn't give a good goddamn. A true bad boy. A rogue. Albeit one who has nevertheless been tamed enough to dutifully pick up his daughter from dance class. He spies me, and although I've never seen him before, a look of recognition passes over his face. Another man. Thank God! A buoy of testosterone in this raging sea of estrogen. He comes over and stands with me.

"That's some rain!" I say, inanely.

"Yeah! It's a fucking monsoon!"

I laugh and nod.

He brushes his sleeves, ringing them of rainwater that forms a puddle on the floor beneath his shoes. He wipes his face in his hands. The adjective *bullish* comes to mind. I notice he has a really cool scar under his left eye and is sporting a Burt Reynolds mustache.

"I'm Will."

"Tom. Tom Harvey."

He offers me his wet hand, and I shake it firmly, as if exhibiting my ability for pulling a wounded man into a life raft. I sense that he requires such proof of my competence. I'm tempted to scratch my balls and spit on the wall, just to prove my indifference to the lady folk in the room, but some civilized part of me takes over just in time.

"My wife usually gets our daughter," I say, as if in apology. "She had something to do."

He nods sympathetically. "Yeah. I've never even been here before."

"Your wife usually comes?"

"*Ex*-wife!" he sneers. "Mona. Mona Mc-something-or-other. I forget what it is now. It's been erased from my brain. She's torturing some other poor bastard now."

"It gets complicated sometimes."

"Let me tell you. But..." He shrugs and holds up his palms. "I'm a free agent these days. My sentence has been served. I can do whatever I please. Eat what I want. Drink what I want." He dips his wet head toward the group of women, gives me a sideways nudge with his elbow, and whispers, "And I can chase all the tail I can handle."

"Sounds like the good life."

"Let me tell you, brother. Let me tell you."

Of course, he doesn't tell me. He just lets my imagination go to work for a minute as I assess the erotic possibilities of the mothers with their backsides all turned our way. None of them appear to be very likely candidates for the sporting pursuit of tail chasing. They've passed beyond that point in their life. They're too satisfied with motherhood. Too fulfilled.

"What do you do?" asks Tom.

This makes me squirm. No matter how many times I'm asked that question, I'm always caught off guard. I used to think it would be satisfying to say I was a writer, but it turns out that it's not as much fun as I had hoped. It's sort of like saying I invent fairytales, like I'm some middle-aged version of Dr. Seuss. It's a trade just a little bit too childish to interest a real man, a little too removed from the grit of reality. Maybe if I were more successful. That might make it easier. Of course, I could tell him about my early years as a technical writer, but then I might be forced to admit I never actually wrote manuals for fighter jets or rocket launchers, just vacuum cleaners and blenders. Alas, the world has changed. Gone are the respected, intrepid days of Hemingway.

"I'm a writer."

"Huh!" he says, bobbing his big wet head. "Anything I've heard of?"

"Doubt it. I wrote a western novel that did all right."

"Is it a movie?"

"Not yet," I explain. "It's in the works."

"Well, let me know when it's out on Netflix. I mean, who has time to read?"

"Pretty busy, are you?"

"Let me tell you. In my line?"

"What do you do?"

"Property management." He fishes in his pocket and brings out a business card, handing it to me. "Commercial mostly. Warehouses. Retail spaces. Some residential real estate."

"Keeps you busy, I'll bet."

"It's a rat race, but..." He pulls a frown that I interpret to mean contentment in the face of great struggle. "... I wouldn't do anything else."

"Satisfying work. That's all a guy needs."

"Yeah." He elbows me, and then points with his chin to one of the more attractive moms. "And a little of that."

The woman is in the back, taller than the others, and is standing on her toes to see over heads through the window. She is wearing a skirt and we can see her legs. Her calves are flexed and nicely shaped, as if she jogs, or rides a bike for exercise. She is pretty, but I can't help but think that she looks a bit too much like my own mother did when I was a kid. Not a very sexy thought.

Tom Harvey emits the muted growl of an aroused tiger.

Class is suddenly over, and the Grande Dame opens the door to let the girls – all squeals and laughter – into the foyer. The Grande Dame herself begins cross-referencing email addresses with the moms. The moms drop to their knees before their daughters, buttoning up coats, and replacing slippers with street shoes. One round little girl waddle-skips over to Tom Harvey.

"Hi, Daddy."

"Hey, darlin'."

I hear in his voice, in those two simple words, that he is smitten. He is suffering that same helplessness I so often feel myself when in the presence of my daughter. But when I look at the man, he avoids meeting my eyes. After all, he has a macho façade to preserve. Can't afford to show another side of who he is. I think of Jekyll and Hyde. Of Roxanne's novel idea. And then I find Ava.

"How was it?" I ask.

"Good."

"You looked great out there."

"Thank you." I take Ava's slippers and place one in each pocket of my coat. She slips into her rubber boots and slicker, and then undoes the bun on top of her head. She takes her loose, dark hair and nimbly twists it into a ponytail, binding it with an elastic band she wears always at the ready on her wrist.

A voice sounds behind me – "Nutclacker?"

When I turn, I am faced with the Grande Dame, a towering, otherworldly creature who goes by Madame Olga and who proudly flaunts her Russian accent in everything she says. "Your Ava will be dancink, da?"

"Uh, yes?" The woman is taller than me, and tougher, I think. She is stern, humorless. A severely erect freak-of-nature she-beast who could eat me for lunch. She is all sinew and teeth.

"I send information," she says, and checks for Jane's email on her phone.

"Thank you. I'll tell my wife to look for it."

Madame Olga turns to Ava. "Good work today, yungk lady. Plactice your *pliers*."

"Yes, Madame."

Then the woman slithers away, poking at her phone like some tech-savvy Baba Yaga. The moment very much resembles a troubling dream. I swallow and turn to Ava. "Shall we go?"

She bobs her head.

We thread our way through the room. The other little girls call out goodbye to one another, and a blond fairy in pigtails flits over and gives Ava a quick hug, kissing her on one cheek, then the other.

I smile to some of the mothers. When we're close to the door, I spy Tom Harvey a few feet away and call over to him. "See you next time, Tom." I wink. "Stay out of trouble."

He stares at me as if he's never seen me before, and gives me a suspicious nod, putting his hand on his daughter's shoulder, as if protecting her from the likes of me.

5

OUTSIDE, the rain has turned to mist, and the city is glazed in the reflections of late afternoon. The red taillights of buses and Ubers flash in the wet street. Neon signs pop in floral brilliance from behind shop windows. Christmas decorations garnish light poles. Steam gushes like swamp fog from vents in the sidewalk. Ava slips into step beside me and we walk hand-in-hand through wonderland.

A pigeon flaps out of an alley and swoops just inches over our heads.

Ava giggles. "Filthy fowl, ugly you, you'll never get me, whatever you do." It's an allusion to the evil owl scene in *Ivan's Island*.

"Shall we get cocoa?" she asks. "Mom and I sometimes do."

"Sure. Where should we go?"

"We usually go to Chez Pearl. It's only two blocks."

A bell rings over the door as we leave the damp air of the street and step into the savory, wrap-around aroma of the bakery. Coffee. Cinnamon. Warm dough.

"Mom and I like to sit there." Ava points. "So we can look out and watch for the horse."

"The horse?"

"The black one who pulls the carriage."

Ava saves our table by the tall window. I fetch two mugs of cocoa, and then sit with her as she diligently watches for the horse.

"We call him Pegasus," she tells me.

"Does he have wings?"

"Not that you can see. They only sprout from his shoulders after midnight, when everyone is asleep. Then he flies off through the stars to other places, to carry dreamers to the other side of the world."

Without taking her eyes from the street, Ava spoons a bit of whipped cream from her cocoa and puts it in her mouth. The gesture is her mother's – the way she turns the spoon over and licks it clean, the way she puckers her lips. I see less of myself in my daughter. Sometimes, as when she suddenly turns to face me, I might catch a glimpse of my own childhood, as if I'm seeing an old, frozen-in-time snapshot. I assume this is because the gesture is my own, and now I'm recognizing it from my past. It's like catching a sidelong glance at my boyhood self in a mirror. But mostly, Ava is Jane. Graceful. Smart. Feminine. I sometimes feel I'm being carried back through time to be granted a glimpse of my wife before I knew her, back when she was just a girl.

"How was school today?"

Ava shrugs. "Good."

"Did you learn anything interesting?"

She thoughtfully sucks her spoon, squinting through the glass. Her eyes widen and she looks at me across the table. "Did you know all the ice is melting at the North Pole and the oceans are getting deeper?"

"I've heard that."

"There are islands that are sinking like boats. The people who live on them have to move somewhere else."

"That's too bad, huh?"

"Nature is all off kilter because of Man's un-sa-ta-bull hungers. We need to not cut down so many trees or drive cars so much, so the smoke doesn't pollute the sky."

I nod. I hate this part of being a parent. I hate that anxiety I feel for my daughter's future. What kind of world awaits her? Nuclear proliferation. Overpopulation. Environmental disasters. What other challenges? I'm sure parents since prehistory have all had their worries, but surely the threats are greater today.

"Toby's mom talked to our class today. She's in an organization – People Who Care About The World Tomorrow, or something like that. She's trying to get parents and kids to do things so the earth won't be so warm. So the ice won't melt."

"That sounds like a good idea."

"She asked us what our parents do for a living, and I told her mom's an attorney, and you write cowboy stories."

"Hmm."

"She asked if you ever wrote anything else, like stuff about the real world." Ava licks her spoon and looks out the window. "I told her, no, he pretty much just makes stuff up."

"It's called fiction," I say, "and some people think it's pretty darn important, that it portrays the truth better than the truth does itself. Some of the world's most revered works of art are just made-up stories full of made-up people. Ask Toby's mom if she's ever heard of *War and Friggin' Peace*."

Ava shrugs again. The thought is over her head. I feel like an ass for getting so defensive.

"Well, Toby's mom is going to call Mom and see if she wants to join her organization. She says she can use someone with her skill set."

Undeniably, my own skill set is pitiful. I can guide a rubber boat down a river that is already running downstream anyway, I can tell you everything there is to know about Japanese Zeros, and I can make up stories about a way of life that no longer exists. The world of tomorrow is in sorry shape if left to the likes of me.

We neither one speak for a minute, just sip our cocoa.

The bell rings, drawing my eye to the door, and I am surprised to see Martine come into Chez Pearl. She has a red umbrella folded under her arm, and she is wearing a backpack with a yoga mat strapped to it. Her bobbed hair is drawn back with a headband, and she is in black tights and running shoes. If a man is a microcosm of the macrocosm – his own little world – I am experiencing a personal surge of global warming. A lump rather curiously forms behind my Adam's apple.

"Pegasus and his driver usually show up by now," says Ava.

"Hmm."

Martine is all business. She seems in a hurry. I can hear her voice as she speaks to the girl behind the counter. An exotic murmur and a laugh. Martine orders a cup of coffee to go, pays, and then steps over to the condiments bar with her thermal travel cup.

"Would you like a straw?" I ask Ava.

"No thanks. Straws are made of plastic and Toby's mom says plastic is killing the oceans."

"I'll get you one."

I leave Ava at her observation post and all but bound over to the counter beside Martine. She is spooning sugar into her black coffee and stirring. The scent of lemon floats around her like an ethereal cloud. It makes me dizzy. I am at a loss. What does one do in such a situation? What is the situation anyway? What the hell am I doing?

Her hands are small and thin. Delicate. Fluttering over her cup like sparrows. She wears a tiny silver hoop through the corner of her lower lip.

"Hello," I say. My voice seems to be coming from far away, as if I'm hailing her from a yonder hilltop.

Martine turns my way, screws the lid on her cup, and lifts it to her mouth, all in one fell move. She takes a sip of her coffee, testing its sweetness, and then licks her lips. "Goodbye," she replies.

And then she leaves.

Simple as that.

She is gone, and I am left to recover from an unmerited wave of adrenaline. She didn't even recognize me, thinks I'm just some predatory sleazeball lurking in a coffee shop. I feel sweat under my arms.

I catch the blur of Martine's figure as she opens her red umbrella and strides past where my daughter is sitting at the table. Ava is waving frantically for me to come quick.

I have forgotten what I am doing. I look at the sugar bowl, at the used spoon container, at the few grains of sugar scattered like a constellation of tiny stars on the black countertop. I drift for a moment through those stars, lost in space.

"Daddy!" Ava whispers loudly for me to come.

I somnambulate across the room and drop back into my seat.

"Ah," she sighs, disgusted. "You just missed him."

I look at her. "Who?"

"Pegasus. He was just here pulling his carriage."

"Oh."

She shakes her head. "He was right there." She points past the sidewalk. "Now he won't come back again until tomorrow."

"Oh."

I have failed my daughter. A pile of vivid green horse manure is steaming in the middle of the street, proof of the fabled horse's earthly visit – the worthless equivalent of a cowboy novel carelessly dropped in the rain.

"Did you get me a straw?"

"A straw?"

"You were going to get me a straw."

"Oh," I say. "No. I thought you said you didn't want one."

6

I am asleep and I am dreaming and I am aware, distantly, that I am asleep and dreaming, but I don't know how to wake myself, and neither do I know how to escape the nightmarish sense of panic and frustration that are the primary elements of this dream.

I am in the midst of a vast, empty ocean, treading water. In every direction, there is nothing but aquamarine waves rolling in the sunlight. A cowboy hat is my only protection. Otherwise, I am naked. Vulnerable. I'm trying to decide which direction to swim but can't. It's all the same. There is no land in sight. I look at the sky – a hopeless blue. And I'm growing weary from the effort.

"Wake up, Kirby," I tell myself. "Wake up!"

But I don't wake up.

Instead, I sense an awful hole of darkness opening up beneath me.

I sense deep-water beasts.

But then I hear a reassuring laughter. A man's. When I turn myself around, I am tickled pink to see none other than Dick Zag rowing a rubber life raft in my direction. He is laughing heartily, putting his back into the oars.

When he is close, he folds the oars into the boat, and leans over the side. That charismatic smile. That rakish twinkle in his steel blue eyes. He lowers a muscular arm.

"Grab hold, buddy."

I can't believe my luck.

I am all grins as I breaststroke to the side of the boat and reach for his hand.

But then... "What the... !" Something grips my ankle and pulls me down; then it lets go.

"Grab hold!"

I try again, but the same thing happens. I feel fingers wrapping around my foot, jerking, and then letting go just when I'm out of reach of my rescuer. I feel like bait on a hook.

"Damn it, man!" cries Zag. "Are you gonna grab hold, or do I leave you for the sharks?"

My mouth is too full of seawater to answer. I cough and splutter. I reach out again, but this time I am pulled completely beneath the surface; the hand holding my foot doesn't let go. What's more, another hand grips my other ankle, and then a pair of arms wraps around my waist.

I am kicking madly, squirming, bubbles streaming from my mouth and nostrils.

Down I go.

And down.

Below me is nothing but darkness. A hollow silence. Liquid terror. It is ungodly cold. I feel it there like some enormous mouth waiting to swallow me up.

I tip back my head and search the receding surface of the sea. The boat is gone. Zag is gone. Just waves and more waves dancing in the sunlight. But wait... Something is floating on the rollers. Some small piece of flotsam.

A miniscule shadow on this everlasting ocean.

A tiny bit of hope.

Then I sadly realize – Oh. It's only my cowboy hat.

———

I don't know when it happened, but I've grown too gun-shy to ever work a dream like that into my fiction. I worry that critics would howl like a pack of self-righteous coyotes. I couldn't take the abuse. Too heavy-handed, they'd yap. Too contrived! But in real life, I have found such dreams are commonplace. My evermore-hackneyed mind just works that way. And although I am certain it is blatantly symbolic – one senses as much – the dream's exact meaning is lost on me as I stare now at the ceiling over the bed.

A wash of weak morning light.

I hear rain outside, but I don't hear the girls.

I slide out of the blankets and into a pair of khakis, and then I go shirtless to the kitchen. Jane has left a note.

Hey Sleepyhead,

Sorry about last night. Let's not fight. (You can't win. Ha!) We'll be late this evening. Extra long dance class to get ready for the show. Could you maybe tidy up and fix dinner? I think there's stuff in the fridge. A good night for soup.

Love you, J
A says, have a good day.

The note seems even more nonsensical than my dream. Perhaps I'm not awake after all. I have no idea what Jane is talking about. Did we fight again last night? What show is she referring to? For a minute, I even wonder who is this A person who wants me to have a good day?

I step over to the French press on the counter and pour myself a cup of coffee. It is cold and viscid as motor oil. I swallow, but it nearly comes back up. "Eww!" It is an ill-advised move, but in an effort to cleanse my palate, I take a bite from the pot of coagulated oatmeal on the stove. Now I have motor oil mixed with wood chips combining alchemically on my tongue to create chilled dog shit.

I go to the glass door and peer out. Our apartment is on the seventh floor, generally offering a pleasant view of the city. But this morning there is nothing to see but a uniform gray. The gray sky has settled over the gray buildings and gray streets where gray men are moving slow as sullen slugs beneath gray umbrellas on the gray sidewalks. The only actual color is, amazingly, the yellow eyes of a large owl sitting on our balcony and ripping apart a mouse she holds in her talons. Entrails and gore dangle from the bird's beak. She tears and gulps the little rodent with a delight that belies the otherwise uninspiring world in which she dwells.

"Filthy fowl," I say, "ugly you."

I shiver in the cold and empty apartment, hugging myself in my own arms. "You'll never get me, whatever you do."

The owl turns her head completely around and grins at me through the glass.

"Oh, yeah?" she seems to say.

7

WHEN I get to the library, Martine is at her desk. She is a bright flower in this otherwise withered garden. She is wearing a chic, but understated, skirt and sweater – surreptitiously sexy, yet conservative enough to suit her job. The sweater is cut tastefully low and is snug and of a shade of blue that matches her eyes. Her lip ring is gone, and I can just barely detect the tiny hole in her tender flesh. One imagines the silver hoop resting in a dish beside her bathroom sink. I feel I know an intimate secret about her; I am savvy to something of her true identity, of who she really is outside of this stifling, bookish environment.

I am determined not to make a fool of myself today. I remind myself that I am a married man with a daughter. I am mature with a capital M. The word *decorum* comes to mind, followed closely by the word *dignity*. But it turns out I am mistaken about my own true character. It turns out, rather surprisingly, that I am actually an awkward thirteen-year-old nincompoop. Albeit one held captive in a middle-aged body.

"*Bonjour!*" I say.

Martine lifts her gaze and stares blankly into my face. "Pardon?"

"Good morning." I smile. "Or rather, good day." The voice that comes out of my face is not my own; it is inordinately high, as if, just before emitting sound, I had taken a hit from a canister of helium, or as if I am suffering a surge of latent, youthful hormones.

Martine tilts her head to the side, unsure.

I consider mentioning our encounter yesterday at Chez Pearl, as a sort of casual icebreaker, but I promptly lose my nerve. Too complicated. The context was obviously all wrong. Why else would Martine have failed to recognize me? I clear my throat.

"I am here to research the notebooks."

"Notebooks?"

"Yes. You remember, the journals of Richard Banal. I am a writer. I was here the other day. I am writing a book about him because I am a writer."

Her blank stare grows blanker. "Banal?"

I shrug, and grin apologetically. "Funny name, huh?"

Martine stares at me, unflinching.

She has an elegant neck – a throat – two collarbones –

"I should properly introduce myself," I say. "I'm Kill Wirby." I chuckle and correct myself. "I mean Kirby. Will Kirby. I wrote a book you might know about. I am a man who is a writer. Like Hemingway. It's called *Western Wind*. It's a western novel that I wrote. Have you heard of it?"

She shakes her head.

"Oh. I thought maybe Roxanne might have shared it with you. She likes it a lot. She's even started something called a fan page for it. It's, like, her favorite book in the whole wide world."

Again, Martine shakes her head.

At the speed of light, this is going nowhere.

"I'm sorry," I say. "What was your name?"

"Martine."

I offer my hand over the desk. Warily, she takes my hand in hers. Her fingers are warm. Muddling buffoon that I am, I hold them a moment beyond what is appropriate. I can't seem to let go.

"*Enchanté,*" I say. "*Tu es francais?*"

"*Francaise,*" she corrects. "*Je suis francaise.*"

Damn! What was I thinking? I should have stuck with English. But then, mysteriously, while in a state of lingual panic, as if some drunken Francophonic demon is channeling through my being, I hear myself say, like a tourist reciting from a French phrase book, "*Le ciel est bleu.*"

Martine melts into an embarrassed and uncomfortable expression, one that might come to the face of a person who suddenly realizes she is talking to a sufferer of mental illness. "The sky?" she asks. "It is blue?"

I want to explain that I am not a moron. I long to erase the last sixty seconds, travel back in time, and start this interaction all over again. I am racking my brain for a way to do this when a nattily dressed old man materializes out of the bookshelves and steps over to Martine's desk. He acknowledges me with a friendly tip of his head.

"Excuse me," he says. "I don't mean to interrupt."

"No," I say, almost grateful. "Not at all."

He thanks me, and then speaks to Martine, prattling off a rambling question in fluent French.

Martine answers in animated fashion, even smiling.

Her perfect teeth, all in a row, appear like an epiphany.

The old man makes a joke in French, and Martine laughs again.

I stand with my laptop under one arm, a grinning Neanderthal, as if I completely understand this good-natured conversation happening before me. In truth, I haven't caught a single word of it. I suspect the codger is showing off.

Martine leaves her desk and steps back to a row of file cabinets some twenty feet away. The old man looks at me and winks. "Charming creature," he says quietly.

I nod in agreement.

"Would that I were young again," he says, a tone of longing in his hushed voice.

I smile, and nod some more. Then we both watch Martine as she bends over the files and searches inside. Her shapely derriere, concealed within the woolen fabric of her tightly stretched skirt, lifts rather deliciously into the air. She seems unaware, but its effect is wreaking havoc. I catch a side glimpse of the old man. He is nodding more vigorously now, wiggling his fingers, smiling like a demented clown. "*Tres charmante!*" He sucks his teeth. "Wonderful!"

I don't necessarily want to be in cahoots with this old fart, but I am at a loss for how to extract myself from his company. I wouldn't want to lose my hard-won connection to Martine – although it is admittedly precarious and thin – so I just wait, regarding Martine's rear end.

———

The truth is, I have absolutely no idea what I am up to at this moment. It's like something has taken me over. What, exactly, do I hope to achieve? What do I foresee? Do I honestly think Martine and I have a destiny? Do I seriously believe that she will become enamored of my charm, shape her entire existence around my own, and become my secret lover? Do I honestly think such a thing is possible, that my family life would allow it, that I could pull it off without any complications, maybe even with Jane's blessing? No. That is absurd. A male fantasy out of control.

A train wreck waiting round the bend.

A meteor speeding toward the Earth.

And yet...

And still...

———

Martine comes back with a folder for the old man. "*Voila,*" she says, and hands it over.

"*Merci bien, ma cherie.*"

He shoots me a wink, and then fades like an enigma of tweed back into the cabinetry.

"You know where are these notebooks?" Martine asks me.

"Uh," I say. "Yes."

"Then you can find them?"

"Uh... Sure."

"Okay." She smiles.

I am dismissed.

I hem.

And then I haw.

"Shouldn't I sign in?" I plead. "Or wouldn't you like to note their condition?"

Martine shakes her head.

"Oh." I step sideways. "Well then, thank you, Martine. It was a pleasure to meet you." I bow slightly, and for some reason click my heels together like a Nazi. At least I overcome my urge to say *merci*. Disaster surely lurks in such an effort. "I hope to see you again."

With the grin of a lovesick cowboy, I take in a deep and intoxicating drag of her lemony scent, turn nonchalantly, and, affecting a swagger, tread toward my boat-sized table through the intervening ocean of books.

"Smooth, Mr. Wirby," I mutter to myself. "Smooth as shit."

8

P AGE 62 of Banal's fourth notebook begins like this –

    I'm reluctant to disclose too much intel about the secret world of Oblivia. And yet, as an explorer, I feel an obligation to share my discoveries with my fellow man. I just hope anyone reading this understands one thing – I'm not your typical flat-footed sap walking down the street. I'm a man who has spent his life confronting all the horrors and beauty of adventure. I've seen and done some things that would easily kill anyone else. I'm an expert on stuff other guys only dream about. Trust me, those dreams can turn into nightmares real fast. Anyone reading this guide needs to follow my advice to a T if he wants to escape with his life. Only by listening to my warnings can you ever hope to penetrate, and then fully withdraw, from the brain-erasing anomaly that is Oblivia. Still, I'm pretty sure that for the right sort of man – for the most ass-kicking and courageous few among us – Oblivia is accessible, and, more importantly, survivable. But as Dante so read the warning posted above the gates of Hell – "Abandon all hope, you poor slobs who enter here!" so, too, will I warn the faint-hearted patsy fool enough to think this secret world is just some sort of amusement park. I warn you, Oblivia is no joy ride. There is everything to lose by entering this realm, but for the fearless few, I would encourage, there is also much to gain. Before you read one line further, you need to ask yourself this – am I man enough for this challenge? Am I worthy and able to endure Oblivia's marriage of Heaven and Hell, to risk having my soul ripped from my spleen if it comes to that, to possibly be tortured and violated and spoon-fed my own testicles if I should fail in my mission?

If your answer is an unflinching and resounding Yes! then I invite you to read on.

Admittedly, *unflinching* and *resounding* might be overstating it. After all, my palms begin to sweat, and I feel a bit sick to my stomach when I consider the more explicit details of Banal's warning. "But dammit!" I whisper to myself. "Am I a man, or a mouse?"

I wipe my palms on my shirt, turn the page, and read on.

Let me begin with the preparations necessary for survival.

———

It is important for any man hoping to survive Oblivia to be in an optimal state of physical and mental readiness. Luckily, I, by my nature and habit, was in top shape on the day I found myself washed onto the shores of this weird atoll. I've always started my day with hard exercise. Push-ups, chin-ups, and running obstacle courses are at the core of any good fitness routine, and any man about to take on a voyage should practice these exercises regularly. Physical stamina and strength are an absolute necessity for Oblivia.

You need to have a good swim stroke too, one that allows you to keep your head up to see any approaching threats. Oblivia is surrounded by ocean, and water is as present in this place as air.

Men turn on each other here, and a combatant's skill is also necessary.

But be warned, bare-knuckling in Oblivia isn't some playground game. It's all well and good to pull your punches when you're in some petty bar fight back home, but you need to be ruthless if you're going to survive a fight here. You're going to need a bag of dirty tricks. Thumbs to the eye, jabs to the groin, and ear-biting all ensure success in these fights to the death. It wouldn't hurt for you to learn how to snap another man's neck, or how to rip his jugular from his throat with a bare hand. I guarantee you, your opponent will not hesitate to use the same tactics on you if you give him half a chance.

Your battles with the non-human brutes of Oblivia are a whole other can of worms. For those you'll need the cunning and dexterity of the most evasive prey, because, buddy, prey is exactly what you'll become if you fail to dodge the beasts of Oblivia. Unfortunately, no amount of warning can prepare you for what lies in wait by way of beastly horrors. These fiends are of that breed that cruise your deepest nightmares. Nasty! I can only advise you to lose that spare tire around your belt, build your strength and quickness, and be damned sure of what you are physically capable. Otherwise, I'm afraid you're a dead man.

The mental preparation needed for Oblivia is even more important than the physical. You'll have to keep your wits at all times, not lose your head. We all have our own ways of getting in touch with our core - that part of us that connects a man to the energy of the universe. You can scoff at this idea if you want, but this is the big battery from which we all draw our power. You're half a man without it. As for myself, I believe strongly in practicing some sort of deep meditation. The brand I personally subscribe to is one shared with a partner of the opposite sex. It seems good ol' Mother Nature has blessed us all with a perfect point of focus, and if a fellow is able to get his hands on a copy of the Kama Sutra, he'll find a form of interactive sexual meditation that is empowering, mind-clearing, and absolutely fantastic. If you don't have an appropriate partner, it's still possible to reach a certain level of focus through deep breathing, preferably in a cold place. Even the best of us has been forced to practice such lone mediation in a pinch. It's nothing to be ashamed of.

Get yourself prepared in the head and the body.

In truth, the mental and physical challenges of Oblivia are nothing more than elaborate exaggerations of the quieter challenges most folks face every day. The differences are only in their degree and extreme manifestation. Daily problems just wear different clothes here, different faces. Reality is only the starting point. For example, in Oblivia you will find yourself confronted by Your Self. This is common enough to all of us as we live our day-to-day lives close to home. To face certain challenges to one's beliefs and general self-image is surely common to every wide-awake person who has ever lived and breathed, even the meekest among us. But in Oblivia, that Other Self one must face is more tangible and basic. You will find Your Self threatening yourself in ways you never imagined were even possible. What's more, your Other will often be a superior version of who you have become through the many wearing years of your life. This is a humiliating and ass-busting experience, and I'll bet my last dime that the number one reason we've never heard from any of the previous visitors to Oblivia is that this other self defeated them in the inevitable battle resulting from such an encounter. Those other shmucks were, in short, killed by their own reflections, as if an old snapshot of their younger and cocksure self had come to life and overpowered them with its eternally youthful strength. A man's survival might well depend on what degree of harmony he can come to between himself and His Self. Of course, it will be impossible for you to understand what the blue blazes I'm talking about so abstractly. Only through an actual visit to Oblivia will these aspects of the place be encountered. I'm only warning you to get as ready as you can before you embark. Know thyself, so it won't be such a damn big surprise when your other self hauls off and busts you in the chops.

Which leads me to the last and most unsettling phenomenon of this odd dominion – its ability to retrogressively scramble and erase the memories of a man's existence as it was lived before entering Oblivia. No buttress of civilization can withstand the primitive power of this awful mind erasure. No person, no matter how secure in society, is capable of surviving its primal vortex of oblivion. It's like a drug. Assuredly, it's more or less powerful depending on its victim. Some guys will last longer than others under its influence. But its complete domination of your brain is inevitable. I have yet to meet a man with character enough to withstand it. I can only advise that when you first begin to feel its symptoms – headaches, lapses in reason – seek your escape. Your window of opportunity is quickly closing. The possibility of forever being trapped grows more sure with every minute you loiter. Remember Dante and his advice to abandon all hope. If you go too far into this forgetfulness, then you will most assuredly be sucked into the deepest most irrevocable wilderness of the soul.

I'll add just one more encouragement and warning before concluding this invitation to adventure. I've traveled all around the globe, from its highest peaks to its most filthy swamps. I've encountered many extraordinary characters and experienced many manly escapades. But the one adventure that beats all the rest is my visit to Oblivia. Nowhere else have I ever felt more free to be a man. Nowhere else have I ever had such a sense of discovering a true Paradise Lost. Nowhere else, to my vast knowledge, can a man find anything to match the extremes of its fleeting bliss. In Oblivia, a man is free to exercise his manliness. The rules of daily life as we're forced to live them at home do not apply here. Things taboo in our daily lives are not frowned upon here with righteous judgment. You can forget yourself here and live your truest life. It is a timeless Eden, to be sure, but as Eden was home to a serpent, understand, so, too, does Oblivia have its terrors. Maybe they're worth the cost. Maybe not. You'll have to decide for yourself.

And so now, my man, you have been instructed.

You have been warned.

And if you're still hell-bent on going, there's nothing left for me to do but show you the secret portal to Oblivia.

The next page is page 69 – the one that has been removed from R. H. Banal's notebook.

9

THE afternoon finds me at The Muscle Factory, my gym of choice. It's only a few blocks from the library and I appreciate its tongue-in-cheek name. It doesn't take itself too seriously, although today I am feeling more serious than ever about my own fitness. I've been inspired by Banal's call for readiness. Of course, I have no idea what I might be preparing for, but I tell myself it never hurts to be primed for battle. To this end, I've strapped myself to a stationary bicycle for an hour – thirty minutes beyond my typical warm-up. I have been lax lately, missing whole weeks of exercise, letting the flab creep in around my middle, and so I need to up my time and effort. I need to lay off the pasta and eat more salad. These machines usually bore me to tears, but today I have closed my eyes and am daydreaming about climbing mountains. It makes the time pass more pleasantly. The techno-pop beat thumping on the gym's sound system fades into my mind's hinter regions and becomes the buffeting wind. The cadenced beep on my bike's electrical console is merely the sound of mountain goats bleating to one another over the boulder fields.

I have had an active imagination all my life. *Inner resources,* my mother always called it. It's a skill I developed early on, while enduring long classes in school and long sermons in church. When I was only about nine or ten, and bored out of my ever-lovin' mind, I used to imagine myself paddling a red canoe down an endless river. Adventures waited at every bend. Sometimes I would rendezvous with Indians; sometimes I would wrestle saber-toothed cave bears or deranged, four-armed gorillas; sometimes I would struggle to navigate my little craft through the most roiling rapids. The preacher would moralize and plead, but I was oblivious to his sermons. I was too far away to hear, lost in my own private wilderness, paddling happily from one adventure to the next.

When adolescence struck, my fantasies evolved. They became more blatantly amatory, not the kind of things a boy should probably be thinking about in Sunday School. Forbidden stuff. Sins of a sort contrary to the societal morality of which I was being instructed. I had one recurring scenario in particular – the last stop of my red canoe – in which I was the lone male trapped on an island of women.

Oh, how they used me!

One after the next.

An endless succession of girls needing my manly services in their Amazonian Utopia. I was their stud slave. Of course, any unworthy males were eliminated. The place was littered with the skulls of lesser boys I had been forced to fight – the defeated and damned. And I was under constant threat of being murdered myself, so jealous were my many mates, so demanding my nightly schedule to perform. I wore a chain on my ankle. I was only allowed to exercise, fight my challengers, and make love. (Never mind that I had only a rudimentary notion of how this latter act was actually performed.) My enslavers were morphs of the various women and girls in the church where I was daydreaming. The prettier moms and their daughters. Their Sunday dresses were replaced with leopard skins, in the style of adventure novels and movies. They all wore their hair down. My favorite was a girl named Louise Townsend, a prim beauty that I sensed held within her developing bosom a lusty heart as sensual as that of the most devoted disciple of the *Kama Sutra*. We conspired to escape this oppressive world of rules and animal behavior. Louise was going to steal the key to my shackles and set me free when it was her turn at my bed, and then we would run away and live a monogamous, blissful existence in the deepest jungles. But until then – Alas! – I was forced, one more time, to service my many mistresses.

As I summit my imaginary mountain, I find myself wondering what Louise, some thirty years later, might look like now. But as good as my imagination is, I am unable to see her as anything but the fresh angel sitting in the pew in front of me at church. She floats in a state of enviably arrested development. Forever young and pure.

My stationary bike beeps its final beep, indicating that I have achieved my cardiovascular goal. I open my eyes, but the scene is blurry. I'm sweating like a pig. A veil of brine impairs my vision. I feel light-headed. I wipe my eyes, lift my gaze, and then, magically, an apparition materializes before me.

Am I truly seeing this?

I am transfixed.

On the far side of the room, beyond the dumbbell racks, beyond the grunting bodies of a half dozen weightlifters, I see none other than Martine. She is behind a wall of Plexiglas, kicking and punching the stuffing out of a heavy-bag hanging by a chain from the ceiling. Her arms move like lightning bolts. Her legs snap and jab like those of a trained assassin. That poor bag.

Richard Henry Banal wrote in his journal some lines that flash to my mind – *Eggheads deem my novels too ironic and fantastic to be believable, but I would argue that when one is in tune with the cosmos, there is no such thing as coincidence and the inexplicable. There is nothing but the alignment of one's self with one's beautiful destiny. This I know for fact – fiction is in league with reality. The fates are putting in our way what we would have.*

I mull these words as I watch Martine.

"Are you awake?"

This voice comes from my left.

I am yanked from my reverie and turn to see a square-shouldered woman with a power drink and a sweat towel standing at my side.

"Sorry?" I say and force a smile.

"I asked if you're done. You've been on that thing forever. How about giving it up for a while?"

"Oh," I say. I look back across the room to Martine kicking her bag. A strategy, slow and sure, develops in my mind.

"Well?"

"No," I tell the woman. "I'm not done. In fact, I'm just getting started."

As the woman walks away, disgruntled, I punch another hour into the console. After that, I tell myself, I'll hit the weights. Then tomorrow I'll swim. Maybe run. Maybe even try kickboxing.

I start in on the bike again, but this time I don't close my eyes. Instead, I watch Martine and pedal like a boy toward his destiny.

10

AS I open the door to our apartment, I am greeted by a tangible tension. It floats on the air with the scent of burnt butter and cheddar cheese. I pull the door closed behind me and walk into the kitchen.

Jane is at the stove, still in her work suit, sleeves rolled up, jabbing at something in the skillet with a spatula.

"Hi," I say.

"Hi."

Her voice comes down like a cold bucket of rain.

"Hi, Daddy." Ava is on the couch watching classic cartoons on the computer propped open on the coffee table. She is already in her pajamas. She waves her hand above her head in my direction but doesn't let her gaze leave the screen.

That's when I spy Jane's note held to the fridge with a magnet – the one asking me to clean house and make soup.

Rats!

"Oh, Jane, I'm sorry. I was late at the gym, and then I had to go to the bookstore. I couldn't find what I wanted downtown, so I had to go all the way over to Southeast, to one of those New Age places, and..." I lift the bag that holds my treasure. "But I found it at last."

My good fortune means nothing to her. Besides that, all of my excuses sound lame, as if I were off playing games while Jane was doing the real work of the world. She flips the food without speaking.

I step forward. "Let me take over."

"It's already done." She lifts the skillet from the burner and slides the food onto two waiting plates. I am ashamed. Grilled cheese sandwiches are a default meal in our house, the kind of meager fare we resort to only when all has gone awry and there is nothing left but to prepare something quick and easy. We've had them a lot lately.

Jane adds steamed broccoli to the plates and carries them over to the couch, handing one of the plates to Ava. Then she sits and watches cartoons. I can tell by the set of her shoulders that I am best advised not to say anything more just yet.

I feel like a semi-worthless jerk.

I take my newly purchased book into the bedroom and slide it under my side of the bed.

I look at myself in the mirror. "Bad boy," I say, as if I'm chastising a poorly behaved schnauzer. Turning sideways, I suck in my gut, prodding my belly with my fingers. My abs are already sore as hell, the result of too many crunches at The Muscle Factory. But it's a satisfying pain, the kind, I assure myself, that indicates progress. I'll be one ripped man-hunk in no time.

Back in the kitchen, I get myself a bowl and heap it full of broccoli. I salt it, but I pass on the black and gooey sandwich left for me in the skillet. It smells delicious – my mouth waters – but I don't want to throw away all that hard work at the gym. I am determined. Starvation is my diet tactic. I'll just live off my love handles for a while. I go and sit on the couch with the girls – me, Ava in the middle, then Jane. Ava gives my knee a loving pat with her fingers, and then laughs at the cartoon.

I am suffering a weird wave of déjà vu. On the screen is an old cartoon about a modern Stone Age family. Two primitive men are playing poker and smoking cigars in the comfort of their living room. Everything is a mix of modern life and some stylized conjecture of what it might have been like in cave man days. A pet brontosaurus snoozes on the rug at their feet. Totally absurd and chronologically amiss. I'm sure I've seen this episode before, maybe as a Saturday morning rerun, but it was eons ago, back in the Pleistocene of my own childhood. "I vaguely remember this one," I tell Ava. "This is from when I was your age."

"It's funny," says Ava. "It's so old-fashioned looking."

I nod and chew broccoli. She's right. Another era.

One of the cavemen draws a straight and slaps his stone cards down on the table. "Yabba dabba doo!" Then the wives, their hair coiffed and both dressed in animal skin miniskirts, come into the room, bringing the boys sandwiches on a tray before going off to take care of their children. The irony – the last century sexism – is not lost on me. Neither is it lost on Jane.

"The good old days," she quips.

I stuff my mouth with more broccoli.

The cartoon has scratched a nerve. I am irrationally peeved. It strikes me as asinine that the show's producers would take the boring stuff of a typical American household, move it back into some fanciful past, and then replay it for the masses. Was that shit really entertaining to people? I realize how much more I am enamored of complete escape. It feels like they've trivialized the subject somehow. I don't want a mirror of my own life, not some dumbass make-believe clad in leopard skins. I want something more. The real deal. Something beyond domesticity and its tedious misunderstandings. I want something truly primal, basic, fantastic, even otherworldly.

"Do you want the rest of my sandwich, Daddy?"

Ava holds up a congealed cheese remnant over my empty broccoli bowl. I lick my lips, nearly drown in a gush of saliva, and swallow. "No, thanks," I say. "I'm full."

The cartoon ends.

"All right, honey." Jane takes Ava's plate. "Off to bed."

Ava gives her mom a hug and a kiss, then she turns to me, "*Ivan's Island?*" She's perfectly capable of reading the book by herself, but this is our tradition held over from when she was little.

"Okay. If you're quick and brush your teeth."

"I'm quick as a shooting star," she says, and scampers out of the room.

I take the plates from Jane and pile them by the sink. "I'll deal with this mess later," I tell her. "Why don't you go take a hot bath?"

She doesn't reply; she's still mad.

———————

I read up to the part in the book where Ivan finds himself hiding in a cave in winter. He's depressed, hypothermic, wounded, sexually frustrated (I infer that part), and lonesome. But it's late, and Ava has school in the morning, so I put the book away and tuck the blankets up to her chin – a gesture no doubt carried out by parents all around the world.

"It feels like we're leaving Ivan in a bad place," says Ava.

"He'll be all right."

"We need to read a little farther, at least to where things get better."

"What makes you think he won't be stuck on his island forever?"

Ava rolls her eyes. "It's a kid's book, Dad. They always end hopeful. The author is supposed to make it happy. That's the difference between grown-up books and kid's books. Grown-up books are gloomy."

"How do you know that?"

She shrugs. "I just guessed by how grown-ups always act."

"Hmm," I say, considering this bit of insight. "Well, Ivan will just have to tough it out for tonight. You need to get your sleep."

I lean and kiss her forehead, and when I do, a spasm of muscle fatigue shoots through my entire body and I momentarily black out. I kind of overdid it at the gym. I need to be careful, not move too fast.

"Sweet dreams."

Then I turn out the light and go to face my last heroic act of the day – marital damage control.

Jane is lying supine on the bed, wrapped in an oversized towel, eyes closed, rubbing her temples. Her face is flushed from the steam of the bath.

"Tough day?" I ask.

"Mmm."

I sit next to her and she opens her eyes and looks at me. I smile sympathetically.

"How about you?" she asks. "How's the book coming?"

"Good!" I lie. "Really great."

She waits for me to elaborate, but I'm afraid of sounding inept, so I just nod.

"Good," she finally says.

As I gaze down at her, a thought occurs to me – Love is a drop of rain in the ocean; it gets diluted with all the other salt drops of life until it's hard to taste.

We stare familiarly at one another.

I am moved to take Jane's hand. A fondness stirs inside of me like the faint pulse of something struggling to stay alive. It makes me sad. My throat tightens. I am admittedly too simple to understand what it is exactly, but I am wise enough not to react. Spontaneity can be fatal in such situations. I need to be cautious, not say something I'll regret. Candor is all well and good, but I'm never very good at it.

"We need to go on a date sometime," says Jane.

"Yeah."

"Just you and me."

"That would be nice."

Jane is still pretty. Granted, she's not the lithe beauty I married twenty-three years ago, not the same person to whom I made all those love-drunk pledges on our wedding day. Even essentially she has changed. She used to hope she could save the world from humanity's foibles. She believed there were certain laws of existence that needed illuminating so that everyone on board could find a general harmony. She's less idealistic now, more haggard in her demeanor. One's enthusiasms inevitably crumble over time. Like the forces of gravity, life tears down the most stalwart among us – from flesh-and-blood women to prehistoric men to fictional mice trapped on miserable islands in kid's storybooks.

"Do you want to mess around?" asks Jane.

This takes me off guard. I am flummoxed. I am somewhere else in my thoughts, somewhere more mortal and subdued. *And* I'm exhausted. But then another thought occurs to me – The *U.S.S. Marital Intercourse* is a boat that rarely drops anchor here. If I ever want a ride, I am best advised to hop aboard before it steams out of port.

"Heave ho," I say. "Yabba dabba doo!"

Jane squeezes my hand and tells me to turn out the lights.

We haven't made love with the lights on for years. I am sensitive enough not to ask why.

———

Things are going pretty well. This is sex as it is performed by veterans of the act. Pleasurable enough. Somewhat predictable. But intimate, like a box lunch shared between old friends.

And yet, let's be honest. One's mind shouldn't drift off to other things. One shouldn't be thinking about tomorrow already and of swimming at The Muscle Factory and about the cold grilled cheese sandwich in the kitchen or the book under the bed and about page 69 of Banal's journal and, it goes without saying, one certainly shouldn't be wondering what it might be like to make out with a pretty French girl wearing a lip ring.

Unaware of my wandering thoughts, Jane is almost there. She's rumbling on the launch pad of fleeting ecstasy. I know the signs, the familiar signals that I should go forward with my own countdown to fulfillment so that it will be assured to coincide with hers. So, I pick up my pace. I begin that animal thrusting thing that a man couldn't stop now even if he wanted to. The horny brontosaurus in me just takes over. I press myself down against Martine's – I mean Jane's – naked body. Martine – I mean Jane – moans. She is there. The ship, for her, has launched.

I, too, am, right, there, on the edge, just waiting to blast off and rise and rise into the sensational vortex of fleeting oblivion... But then something happens I'm not expecting.

"Aah!" I cry.

An assassin jumps out of the shadows behind me and stabs an icepick into my right hamstring.

Or at least I think so.

"Aaah!"

My body tenses and my legs shoot out straight.

"What?" asks Jane.

"Ahh!" I can't speak. "Aaah!"

"What? What?"

I roll off of her and clutch the back of my thigh. "Ahh, damn!"

"Is it your heart?" Jane sounds worried; she scrambles to her knees and lays a palm on my chest, preparing to perform CPR.

"No, God!" I moan. And then I sort of start laughing.

"What?"

The comedy of the situation overwhelms me.

"Oh, Jane." I laugh through my tears, rubbing my leg. "That's absolutely the worst charley horse I've ever had in my life."

She just stares down at me. Even in the near darkness, I sense her incredulity. "You're kidding."

"No," I grimace. "I am not."

Jane sits back on her heels. "Jesus, Will. That's just a little bit weird."

I don't bother to explain that I'm suffering from the side effects of enacting the overzealous exercise routine of Richard Henry Banal, the one devised for a man about to embark on a journey to the enchanted isle of Oblivia. I sense, in this particular moment, that such a divulgence is ill-advised. "Sorry," I say. "Maybe I'm just... I don't know... dehydrated, or low on electrolytes or something."

"Mommy?"

It's Ava at the bedroom door.

Jane quick slips into her nightgown and throws a blanket over me. For some reason – even though it's a natural, beautiful thing – it's not okay for a daughter to see her parents naked and humping like buffalo. Jane flips on the light by the bed and steps over to Ava, kneeling before her.

"What is it, honey?"

"I heard scary noises."

She brushes the hair out of Ava's eyes and takes her hand, kneeling before her on the floor. "Oh. Well, Daddy and I were just talking."

"I had a bad dream."

Jane hugs Ava. "Oh, that's no fun."

Jane glances over her shoulder and gives me the signal that I should get decent. I sneak out of bed and put on some boxers and a t-shirt.

"Can I sleep with you and Dad tonight."

Remembering our own vivid nightmares of childhood, Jane and I have never said no to this request. So, Ava hops up and snuggles beneath the blankets in the center of the bed. Jane slides in beside her and turns off the light.

I just sit there for a moment. The plot of the evening has changed so rapidly that my head spins. Coitus interruptus to the maximus. How did we get here from where we were just few a minutes ago? It's like an abridged account of my entire married life. Bewildered, cautious, I gently knead the back of my thigh. When I believe the charley horse has gone, I slide beneath the blankets.

Ava, nestled up close to her mom, reaches over and takes my hand.

"I love you, Daddy."

"Hm." I squeeze her small fingers. "I love you too, honey."

We all three lie there in the bed.

My stomach growls.

On the dark ceiling I watch the scene of a vast ocean slopping with waves. Far away, almost at that point where it is about to disappear over the horizon, I spy a boat sailing away.

The sky above is blue.

II

WHEN I wake, everything hurts. Everything! My body is a medium for pain. My muscles are pulsing strands of agony. Even my eyelids ache. My individual cells. My cytoplasm.

"Wow," I mumble.

Was I beaten with a pipe?

Was I trampled by a stampeding herd of cattle?

I move slowly, cautiously, beneath the blankets, spreading my toes, then my fingers. I stretch my legs, oh so gingerly, and groan.

"Holy Mother of God!"

Of course, I probably should have eased into it yesterday at the gym. I basically did an entire month's workout in an afternoon. And that after weeks of sitting on my ass. Serves me right, I suppose.

I lie there, listening for the girls, but all I hear is the rain and the muffled swish of traffic in the street below our building. Jane and Ava have gone. How do they sneak away so silently? Am I that lost to the world when I sleep, that close to a coma? I seem to remember, in my whitewater days, being more finely attuned to my surroundings. I used to sleep, as the saying goes, with one eye open. Like some great jungle cat. My senses used to be sharper. I had the spatial awareness of Jason Bourne. I used to be able to hear the stars grating across the heavens. I used to be able to taste the coming of a storm on the breeze. I used to be able to smell... I breathe in.

"Chez Pearl?"

My nose draws me to the nightstand beside the bed. There's a note from Ava, written in crayon.

> *Daddy,*
> *Mommy and me bought you a surprise.*
> *Have a nice day.*

She's drawn a red flower and a smiling sun at the bottom of the paper.

Behind the note lurk a thermos-cup of hot coffee and the biggest, gooiest raspberry and sweet-cheese Danish in the world. My favorite, as they well know.

My belly roars like a starved beast.

I sigh and, with effort, wrestle myself upright in the bed. The room is full of gloomy shadow, and so I switch on the lamp. I rest against a stack of pillows, considering what the universe has brought me, what the fates have put in my way. I taste the coffee. It's good. I look sidelong at the Danish. Then I lean over the edge of the bed, reach beneath, and, with a painful stretch, pull out my newly purchased book. It's a fairly pathetic scene. I sense as much. I see myself as if hovering above myself, like a puppet master trying to decide what to make his dummy do next.

How did I get here?

What have I become?

The framed photo of yester-me regards now-me with a condescending smirk. "What the hell are you looking at, punk?" I say, and then I turn him face down on the table.

The rest of the world moves on with its evolution. Tom Harvey is no doubt already managing property somewhere before heading downtown to chase a little tail. Madame Olga, after a nourishing breakfast of human bones, is practicing her leaps and twirls. Toby's mom is organizing her committee according to the skill sets of its various members who care about tomorrow's world. Jane is at work sorting legal matters with a client. Even Ava is in school, learning how to work well with others for the common good of humanity.

But me? Well, I'm just a truant little boy – a malingerer camped out in bed on a rainy morning, eating my pastry with a primitive gusto. I lick the sticky fingers on my one hand, while thumbing with the other through the erotic illustrations of *The First Modern Translation of the Kama Sutra.*

12

"WHAT do you think of that?"
Roxanne has just handed me a poster and is waiting with an expectant grin for my reaction. The poster is illustrated with the silhouette of a lone cowboy atop a plucky horse on a high bluff overlooking a valley dotted with cows. It says –

**Spend an evening with Acclaimed Novelist and
Cult Sensation**

**WILL KIRBY
as he reads from
WESTERN WIND
Saturday, 18 December, 7 p.m.
City Center Library
(Reception to follow reading.)**

My palms sweat in an instant; my heart begins to drum roll.

"Oh," I say.

"Do you like it?"

"Yes. It's... It's inspirational."

"I cleared it with the Head Office. We can use the auditorium. Everything's a go." Roxanne shimmies with glee. "It's so exciting. I can't *wait* to hear you read."

Distantly, from the parting fogs of my memory, I see myself months before talking with Roxanne about possibly doing a reading at the library this winter. I hear myself saying yes to certain dates. And now, horrified, I realize that this is the upshot of that seemingly benign conversation.

"I wanted to surprise you," she says.

She has.

"I've hung these posters in the best places all over town. I'm spreading the word. And I've posted a shout out on your fan page. It should be an awesome turnout."

If I were to die right now, I would be fine with that. I've always hated doing readings. I loathe the sound of my voice when I'm nervous and speaking before a group – a creepy mix of Adolf Hitler and Huckleberry Hound. Sure, it's an important part of the job, but not my favorite. And right now, I'm so caught off guard, so psychologically unprepared, that I feel a faint coming on. The blood has evacuated my brain. It's suddenly hard to breathe.

Impulsively, Roxanne gives me an enthusiastic hug. I swallow, and put one arm around her, holding on for dear life, lightly petting the small of her back. The poster is getting crunched between us. The embrace seems to last forever. I have time to think about Stromboli, about swimming with Roxanne in the amorous sea, about the Congress of the Cow.

When Roxanne finally pulls away, her glasses are askew. She is blushing. It's the strangest thing. I am astonished, while trying not to show it. But almost instantly, I'm sporting an erection. I feel it springing to life in my boxers.

I lower the poster over my front, and, like a maniac, sort of chuckle.

Roxanne readjusts her glasses. She smooths her skirt. Something bizarre is happening between us, something primal and, well, erotic.

Flustered, I can find no escape. Distracted, I can think of nothing intelligent to say. I can't help it, but I imagine Roxanne standing before me naked. I can't stop grinning.

Having already crossed certain lines of etiquette with an older man, Roxanne has become emboldened. I feel I'm glimpsing another side of her. She steps close and reaches up with both hands, placing the tips of her thumbs together on my forehead, and then wraps her palms along my temples, measuring my head. I find it unbearable. She doesn't bother to explain what she's doing, just prattles on in an oddly sexy voice about what a great evening it's going to be. "The event of the season." I am only distantly able to understand what the hell she's talking about. It's all gobbledygook in my head. I'm too preoccupied with my boner, and by how, when Roxanne leans toward me to measure the back of my head, her breasts smash ever so lightly against my ribs.

———————

Now there are certain aspects of life that are dictated by societal systems and customs. These, it is understood, are necessary for the smooth running of civilization. These are the rules and commandments taught to us as children by our teachers and parents. They're wired into us from the get-go. They're presented in Bible stories and hygiene films and the other morality tales anthologized in Dr. Seuss, Aesop's Fables, and even classic cartoons – those oblique mainstays of proper behavior.

But then, contrarily, there is that other more animal side of a human being. This is the part that causes a boy to fantasize about being a love slave for the Wild Women of Wongo. This is that secret part you read about in newspapers after it has risen up like a beast in the lives of evangelists and politicians wearing dark glasses and trench coats caught flashing teenage girls at the mall, or frolicking with hookers in seedy motels. This is the Mr. Hyde part of a man that cannot help but assess the sexual assets of every woman he passes on the street. It's that natural, God-given wiring in a man designed to propagate the species. (Women must surely have their equivalent urges.) Granted, society cannot run smoothly if these base tendencies are left unarrested. What then would be the difference between us and the beasts of the wild? How would we ever perform the business of the day? Economies would crumble. The Gross National Product would plummet. Infrastructures would collapse. But that doesn't mean these wild sides aren't there. They're simply held in check, hobbled like an ornery bull, herded together like a band of restless cattle. Still, in spite of our best intentions, they occasionally run amuck. Sometimes they rear their heads and, as it were, stampede.

———

I blame my near miss with Jane from last night. I blame my morning overdose of caffeine and sugar and the *Kama Sutra* for priming my virile pump. But right then, as Roxanne is sizing the girth of my head, that restrained and hidden animal part of me lets go in my shorts. I am experiencing an untimely wet waking dream the likes of which I haven't known since I was tossed upon the confusing sea of adolescence.

Roxanne steps away from me, just watching, a grin on her slightly parted lips.

My eyes cross and my vision blurs; I clench, relax, and clench and clench again. Although my mouth is clamped shut tight, a helpless whimper escapes through my nose.

Does this erogenous little advocate of the Dewey Decimal System have any idea what she has just done to me?

When I'm all played out, I just stand there, sort of hunched and quivering like a cur suffering from distemper.

It's incongruous, but my first lucid thought is of Ava, of her watching out the window for Pegasus, and of how I've somehow failed her. Then I think of Jane. Have I just cheated on my wife? And then I get angry. Defiant. I'm a man, goddammit! Although I'm too addled to know exactly what I mean by this declaration. It's as if some submerged part of me is coming to life and rising to this waking world, wanting to proclaim its existence.

"Well," says Roxanne. She's still grinning, but I can't read her look.

"Well," I say, and shrug like a dimwit.

She takes the poster and lays it on her desk, pressing out the wrinkles. "Are you doing research on the notebooks today?"

"Notebooks?"

"Banal," she laughs. "Are you here to work on your book?"

She obviously doesn't realize what's just happened.

"Oh... No. I just came..." I swallow and shake my head. "I mean, I just stopped by to say howdy."

"Oh," she says. "Nice." She reaches behind the desk and opens a drawer, pulling out a pink sticky note. "Before I forget." She hands me the note. "A bit of intrigue." She raises an eyebrow.

When I look at the paper, all I see is a telephone number. I turn it over, but there's nothing else. "What is it?"

"Mmm," says Roxanne. "You'll have to call the number and find out." She leans forward and whispers in the playful accent of a British agent. "But you must follow these instructions to a T – you must tell the person on the other end your name, and you must tell her that Roxanne has sent you her direction."

"Who is it?"

Roxanne places her finger to her lips. "Shhhh!" she says playfully, and peers suspiciously into the corners of the room. "You'll find out if you make the call. And I suggest very much that you do, Mr. Kirby. I suggest very much that you do."

My mind jumps all over the place. I can't imagine who it might be. But no. That's not entirely true. Some unreasonable part of me thinks – indeed, hopes – that the number is Martine's, that she has asked Roxanne to give it to me out of her shyness, like in the manner of high school girls working together on the project of fulfilling a secret crush. Why this would be the case is beyond my retarded grasp of probabilities. I casually fold the paper and slip it into my back pocket.

"Well," I say.

Can this moment get any more bizarre? I turn and pick up my computer from where it sits on the desk, and then I hold it with both hands in front of me.

"Okay, Roxanne. This is pretty exciting stuff. Thanks for your services... I mean, you know, about the reading and the posters and all."

"My pleasure," she says. She slides her glasses up higher onto her nose with a fingertip, and then flashes her green eyes through the oval windows housed within the horned rims.

By default, I say, I love you, but – thank God – not out loud.

And then, before I commit another more irrevocable faux pas, I walk quickly away, through all the many rows of books – past the poetry, the stale dictums, the overabundance of novels – out the front door into the face-slappingly fresh air and onto the long ramp of cement steps dropping to the street puddled with the perpetual winter rains.

13

"OKAY," I wheeze. "Maybe I couldn't... cross an ocean... full of mutant sea beasts... on this particular day."

I am clutching the side of the pool at The Muscle Factory, gasping. I had decided that swimming was probably the best workout for me today since I am too sore to engage in anything involving the unhindered forces of gravity. Buoyancy is key. But it turns out I can do little but bob around and move my aching limbs in a slow and spastic breaststroke. I am like a chubby, geriatric dugong in a sea of supple marlin.

The rest of the lap pool is a froth of flashing arms as the super-fit go about their routines. Crawls, butterflies, backstrokes. I used to be one of these merpeople. I used to tirelessly swim through wild rapids, a fearless grin on my face. I had gills. I was a completely superior river god, the veritable spawn of Aquaman.

Was that so long ago?

How did I become this floundering thing that I am?

I belch chlorinated bile with an essence of raspberry sweet-cheese Danish.

To say that I am disheartened is an understatement.

"Excuse me, sir. Do you need some help?"

It's a lank, young guy in a Speedo peering down at me from on high. He is wearing a black swim cap and goggles with those opaque tinfoil lenses that make him look like a sci-fi action figure. He has some cool pictogram tattooed on his chest, probably a secret emblem from the planet where he was manufactured. He no doubt dedicates long hours to shaving his body. Is he what I would be if I were young in this day and age? I'll bet I could have kicked his ass when in my prime.

"No." I smile. "Just taking a breather."

He nods, doubtful. "Well, the pool's pretty crowded today. Do you mind if I share this lane with you?"

The idea of sharing a lane with this streamlined cyborg is too depressing to contemplate. I've only swum three laps of my planned fifty, but, "Oh," I say. "I just finished up. It's all yours."

"Awesome," he says, and launches over my head into the pool. I don't bother to watch. Instead, I work my way to the ladder, heave myself out of the water, and limp to the showers.

"Dammit."

———

As I leave the locker room, I tell myself, okay, Kirby, you have two choices. One – you can lie down and die, or Two – you can try harder.

Honestly, lying down sounds very pleasant right now. I have a headache, and I keep nearly blacking out. But I chastise myself for my lapse in courage. After all, what would Richard Henry Banal do?

And that's when I spy Martine.

She is just leaving the building and heading out into the street. I only see her from behind, but I recognize the back of her head, and, of course, her derriere. I pause, not sure what to do. A subtle vitality surges through my being. In an instant, I am recharged. I reach into my back pocket and pull out the pink Post-it that Roxanne gave me at the library. I study the number on the paper, bite my lip, and then nod, scurrying out of the building after Martine.

My intention is not to catch her, but merely to get close enough to observe her. I want to see how she reacts when she is talking with me on her phone. Will she blush? Will she place that loose strand of hair behind her ear in that way she does with her middle finger? I'm looking for those telltale signs of her true intentions. Why I still think the number is even possibly Martine's is something I could never explain to a sane person. Let's just say that I devoutly believe in destiny and the great ironic and wisdom-driven gears powering the inexplicable plot of the cosmos. Or anyway, something like that.

I rush down the sidewalk, trying to get close to Martine. It's not easy to do. The girl moves fast, weaving her way among the horde of pedestrians. I have new respect for those gumshoes in old detective novels. Shadowing a suspect is harder than it sounds.

Finally, Martine has stopped at a crosswalk, waiting for the light to turn. I step behind a bus kiosk, pull out my phone, quickly tap in the number, and watch.

Pigeons flap over the street in slow motion.

Traffic moves by as if in a dream.

I hear the ringtone in my ear – once – twice – three times –

And then, on cue, Martine reaches into her coat pocket, pulls out her phone, and stares at it.

The ringing stops on the other end, and, magically, a voice says, "Hello?"

I watch as Martine places her phone to her ear.

I sense, distantly, that something is not quite right about this – the sequence is somehow out of whack. *Hello* should not come before her lips are to the mouthpiece, right? And yet, I'm too muddled to entirely understand what's happening. Have we perhaps entered some sort of peculiar sphere where time lapses back over onto itself like a wave lapping onto and onto a beach?

"Hello?" comes the voice again.

Maybe it's just the street noise, but Martine's voice sounds very different than I remember.

A long and confusing moment passes; I can't make myself respond.

Martine puts her phone back into her pocket.

The light turns green, and Martine crosses the street.

It occurs to me then that half the people in the city are either looking at a phone or holding one to the side of their head. I could be talking to any one of them.

"Is someone there?"

Martine disappears around a distant corner.

Shaken, I finally reply to the voice in my ear. "Oh, hello, are you there?"

"Yes. Who is this please?" The voice belongs to a mature woman. It has a faintly seductive scratch in it.

"This is Will Kirby." I gather my wits. "Roxanne at the City Center Library gave me your number. She said I should call."

"Oh, yes, Roxanne. Sweet girl. And did she tell you who I am?"

"No. To tell the truth, she was very secretive about it."

"Good for her." The woman laughs. "Well, Mr. Kirby, I understand you are writing a book about Richard Banal."

This jars me. Why would Roxanne give out my secret? "Yes," I confess. "I am."

"Well, if you would like, I think I might be able to help you with your research."

"Oh?" I try not to sound doubtful, but that's my first reaction. "And who, may I ask, are you?"

"My name is Hadley Allsworth," says the woman. "But my maiden name was Banal. Dick, you see, was my father."

––––––––

I used to have an infatuation with Suzy Salinger – the radio announcer from the weekly public radio program *Let's Talk Adventure*, the one who interviews all those risk-taking personalities – alpinists, astronauts, spelunkers. I had never actually seen a picture of Ms.

Salinger, but that didn't matter. I had managed to create a complete character in my imagination built from nothing but the sultry, intelligent voice I listened to every week over the airwaves. I was pretty certain that Suzy was blond, tall, had good posture, and was missing the ring finger on her left hand. This last detail, I reasoned, was a memento from her early days as a war correspondent. Shrapnel from a grenade had plucked a digit. This feature made her more real and singular somehow, more vulnerable and endearing. Anyway, this was the woman I saw in my mind every time I heard *Let's Talk Adventure*.

And then one day I was thumbing through a magazine and came across an article about my favorite radio presenter. It came complete with a photo. As I looked at that photo, I suffered a weird spasm between my temples. Something was at battle with something else in my inner being. Call it, Imagination versus Reality.

It turned out Ms. Salinger was not blond. She was not tall. She had the posture of a bowl of Jell-O. And she still possessed all ten of her fingers. In short, she had none of the characteristics I had given her. In fact, if I had to describe her physical appearance accurately, I would have to say she looked very much like the twin sister of none other than Elmer Fudd.

Now, standing in the street, my phone to my ear, having just heard that Richard Henry Banal had a daughter – that he might be somewhat different than I imagined him – I am suffering a similar spasm in my cerebral cortex.

I cannot speak.

I am speechless.

"Mr. Kirby? Are you there?"

"Erm."

"Perhaps we should meet some time so we can talk."

"Of course," I finally manage. "That would be wonderful."

Hadley Allsworth gives me her address and we set up an appointment to meet at her home to discuss her intrepid father.

I feel I am levitating a few inches above the sidewalk, slowly turning upside down. Not in that lovesick way of old romantic comedies, but more like I am leaving my body because I am dying.

"Well, Mr. Kirby, until then."

"Yes," I manage. "I look forward to meeting you."

And then she hangs up.

I return to my upright position. My heels settle back onto the sidewalk. I slip my phone into my pocket. I notice it is raining hard. Another one of those mysterious piles of horse manure is steaming in the street. People pass on all sides of me, surging like a tide of humanity engulfing a man-shaped island of personified bewilderment.

14

I am *not* an idiot.

At least, I'm pretty sure I'm not.

When I am clear-headed and objective – as I am now, while preparing dinner for my wife and daughter, who are due home any minute – I see very clearly that I am suffering from some sort of delusional-male-fantasy-arrested-development-personality-disorder-syndrome. Psychologists probably have an even more demeaning name for it. There might even be medication available. Something like Boyopine, or maybe Infantilismazan. Shock therapy is surely an option. Or a lobotomy. But I eschew all professional treatment and instead choose to self-administer a large dose of sober reasoning. To this end, I use that surefire method so often practiced by ancient philosophers, lonely cowboys, or astronauts who find their spaceship malfunctioning in orbit on the dark side of the moon. That is to say, I talk to myself. Sometimes it just helps to hear the argument out loud.

"You do still have the hots for Jane, don't you?"

"Absolutely!" I guffaw. "We go way back. She's an amazing

woman, an amazing mother. I mean, sure, she's become a little domineering, but I respect her opinion more than anyone I've ever known."

"And so, you don't have any desire to call it kaput with her, correct?"

"Shucks no! Not really."

"So, bub, what, exactly, are you hoping for?"

I feel myself blush. "Well," I say, "between you and me, I suppose I'm hoping for Jane to grant me some sort of temporary pardon from our marriage, or at least a little holiday. I guess I'm hoping for something like what the writer Jean-Paul Sartre enjoyed with his partner Simone de Beauvoir."

"Which was?"

"Well," I chuckle, "I read that Simone allowed Jean-Paul to have other lovers, that she even brought them home for him when she found some girl she thought he might enjoy in bed."

"So, you just want more humpy-humpy with the dames?"

"Oh, no! Gosh no! I mean, don't get me wrong, sure, more would be awesome. But I'm willing to be reasonable. I just crave, you know, variety and a little adventure, a break from the routine. I want to live life more like Dick Banal. He was quite a guy. I'd really like to get back to that more fancy-free way I was pre-Jane, maybe travel with Martine to some exotic place and... you know..."

I shrug.

"And would you be willing to allow the same for your wife? After all, what's fair for the bull is fair for the heifer. Would you let her hook up with someone like that cyborg from the pool today, maybe send them off on a holiday together with your blessing, maybe let her roll around for a while in the tangle of his hairless, well-toned limbs?"

An unsettling image flits in my head. I take a breath. "Well, it's different for a woman, isn't it? I mean, Jane's a mother. She's already satisfied her biological needs. To put it crudely, she's past her prime."

"And you're not?"

"Well..." I hold up my palms. "I may be older, but men are born with certain requirements. We're insatiable. It's just how we're put together. It's Nature's way. Survival of the species, and all that. It's nobody's fault. Besides, I doubt Jane really wants something like that anyway. I mean, anymore, I get the feeling she doesn't even like sex."

"Maybe it's just sex with *you* she doesn't like. Charley horses can throw ice water on a gal's passion, you know. What if you were young and lean and able to accomplish some of those circus tricks in the *Kama Sutra*?"

"Like in the old days." I think of the photo of my river guide self on the table beside our bed. "Like back when we first met."

"I bet the cyborg could fornicate on his head while juggling coconuts."

"Well, Jane and I have something more than that, don't we? Something deeper. We have years together, a bond. *And* we have Ava."

"So why ain't that enough?"

I don't have an immediate answer for myself; I'm momentarily confused as to whose side I'm on. I feel tricked. I set three dinner plates on the table and then look at them.

"Hey, you dope, I said, why isn't an enviably happy home life enough for you?"

I stare out the glass door to the balcony. It is streaked with rain. The lights of the city are glowing on the other side in an abstract blur. I murmur, "I don't know."

"You must realize that Martine probably farts too."

"What!?"

"I'm just saying, once you get to know her, she's probably much different than you imagine, and not the perfect French hottie of your adolescent dreams. She probably has disturbing, real-world flaws."

"Yes, of course. I know that. But she's so damn chic and lemony-scented. It's just hard to imagine what those flaws might be."

"That's because you're suffering from delusional-male-fantasy-arrested-development-personality-disorder-syndrome."

I snort in reply.

"Besides, you must realize, Martine has no interest in you whatsoever. You're timeworn and flabby, a male chauvinist in denial, and you have no attention-grabbing tattoos or piercings. What could a bozo like you possibly offer a girl like her?"

"I'm a man with life experience. That has to be appealing to any woman, especially one far away from her home. I could be her guide while she's here in a foreign land. She just needs to get to know me."

"An older man with a young girl is a bit too *Lolita*, don't you think?"

"We could be happy together."

"How would you feel if Ava got all hot and romantic with a senior citizen?"

I don't reply.

"Not to mention, you speak French like a duck."

"Now you're just being mean."

"I'm just being realistic."

"Well, I have my own ideas about realism."

"That's because you're suffering from delu..."

"Oh, shut up!"

"Who are you talking to?"

This last voice is different.

It's not mine, or, for that matter, mine.

It's Jane's.

I whirl around and there's my wife coming through the front door with Ava.

"Oh," I squeak. "You're home."

Jane is cradling a wet paper bag in her arms and is struggling to keep it from bursting apart. Ava is wearing her pink Ballet Princess backpack and carrying Jane's briefcase. Jane is also wearing an amused, if concerned, grin.

I rush over to help.

"Who are you talking to, Daddy?"

"Oh, feedle-dee," I reply, and just sort of flap my hands in the air and waggle my head like a deranged marionette. "Let me help you there. Come in. Come in." I take the bag from Jane and kiss her rain-dampened cheek without meeting her gaze. I put the bag on the counter.

The girls – a couple of lovely wet birds – shed their coats and shoes and various other soggy burdens.

"Dinner's all ready," I boast. I am especially proud of myself for having accomplished this heroic feat of domesticity. It surely makes up for my other evenings of grilled cheese sandwiches. But when I turn back around, I don't recognize happiness as the overriding expression on my wife's face. No. Instead I see confusion, disbelief, mixed with something verging on exasperation.

"Will!" she says.

"What?"

"Don't you remember our conversation from last night?"

I smile sheepishly and hunch my shoulders. I recall no conversation of any consequence.

"Daddy," says Ava. "We brought home Indian food from Shiva's."

And then I remember.

"Oh."

Since I've been so *busy* lately with my research and have therefore become so lame about getting supper ready, and because Jane and Ava were going to be late this evening anyway, we all decided that they should pick up some take-out on their way home.

Only I forgot.

"Well," I say, and try to smile. "Why can't we have both?"

Jane, unabashedly peeved, just shakes her head in disbelief, as if asking herself how the hell she ever let herself get saddled with such an idiot.

———

We gather around the dinner table, the perfect picture of familial bliss. One is reminded of a contemporary reworking of an old Norman Rockwell painting. Before us are open cartons of alu saag and naan and pakora alongside my offerings of quiche Lorraine and salade nicoise. I've poured pinot noir for me and Jane, and a glass of Perrier for Ava – what she calls "bubbly water." I have mousse au chocolat chilling in the fridge. I've decided to suspend my diet for the evening. After all, a man needs his strength.

"Why the French menu?" asks Jane.

"Oh." I reach for the naan, and tear a piece in two, dipping it into my food. "It just sounded tasty."

Jane nods, suspiciously, I think.

"It's good, Daddy." Ava has smeared a large dollop of curry onto her quiche and is devouring it with the indiscriminate enthusiasm of a half-starved ballerina.

"So, how was everyone's day?" I ask.

"Toby's mom asked Mom to join her club for People Who Care About The World Tomorrow."

I look at Jane. "Are you going to do it?"

Jane nods. "It's certainly a good cause. And I think I can help them work out some of their issues. I was wondering..." She winces at some ethnically incompatible flavor explosion happening on her tongue. "I was wondering if you wouldn't want to help them with their writing. They need copy for fliers and blogs, and maybe you could even write an essay on imbalances in Nature and climate change, or something."

"Dad only writes *friction*, Mom. Some people think cowboy stories tell the truth better than the friggin' truth." Ava smiles at me, and winks.

I grow warm.

"Of course, honey." Jane shoots me a what-the-hell-are-you-teaching-our-daughter look. "But this might lead to some good opportunities for your father. And I'm not asking him to give up his other projects."

Jane has always been supportive of my so-called career. She's suffered through our many lean years, eventually getting herself a real job to keep us financially afloat, forever assuring me that it's worth my while to keep at it even when the world doesn't seem to give a damn. But there's something new in her tone this evening, a subtext, something suggestive of pity. Am I imagining this? Or am I just feeling insecure because my Banal project is moving so slowly?

"I just think Daddy might be spending too much time alone," continues Jane. "This might be a chance for him to get out in the world, make some friends, and work with other people toward something that's truly worthwhile. Maybe it would give him a broader perspective."

Worthwhile! I think. *Perspective!* So, suddenly what I do lacks perspective and isn't worthwhile!

"Well, I'm pretty busy," I say. This sounds unconvincing. I gulp some wine and clear my throat. "I've uncovered some new information about Richard Banal that could lead to a real breakthrough."

Jane nods, forks a bit of *pakora* onto her plate. "Wonderful."

I consider telling the girls about my upcoming reading at the library, just to earn myself a few brownie points in the credibility department, but I am still halfway hoping to get out of that obligation so I don't say anything.

We chew our culturally mismatched meal.

The rain dumps onto the city outside.

"I made reservations for our trip today," says Jane. "We'll be staying at a hotel right near the auditorium."

"Great!" I pour myself some more wine. I have absolutely no idea what trip Jane is talking about, but I am hoping that she will give me clues that will jog my memory, so I won't have to reveal my ignorance.

"I thought we'd take the train. Might as well leave the car home and support public transportation."

"I like trains," says Ava.

I gulp wine.

Ava leans over to her mother and whispers, "Should I tell him my surprise now?"

"Yes."

"Daddy..." Ava is suddenly shy; her cheeks turn endearingly pink; her voice is soft. "Today at ballet Madame Olga chose which one of us dancers gets to be the Blue Star in the production. And anyway..." Ava shrugs. "She chose me!"

I sense that this is a good thing and say, "Wow!" She reaches over and we lace our fingers together, giving our hands a little shake. "Good job!"

"It's quite an honor," says Jane. "Madame told me that Ava has worked harder than anyone and is the most deserving girl in the class."

"Can I show Dad my light?"

"Of course."

Ava pushes away from the table and scampers over to her backpack, pulling out a tiara that she scrunches down onto her head. "You and Mom need to sit on the couch."

Jane and I do as we are told.

Ava turns out the lights around the apartment, and then stands on the far side of the room in silhouette against the glass doors. "Turn on the music, Mom."

Jane taps a button on her phone and sets it on the coffee table. A tinny little orchestra plays Tchaikovsky. When the ensemble finishes its brief overture, Ava reaches up and flips a switch on her tiara, causing a blue light to flicker to life atop her head. Ava twirls and leaps. She moves this way and that, dipping and swaying. The blue light blazes like a star marking a trail through the darkened galaxy of our home.

This is not the Bolshoi Ballet. Far from it. It is just an eager little girl dancing awkwardly for her parents. But for some reason I find it more beautiful than anything I've seen in my life. A lump forms in my throat. No doubt I am suffering from a severe case of parental pride. A whole sea full of confused emotions tosses inside of me. The macrocosmic world beyond our microcosmic living room is surely oblivious to this magical epiphany of nymphet elegance, this pure example of unadulterated innocence and loveliness. It is for us alone. Nothing else matters. We are abruptly happy. Content.

Jane takes my hand, and we watch our daughter – our most sublime joint venture – dance, come to a balanced halt before us, and curtsy.

The music stops.

The blue light goes out.

The sound of rain pours down beyond the windows.

Our little girl skips over and flips on the lights. A big smile on her face. She bows again and laughs as Jane and I clap and shout, "Bravo!" Then Ava squeezes in between us on the couch, accepting our hugs and kisses.

My eyes are misted over with fatherly love and adoration.

———

After we eat our mousse, I put Ava to bed. It's too late for *Ivan's Island*, leaving that unfortunate rodent to suffer through another lonely night in his gloomy circumstances.

"I don't remember a Blue Star in *The Nutcracker*," I say, as I come into our bedroom.

Jane is already under the covers. She is smiling. "It's sort of a new interpretation."

"I didn't think anyone ever dared to rewrite that particular bastion of Christmas tradition."

"We live in a brave new world."

It's nice to see my wife happy. Our daughter has made her that way. I take off my shoes.

"So, my little Bodhisattva," says Jane, "what's this?"

When I turn around, Jane is holding up my *Kama Sutra*.

I feel like I did as a kid when my mom found my stash of *Playboy* magazines. "Oh, that." I feign nonchalance. "Believe it or not, that's research."

Jane arches an eyebrow. "Hmm," she says, and grins. She thumbs through the pages. "Interesting."

"Yeah. Banal mentions it in his journals, so I thought I better take a look."

Jane studies the ancient text of sexual positions. "God," she says, and pulls a face. "Some of these circus tricks could only be imagined in the land of yoga."

I smile self-consciously, standing next to the bed. I guess I'm a little embarrassed.

"What's so special about this one?" Jane holds up the book to the page where I have placed Tom Harvey's business card as a bookmark.

I shrug and shake my head.

"Congress of the Cow," says Jane. "Hmm." She looks at me. "Well, maybe I could help you with your research. Besides, didn't you fail to reach Nirvana our last go round?" She gives me what's supposed to be a sexy look, but she can't hide her amusement, and so it comes across sort of comical and slightly patronizing. "Shall we give it a try?"

That the U.S.S. *Marital Intercourse* has so soon returned to port is almost unfathomable to me. Sometimes it's out stranded in the doldrums for weeks on end. That Jane wants to leave the sidelight on so we can see the pictures in the book while we do it is also intriguingly kinky and unbelievable.

"Just lock the door," she says.

I do what I'm told, and then quick get undressed.

"Do you think you can do this Cow Congress thing," she asks, "without going into one of your seizures?"

"Absolutely!" I reply. "Mroooo!"

———

Now most people would agree that the sexual act, when performed as Nature intended, is a team sport. They would argue that it takes at least two partners – traditionally a male and a female – both working in tandem toward a common goal. I agree with this, generally. But what I don't think women appreciate is that it also takes a certain amount of teamwork between a man and his penis. One is pretty worthless without the complete participation of the other. As a consequence, a twosome is, in reality, a threesome.

I'm doing my part, showing up for the game, so to speak, and Jane is doing hers, but Ol' Sputnik (Don't we all have clever names for our sidekicks?) seems to have aborted the mission.

"What the hell?" I mutter.

I grit my teeth and try harder. But there's Me, and there's Sputnik, and I seem to be the only one interested.

Jane is valiant, kind, patient, but after a while, even she gives up. She rolls over and sighs. "Everything all right?"

"I don't know." I stare at the pillows. "Maybe I just had too much wine."

"Well," she pats my thigh. "At least we know your electrolytes are okay."

I know this is supposed to be a good-natured joke, something to lighten the mood and alleviate my frustration, but it doesn't work that way on my ego.

Jane yawns and takes up the *Kama Sutra*, flipping through the pages. All the men in the illustrations seem to have members the size and rigidity of two-by-fours.

"I'm sorry," I say.

"We'll try again some other time." She yawns. "It's no big deal."

A man who is suffering whiskey dick, while his wife studies photos of well-endowed sex acrobats, does not like to hear the phrase – "no big deal." It smacks of a Freudian slip. It resounds of double entendre, as if she's referring to the inadequately equipped and limply flopping machinery of my manhood.

I seem to remember being able to go at it all night long. Was that so long ago? I used to be – to employ a masculine metaphor – a well-oiled six-shooter. But now my tool is more like one of those quaint cap-and-ball single shot pistols from the days of yore, the kind you see in old pirate movies, the kind that takes a while to reload after it has been fired. I blame my earlier encounter with Roxanne for this unfortunate evening. My misfire at the library is surely behind my physiological inability to impress now. That feels just a little bit pitiful. I know there are pills for this problem. I've seen the advertisements featuring the swaggering, medicated, silver-haired man walking hand-in-hand on the beach with his smiling, dazed, and superbly satisfied helpmate. But to go that route would be to admit something that I'm not yet willing to admit. No, gosh dang it! I can do this. I can.

I glance over at the old photo of perfect me in the days of yore – that supercilious smirk, those perfect muscles, that full head of sun-bleached hair. That kid sure never knew this problem.

I peek down at my fellow traveler.

Dang it!

Jane closes her book, turns out the light, and snuggles down under the covers. I'm lying on my back, watching the dark ceiling. My wife searches for my hand under the blankets and pats my fingers. We listen to the rain beat against the window.

"Who's Martine?" asks Jane.

My heart leaps like a fish. "What?"

"Last night you were talking in your sleep. You very distinctly said the name Martine."

"I did?"

"Uh-huh. Someone you know?"

"No."

"Well, she was making you very happy. It was pretty hilarious listening to you laugh like that in your sleep."

"Oh, that's funny." I swallow. "I can't think who it might be."

"Hmm."

"Oh, hold it," I say. "Wait. Yeah. There is someone – a girl at the library. I think her name might be Martine. But I don't really know her."

"Is she pretty?"

"I guess so, to a certain kind of guy. I think she has a lip ring."

"Well, you sure seemed like old chums in your dreams. Is she French?"

"Maybe."

"It sounded like you were trying to speak French to her."

"Oh. Heh-heh. Funny."

"Martine's a French name, isn't it?"

"I don't know. Maybe it's Czech, or something."

Jane laughs. "Sounds pretty French to me."

"Yeah," I say. "Probably."

Jane leans over and gives me a peck on the cheek. "Sweet dreams."

"Uh-huh."

She adjusts her pillow and rolls over with her back to me. "*Bonne nuit, mon mari.*"

"Yeah," I say. "Good night."

Jane is asleep almost at once. But not me. I don't dare let myself slide into some sort of self-incriminating, imbecilic, sleep-talk mode. Instead, I lie there with my eyes wide open to the darkness, insecure, thinking about Ava's dance, thinking of Martine, thinking of Jane, and going mad with all the frustration and guilt of a man having an illicit liaison without enjoying any of its more savory rewards.

15

UNDENIABLY, I am in a rut. I am a man on a treadmill moving through the same motions as yesterday, and the day before that, and before that, as far back as that foggy portal between a more favorable way I was, and this depreciated character I have become. I rise from my bed, dress, eat an all-too-familiar piece of toast, drink a habitual cup of coffee, gather my kit, and take the elevator downstairs. I leave our building and step onto the sidewalk where it is inevitably raining. I plod the thirteen blocks to the City Central Library, following the same route, day after boring day. Nothing changes. I have time to ruminate. In the course of my walk, I am afforded the leisure to envision more adventurous alternatives to this monotony in which I feel trapped. Is it any wonder I am hounded by fanciful daydreams, that I all but sink into an altered idea of reality?

As I move closer to downtown, I merge with the throngs of other automatons shuffling along in their own private ruts. We all intermingle like the squiggly emasculated splotches of a Jackson Pollock painting. Of course, there are women too, but it's my fellow men who make me most curious. How many of them are happy with their civilized lives? How many are fulfilled? And how many are like me? This everyguy passing here, for instance – clean-shaven, sharply dressed, a roll of dough hanging over his belt, and a submerged anxiety apparent in his somewhat waddling gait – did he have failed sex with his wife last night? Does he have a girl on the side? Has he ever chopped down a tree, swum across an ocean, or killed an evil adversary with his bare hands? Or, like me, does he only just dream about such heroic acts of manliness?

Many years ago, in my river guide days, I used to take fellows like him on weeklong trips through the wilderness. It was amusing to watch them transform from timid, sunscreen-slathered urbanites into bare-chested he-men howling at the moon. All in the course of a few days. It was as if the many chains of society – the well-honed manners, the repression, the quiet desperation – all magically washed away with every splash of the river's rejuvenating waters. A progressive devolution occurred, a speedy return to that thing primitive held seething and caged in the depths of every man's secret soul.

Thus, my fascination with Banal; he was able to cast off society's strictures. He was able to exercise his manhood with a grace and bravado that I crave. I want to know how he did it. I want to model myself after this heroic, charismatic figure who was so capable of stylishly embracing taboo. I recognize that it is a boyish idolatry, but I *want* to *be* like *Dick*. I long to smash my cell phone, rend my clothes, and sail away to the sun-washed shores of Oblivia.

But then – goddammit! – I think of my wife and daughter.

I recall Ava's Blue Star dance last night and the whelming pride and tenderness I feel for her. I remember my long history with Jane, the many hurdles we've overcome as a team in the course of our married life. These are important things. I'm smart enough to know this. Surely, I am. They're not something to just throw away on impulse. In my more lucid moments, I understand that I have something very worthwhile to preserve and protect. I have love, and a fruition of that love. Is it as fragile as I fear? Am I so capable of being an idiot? Will my fairytale daydreams torture me to distraction, overcome me, and finally lead me down a rabbit hole of irrevocable folly?

(And just how far is irrevocable, anyway?)

I stop at the steps leading up to the great doors of the library.

The rain comes down cold on my head; it runs down my collar.

I know that either Martine or Roxanne is waiting beyond the threshold. I know that Martine will be aloofly chic and smell tantalizingly of sweet lemons, or that Roxanne's breasts will somehow find a way to invade my personal space and solicit from me something that I am all too willing to offer up. Either way, I know that this morning I am so teetering on the edge of civilized sanity that either one of those femme fatale intrusions is enough to plunge me into an unadulterated state of Mr. Hyde-like primality. So tenuous is my grasp on realism. So precarious is my ability to reconcile my will with my self.

I wipe the rain from my face.

I feel an ever-widening black hole opening up beneath me. Hideous beasts lurk therein.

And then, with the last of my waning intelligence and fortitude, I turn on my heel and deliberately walk away.

Then I break into a run.

As if I'm being pursued.

I don't care what the people around me might think. On some level, they probably understand.

I run and run, past the men and women – the automatons and the automatines – all the way to The Muscle Factory, where I hope to escape my frustration through physical exertion.

I plug myself in and run for half an hour, and then another, lumbering along in my shambling stride, chasing after something while simultaneously fleeing something else. My feet pound a rhythm that coincides with a techno jungle beat thumping over the whir and beep of my state-of-the-art stainless-steel treadmill.

16

WHEN I'm finished at the gym, I take the bus home. I'm too spent to haul my sorry ass all the way up the hill to our building. Besides, my knee joints are creaking, and I think I've developed bunions. I dare not pass the library for fear it will suck me into its siren-populated, brain-erasing maw. And anyway, annoyingly, I keep almost passing out.

Stars drift across my vision.

I can't stop sweating.

"No quick moves, Kirby. Steady as she goes."

When I stand to get off the bus, I have to hold onto the rail for a moment while everything wanes to darkness... like an iris-fade in an old movie... before the gray world brightens and more-or-less comes back into focus.

Maybe I've been overdoing it at the gym, but how am I supposed to reach my physically superior state of being if I don't kick it in gear and replace this belly fat with some seriously lean muscle mass?

Maybe I'm just coming down with a bug, or just didn't get enough sleep.

I warily ease myself from the bus and step onto the wet sidewalk.
The door closes behind me.

The bus hisses and rumbles away.

It feels like someone has switched on a tiny vacuum inside my
head.

———————

The apartment is chilly. I go to the bedroom, undress, towel off
my damp, shivering body, and then put on some different clothes.

I go to the kitchen and nibble on some pumpkin seeds. (They're
said to bolster a man's libido.)

Then I go to the bookshelf and find *Western Wind*. I turn on the
reading light, stretch myself out on the couch under an afghan, and
open up to the first page. My intention is to forget Banal for a while
and spend the afternoon practicing for my upcoming reading gig on
the eighteenth.

I've quoted an old poem in my novel's opening. It's one that a
lot of great writers have used over the years – Virginia Woolf, Brian
Kindall. I think Hemingway even alluded to it in *A Farewell to Arms*.
It's by our old friend Anonymous, and now, even after all these
intervening centuries, it is still decidedly perfect in its tone and
nuance. Attaching it to one's work is merely a way to hopefully – in
the parasitic manner of a talentless leech – become connected with
that enduring, pre-digital era perfection.

I lick my lips, clear my throat, and read –

> *"Western wind, when wilt thou blow*
> *The small rain down doth rain*
> *Christ, that my love were in my arms*
> *And I in my bed again"*

I stare at the words – those magical little glyphs so full of
nostalgia and latent emotion. They fall out of order as I'm watching.

They swim before my eyes, scattering, regrouping, as if I'm zooming into the depths of the galaxy as my space capsule reaches warp speed.

And that's as far as I get.

The g-forces are too much for me.

An unexpected tightness squeezes between my ears and I begin, rather uncontrollably, to sob. I am at a loss.

The rain beats at the glass doors.

Over it all, I hear the soggy, flapping wings of a patiently patrolling owl.

I close my book.

Everything goes black.

———

Next thing I know, I am being shaken back to life with small hands.

A Mack truck is parked on my forehead.

"Daddy?" someone says, as if from over a wide body of water. "Daddy?"

Her voice is distant birdsong.

My eyes flutter open and there is Ava, leaning in close. She smiles angelically and pats me lovingly with her fingers. "Daddy, supper's ready."

Sure enough, I know by the familiar indicators that it's true.

The apartment is made claustrophobic with the oppressive air of my ineptitude.

The room is filled with the ominous, nauseating, and yet slightly reassuring odors of grilled bread, burnt butter, and cheddar cheese.

17

A few days later, once I've recharged my courage battery, I push through the front doors of the library. I am greeted by the oppressive potpourri of polished marble, hot reading lamps, and moldering paper. But also, stirred into the mix – the faint and heady scent of lemons. Even as I boldly stalk between the bookshelves, my simmering animal senses tell me that Martine is in the vicinity.

I mutter to myself, "Okay, Kirby, forget it. Get real, get focused, and grow the hell up."

My unreciprocated preoccupation with Martine is obviously inflicting chaos into my life. I'm losing sleep; I'm not getting any work done; I'm alienating my wife and daughter. I've developed a severe case of selective amnesia. On top of that, I seem to be on the verge of some sort of nervous breakdown.

And for what? A pipe dream? A juvenile whimsy?

But no more. This whole male fantasy thing has got to stop.

"Today!"

I suck breath through my teeth.

(The zesty, airborne flavor of Martine's skin settles lightly on my tongue.)

I resolutely step around the corner and...

... it's as if the clouds have parted and the sky has abruptly – wondrously – turned blue.

Martine greets me with a sunny smile as I mosey over to her desk.

"*Bonjour,* Will."

(She remembers my name!)

"Hi, Martine." My voice is surprisingly confident and suave. I sound like Steve McQueen. "How are you today?"

"*Bien.*" She places a loose strand of hair behind her ear with a middle finger. "How are you?"

"Good."

All of my previous resolve melts away like a snowball tossed into a blast furnace. Never in my life do I remember having a more stimulating and enjoyable conversation. I'm cool as a cucumber. My knees quit hurting. My bald spot sprouts hair. I feel handsome. I am aware of the cosmic round, of the stars shuffling into place on my behalf. I hear orbiting asteroids, singing whales, glaciers calving at the polar ice caps.

Then my phone dings in my pocket; I ignore it.

Next, Martine does something that surprises me. She holds up the book she has on her desk and tells me, "Roxanne gives me your *Western Wind* for to read." Her fingers wrapped around my novel makes for the most sensual and evocative image I have ever beheld.

"Oh!" I say. "Excellent!"

"It is very good," she tells me.

"Thank you. I'm glad you like it. How far along are you?"

In answer, she opens up the book and begins to read – "*The sun beat down hot and merciless on the plain. Vultures circled in the jaundiced sky. Buck dropped to his knees in the dirt behind the heifer. He hung his hat on a sagebrush, rolled up his sleeves, and wiped the sweat from his brow. The cow was sprawled on her side and lowing mournfully, obviously suffering. A pair of small black hooves stuck out her backside, but the calf was twisted and not coming out the way Nature intended.*

"'*Well, ol' girl," said the weary cowboy. "Looks like you could use a hand.'"*

Martine closes the book. "How do you know birth?"

"Oh," I shrug.

An image flashes in my head – the scene of Jane delivering Ava in homebirth. Snowflakes are falling past the windows. Candles are burning. The midwife is humming serenely while damping Jane's brow with a cool cloth. I am positioned between my wife's spread-open legs, as if kneeling at an altar, or tending the controls of some weird spaceship, preparing myself psychologically for what is known as *catching the baby*. We are poised on the brink of that moment from which all involved can never return unchanged.

"Oh," I tell Martine, and shake the scene from my head. "I just did a little deep research."

She nods.

I gaze into her eyes.

A solar flare plumes from the surface of the sun.

My phone dings again and I pull it out of my pocket and turn it off without looking at it. "Sorry," I say. "I hate these dumb things."

"Would you write for me in your book?" asks Martine.

"You mean sign it?"

She hands me the book and nods demurely. "*S'il vous plâit.*"

"Of course. My pleasure."

I recognize this as an opportunity proffered me by the fates. Would that I could take the book away with me, spend some time, and compose a flowing, perfect poem full of innuendos and invitations for this lovely young girl for whom I would gladly do battle with dragons. But that's not the situation, and so I decide, instead, to call on my inner Zag. I feel, through poring over his notebooks, that Banal's chivalrous and undaunted talents have permeated my being like a drug. I'm almost sure of it. Perhaps his very own soul has reincarnated itself in me. I need only trust that it is so. I need only allow myself to be a conduit for his manly eloquence.

Martine gives me her seat and offers me a pen.

I sit at her desk. Her lingering warmth soaks into the back of my thighs, charging me with bonus power. I flip open the novel to the title page, and, wholly giving myself over to unseen forces, begin to write.

> *Martine –*
> *As the small rain down doth rain, I drive my pen to ecstatic paroxysms of fanciful passion, inspired by you, O, gentle guardian of spiral-bound sutras, O, blue-eyed keeper of secrets held captive within the most private pith of my fondest desiring. Thank you for the purpose you serve in my work and striving. You can never know how much you mean.*
> *Will Kirby*

I don't reread it; I don't dare.

I am riding a wave, after all, trusting that my Anonymous-meets-Valentino-meets-Zag gush of spontaneity might somehow speak to Martine on a deeper level, while hopefully not scaring the bejeebies out of her.

Fortune, I remind myself, favors the bold.

I return the book with a smile.

She opens it to the inscription. Her lips move as she silently reads.

I am hoping, indeed praying, that my words are working like primordial jazz, penetrating to the feminine seat of Martine's solar plexus and lodging there like a seed with the power of an oblique, musical nonsense that will ultimately bloom in her dreams and stir her inner cave girl to a passion. She is French, after all, from that land of flowery poésie. Surely, if anyone is susceptible to such poetic flights of fancy, it is this lovely demoiselle standing before me. I remind myself that any complete man must be master of two languages, the monosyllabic one he speaks with his fellows – that macho jargon full of curses and grunts – and that other more tender patois he reserves for talking privately to his lady friends – what Banal might have whispered when joining with lovely Indira in the

Congress of the Cow. It is this latter variety I hope to have employed in my inscription.

Martine closes the book and studies me curiously. At first, I find it impossible to read her look. She is sort of smiling, sort of not. Is she alarmed, or intrigued?

Then she laughs softly, and I sense that something has shifted between us; we have grown more familiar; we are on our way to becoming fast friends.

"Ecstatic paroxysms," she mumbles with a grin.

The words roll in her mouth like fruit.

18

SO bolstered am I by my latest interaction with Martine that I allow my derring-do to run free and go all out rogue. Of course, I'm only acting the way any self-respecting real man should be acting in the first place. These are not unreasonable aspirations you're entertaining, I assure myself. This is merely genuine masculinity in action – that same marvelous manliness of the insuperable Dick Banal.

You can do this, I tell myself. You are perfectly designed for living two lives at once.

Martine has reminded me that I am invincible.

I stride through the city, laughing at the rain.

"Hell, Kirby! It's not too late. A man like you can live as many lives as he wants!"

Granted, the logistics might appear contrary to this notion. After all, I'm no spring chicken. And my family-man status is obviously a major impediment to my otherwise glorious ambitions. But I look at my developing clandestine identity the way a spy might look at his secret cover. Through it I will dwell simultaneously on two separate planes as I walk through two different spheres of existence, two simultaneous dimensions. Sure, I may be a touch delusional, but I figure it's this very ability to stifle my doubts and ignore reality that separates me from all these other impotent, robotic schmucks walking down the street beside me. I'm more daring than they are. More courageous. And because of this, the rewards will be greater.

Yes, yes, true enough, there are a few complications to work out. But I'm not concentrating on those particular glitches right now. I'm charging forward. I'm thinking, instead, about brushing up on my French. I'm thinking about taking up deer hunting. And I'm trying to decide on the all-important issue of whether to get a tattoo that says Wild One, or maybe an image of a topless mermaid.

"Shoot!" I laugh. "You've got two arms, my man, why not get one on each biceps?"

While I'm at it, maybe it's time to come up with a catchy penname to use for the many cool books I plan to produce. Something like Zag, only with a little more edge to it.

Maybe I'll ask Martine what she thinks.

But first I'm off to The Muscle Factory for a kickboxing class. I need to get myself in top-notch shape. After all, a man never knows when he might be called upon to kick some serious ass.

19

CLASS went remarkably well. I'm no Bruce Lee, but at least I seem to have moved past my muscle soreness. I might finally be whipping myself into shape. I was able to kick and punch the heavy bag without throwing up, passing out, or sprouting a hernia. That's progress. It was even kind of fun. I'm rather proud of myself. No doubt Martine has me energized.

Now I'm home sprawled on the couch, nursing a couple of well-earned bottles of beer (Only wussies count their carbs.), while studying Ultimate Fighting videos on YouTube. I'm hoping to pick up a few tricks from the masters. This particular video is called *The Great Cage Fight Rallies.*

On my computer screen is a muscled-up fighter by the name of Lester Jinks. He has just sprung into the air and thrown his legs around his opponent's neck, driving the poor man's head into the mat like a ballpeen hammer. Conk! Now Jinks has him in a vice hold, locking his ankles and squeezing the other man's head between his knees like a pecan in a nutcracker. The camera moves in for a closer shot of the action. Jinks' victim – one Kyle Tull – is turning purple in the face. His eyes are popping.

I was in a couple fisticuffs on the playground when I was a kid – got a fat lip once, and a black eye – but they were nothing compared to this. I open a third beer, take a couple swigs, and lean in closer to the screen. "Yikes!"

Tull has the look of a man about to meet his maker. But before he does, Jane rattles into the apartment with Ava.

I kill the volume and then stand to greet my roommates. It takes all of one eye blink for me to see that something's wrong. Ava's cheeks are smeared with tears. Jane, on the other hand, looks like... well, it strikes me that she looks curiously like a cage fighter, albeit one in a skirt and heels. She is clenching her jaw.

That's when it occurs to me that I have inadvertently assumed my purest oblivious-male pose – sock-footed, a half-consumed beer in one hand while scratching my belly with the other. I can't help myself; I frown like a gomer and ask, "What's up?"

Jane slams her briefcase on the counter and stares at me, seething.

I redirect my attention to Ava and shrug, wordlessly asking her what's bitten her mother on the ass.

Ava juts her mouth into a pout and then, after quickly shucking her coat and boots, she scurries over and hops onto the couch, drawing up her knees and hugging them to her chest. She utters a single, pitiful sob.

Jane glares at me, but then her gaze drops, and she holds up her palms and points near my knees. "Jesus, Will!"

I am utterly baffled. So many threats are coming at me at once. I feel like a pet dog who has done something heinous – maybe rolled in a dead fish, or possibly despoiled the neighbor's purebred bitch with my mongrel bloodline – but I don't really understand what my crime is, or why I'm being whipped.

Jane points more forcefully toward my knees.

When I look down, I see Ava has her eyes fixed in horror on my computer screen.

Alas, the tide has turned for Lester Jinks!

Somehow, while I was distracted by Jane's fury, Tull has managed to squirm out of Jinks' death hold and has taken the advantage over his rival. Jinks is now flat on his back with Tull astraddle his chest and pummeling him about the head. A bombardment of fists is raining down on the now grotesquely distorted face of Lester Jinks. Blood geysers from his nose, splattering across the mat with each of Tull's driving blows. Both men are drenched in gore. Jinks' mouth guard goes skittering across the mat. The referee is struggling in vain to pry Tull off Jinks before he kills him. Droplets of blood spray over the lens of the camera capturing all of this gritty action. It is very vivid and fascinating, and yet probably *not* appropriate entertainment for an eight-year-old ballerina.

I understand this and move to intercede, but because things are not going quite badly enough for me right now, I drop my beer.

My first reaction is to lurch forward and try to catch it, but in my slightly inebriated state, I arrive minutes late. The bottle hits the table and explodes into a burst of shard-laced suds.

Then I step on some glass.

"#*∧`!"

By now, Jane has leapt across the room and closed my computer, so Ava won't have to endure any more carnage.

I hop on one foot a time or two, and then fall to my butt on the floor, squeezing my lacerated heel in both hands. My sock rapidly fills with blood.

Ava stares at me, horrified. No doubt this is exactly the kind of repressed, traumatic moment for which she will someday need therapy. She appears on the verge of a scream.

Jane – now posing as Wonder Woman – leaps back to the kitchen counter, grabs a dishtowel, and before my sock reaches saturation point and drips blood all over the rug, she rips it off and has my foot wrapped up tight with a field dressing. She's like a friggin' war zone medic!

"Thanks," I grunt.

Jane rather forcefully lifts my bandaged foot and then indelicately drops it on a cushion she has pulled from the couch. "Just keep it elevated. And *don't* bleed on anything!" There is absolutely zero tenderness in her voice. "I'll go get the car."

Jane leaves me alone with Ava.

I'm on the floor on my backside, propped up on my elbows, my head spinning, suffering from psychological whiplash. How do things change direction so fast?

My little girl sits on the edge of the couch with her hands folded in her lap.

Rain doth lash down against the glass doors across the room.

I try to smile, but it comes off as a grimace.

"So," I shrug. "How was your day?"

20

EIGHT stitches later, we've all returned home from the Emergency Room.

I am back on the couch with my bandaged heel propped up on a pillow.

Jane is kneeling before me, plucking slivers of glass out of the carpet and scrubbing at the beer stain with a rag and some kind of squirt-bottle cleanser. She carries a handful of brown shards to the kitchen and dumps it tinkling into the trashcan under the sink.

Tension hangs over our heads like a cloud of nuclear fallout.

Ava is silently orbiting on the perimeter, watching her parents from a safe distance.

"Honey," says Jane. "Why don't you go take a warm bath and then get into your pajamas while I make supper?"

"Okay." Ava's voice is weak and quavering. She is still traumatized. She goes to the bathroom and soon I hear the sound of water running into the tub.

My wife and I are left alone.

The local anesthesia has worn off, and the beer, and my foot hurts like hell. My dignity, too, is badly bruised and throbbing. To my memory, I've never felt more worthless and reprehensible than I do right now.

But hang on, it gets worse.

Jane sits in the armchair across from me and then leans back with her elbows on the armrests, tapping her fingertips together, regarding me. I can't decide if the look in her eye is more like that of an owl studying a wounded mouse, or a KGB agent about to extract my toenails as punishment for my many crimes against the state.

I wait.

"So," she finally says. "Don't you ever check your phone?"

"My phone?"

Jane nods.

When it becomes obvious that she's not simply going to explain what she's talking about, I reach into my pocket and pull out my phone. I tap the screen, let it identify my hangdog face, and then watch as the long list of missed calls and text messages materializes before my eyes. All of them appear to be from Jane. Sweat droplets form behind my ears along the edge of my scalp as I suspect these are not merely love notes from an adoring sweetheart.

Jane says nothing, putting me through the excruciating process of checking her communications.

Message number one reads – *Will, you'll have to get Ava from ballet. We're having a crisis here at work and I can't get away.*

Message number two reads – *Will! Please call me! ASAP!*

Message number three reads – *Mayday! Mayday!*

There's no reason to read further or listen to those messages she tried leaving in my voicemail. No doubt they only escalate in intensity and impatience as Jane pleads for me to take on the mantle of parenthood. I sigh and then look sheepishly at my wife. "Sorry. I must have turned it off at the library so it wouldn't bother anyone."

"Well, they're fairly worthless if you never look at them."

I recall then – like a distantly remembered dream – the ding of my phone as I was channeling Steve McQueen at the library; I recall ignoring it; I recall turning off the phone without even looking at it as I chatted with Martine about the birthing scene in *Western Wind.*

My guilt deflates me. "So..." I swallow. "What happened?"

"Well, I foolishly thought you'd get back to me, so I waited too long to get ahold of any of the other mothers before they left the dance studio. I had to call and ask Madame Olga to bring Ava by the office, which she couldn't do until she had finished teaching her last class." Jane glares at me, eyes narrowed. "A damn awkward situation." Her voice is measured, controlled, like that of a prosecutor about to convict a deadbeat dad for the deplorable offense of unreliability. "I don't appreciate it, Will. And I'm sure Ava doesn't either. You undermine your daughter's trust when you pull that kind of bullshit."

Ouch.

"And I'll tell you, Olga might be a great dance teacher, but she can turn into a real she-bitch monster when she's annoyed. She was obviously put out. And then Ava had to wait while I finished at work. I was dealing with an angry client in one room and a weeping little girl in another."

I consider suggesting that a bit of adversity might help build Ava's character. Kids these days are so coddled. Parents all but swaddle them in bubble wrap before taking them out to play. A few hard knocks are good for a youngster. I sure never wore a bike helmet when I was a boy. And blar blar blar, etcetera, etcetera, and more of that sort of childhood hardship speech. But before I launch in with this stratagem, my limited intelligence kicks in and I bite my tongue.

"I'm sorry," I say. "I guess I screwed up."

"It's not just today, Will. I need you to engage and help me out here."

"What's that supposed to mean?"

"I'm just saying, sometimes I feel like a single mom with two little kids." Her voice becomes less controlled, more emotional. "I just..." She looks away, pursing her lips. "I'll be honest, Will, I just don't understand what it is you're up to that takes so much of your time and attention. You seem so far away. It's like we don't even speak the same language anymore. I swear you only hear about half of what I tell you."

"Well, I'm pretty busy with my project."

"Great! But why don't we ever see any results from all this supposed hard work? It's kind of hard to believe you're doing anything but hanging out all day watching YouTube and going to the gym."

"Writing's not exactly a spectator sport. It takes concentration. I spend a lot of time just sorting things out in my head. And I only go to the gym to balance out the stress of all that cerebral stuff with a little physical activity. You don't want me having a stroke or something, do you?"

"Of course not. I understand it's difficult. Haven't I always encouraged you? But God, Will! You never seem to produce anything!"

I inadvertently snort. "That's not true."

"Yes, it is!"

The water stops running in the bathroom, and Jane and I both automatically dial back our volume so Ava won't hear us arguing. Now we're just whispering loudly.

Jane sounds like an irate rattlesnake.

I, on the other hand, sound more like a dump truck tire with a slow leak.

"You've written one book, Will, and that was nearly seven years ago!"

"It hasn't been seven years."

"Do the math!"

I feel dumb doing it in front of her, but I calculate the publication date of *Western Wind*, tallying up the intervening years on my fingers, and then... Dang! She's right. Where the hell did all that time go?

"Well," I whisper, "Tolstoy took seven years to write *Anna Karenina*."

"Wonderful! And so, do you have the world's next literary masterpiece about ready for us to proofread?"

I consider what I have in rough draft form for my book about Banal – a few paltry pages of scribbled phrases and quotes from his notebooks. "Almost."

"That's great, Will. But until you get it finished, why don't you think about trying something else? What about going back to your technical writing for a while? Or what about getting involved in other things? You could write something for People Who Care About Tomorrow's World. That would be *so* worthwhile, Will. You would even be working to improve your daughter's future. She's the one who's going to inherit this whole global mess. You could meet new people, exchange ideas, maybe even make a difference in the world."

"Well, I like to think what I do might make a difference to someone."

"Of course. I'm only suggesting you try doing something more immediate, something more involved with what's happening right now, today, instead of..." She waves her hand in the air.

I almost don't want to ask. "Instead of what?"

She shakes her head and sighs. "Instead of writing obsolete cowboy stories, or books about dead pulp writers that nobody gives a damn about but you."

Ouch again. She's good at this. Obviously, far better than me. A scrappy, calculating character assassin. As Jane continues on this course, it becomes very clear that I am best advised to forfeit this fight and escape with what little self-esteem I have left. Granted, if I weren't wounded, I might jump up and stomp out of the room, maybe go prowl the streets until dawn, hang out in a bar, or even leave town for a while and travel cross-country on my Triumph motorcycle – that is, if I actually had a Triumph motorcycle. That's probably what a real man should do in this situation. But my foot hurts, and even the most timorous stomping would doubtless bust out my stitches. I am trapped on this couch with the quandary of how to endure my defeat with any grace. As usual, complete surrender seems the best tactic. My gut tells me, once again, it's time to just give up.

"Okay," I mumble.

"Okay what?"

Jane's not going to make this easy for me – a little payback for leaving her hanging today with Ava. She dons the blank forbearance of the most consummate lawyer. But I know her better than most people. I detect – right there, in the corner of her mouth – the slightest twitch of self-satisfaction. Behind that poker face is a gambler who knows she holds a winning hand. She exudes victory.

"Okay." I feel like a scolded little boy. "I'll consider finding something else to do – something in the *real* world."

Before Jane has a chance to celebrate, Ava comes back into the room.

"Is supper ready?" she asks. "I'm hungry."

Jane smiles broadly, slaps her knees with enthusiasm, and stands. "I was just about to start cooking."

There is an unmistakable note of glee in her voice. She clearly feels she's made some progress this evening. Through deliberate reasoning and strategic coercion, her unruly husband has been collared, castrated, and cowed.

21

IT is decided that I will sleep on the couch. Jane wouldn't want to accidentally bump my sore foot in the night. I'm fine with this idea. To be honest, the last place in the world I want to be right now is in bed with a gloating dominatrix. It is no doubt churlish and puerile of me, but I don't relish the thought of lying next to her as she dreams the exultant, glorious dreams of a conquering female.

After Ava brushes her teeth, she comes in to tell me goodnight. Her demeanor is reserved. She leans in and gives me a perfunctory kiss on the cheek. It is a palpably distant gesture. Have I become some sort of beer-breathed, bloody-socked monster in her eyes? I would like to read to her for a while, maybe reconnect over the fictional trials of destitute Ivan on his island in an attempt to reach across this ocean that has deepened between us. But it has gotten very late and Ava just needs to go to bed.

"Sweet dreams," I say, and muster a fatherly smile. "Love you."

Ava only nods and wanders off to her room.

A tiny dagger twists in the center of my heart.

Jane turns off the living room lights and poses in voluptuous silhouette on the threshold to our bedroom. She resembles some sort of vamp out of film noir cinema. Why does it feel like she's taunting me?

"See you in the morning," she says, and then, in what strikes me as an inappropriately sensual manner, she closes the door with a suggestive click.

I imagine her in there now, lights turned low, eagerly perusing my *Kama Sutra.*

I sigh.

My foot throbs with little jabs of pain that syncopate with my pulse.

I carefully roll onto my side and watch the gloom of the city illuminating the doors to the balcony. The rain beats incessantly against the glass. The nauseating odors of stale beer and cleaning agent drift up from the carpet and work into my nostrils like a drug that bores into the dustiest catacombs of my brain, causing me to reflect, to mull, to remember.

Ava's arrival in our life was a shock to me. It was not what I had intended, not a plot twist I had ever anticipated when creating the outline for my marriage to Jane. No, according to *my* plan, we were to continue on to the end of our connubial sojourn as a blissfully childless couple. And thanks to the freedom afforded by that arrangement, we were going to experience extraordinary adventures along the way. Once Jane finally finished law school, we were maybe going to travel the South Seas in a sailboat, maybe trek in the Himalayas, maybe... hell, I don't know... maybe become Space Travelers and go camping on Mars. At any rate, we were sure as hell never going to join the breeders of the world – that hapless, swollen horde we saw overpopulating the planet with the parasitic spawn of their contraceptive mishaps.

And then it happened to us.

Jane, being noble and wise and intrinsically maternal, took motherhood in stride. For her it was only a slight complication, a minor detour, a barely noticeable bump in the road on her original course toward making the world a better place.

For me, conversely, it was a sucker punch to the nuts.

(Who knew passion could have such ramifications?)

I balked.

There was some serious talk of me leaving.

"If you're not man enough to handle it," Jane told me, after she had grown sick of my pouting, "consider yourself free to go."

And I might have, too, except for one thing – I fell in love with my daughter. It felt like yet another ruthless trick played out on me by Mother Nature, that same species-preserving wiring thing that keeps daddy bears from devouring their cubs. I felt helpless, smitten in ways I had never known. Every time I held Ava's squirming little body, every time I looked into her face, my cold heart melted like an ice cube tossed onto hot asphalt.

So, Jane and I worked out a deal. She would pursue her career – she had just taken a position in the city with a firm representing socially responsible cases – and I would quit my job writing owner's manuals for household appliances and stay home with Ava, taking on the role of Mr. Mom. Hence, I entered unto that diaper-laden realm of binkies, spit-up rags, and sippy-cups. The idea was that this arrangement would give me time to write a novel.

It worked.

Miraculously.

After years of false starts and lugubrious bouts of writer's block, a wordy dam burst open in me and poured forth like a raging storm-fed river.

Ava's advent had triggered something. It allowed just enough tension to keep me hungry, and just enough time for me to alleviate that tension at my desk. When the baby napped, I worked. The inspiration came in these spasms of creative opportunity. I was able to overcome my essentially emasculating circumstances and transform them into a novel that was original, even daring to the point of tour-de-force defiant. And although I would like to take credit for their creation, it was more like those chapters were channeling through me by way of some other personality. It was as if Ava's birth had birthed a corresponding force in me. She was an alien messenger from the stars sent to earth to deliver this novelistic message so that I, the chosen agent, might bring it to light in the world.

Or anyway, something like that.

It felt pretty amazing, the purest creative experience I had ever enjoyed. When it was all said and done – when the last period had been typed on that last sentence – I held in my hands what would come to be known as *Western Wind*.

The book did all right.

The few reviewers of note who read it said that it held "revisionist western tendencies tinged with refreshing hints of magical realism." One called it a *Rawhide Redux*. They all agreed that it might have been more popular had it not been such a cliché housed in a dead genre.

"Westerns," as one mainstream critic put it, "have gone the way of Roy Rogers and John Wayne, whose happy trails have long since been paved over and forgotten beneath the highways and high rises of modern sensibilities."

And yet, in spite of this postmodern postmortem, my novel gained a following with a certain faction of eccentric youngish readers hungry for more than the pretentious, cookie-cutter tripe offered up by the big publishing houses unwilling to risk paper and advertising on anything edgy. One underground reviewer claimed that *Western Wind* was the first novel she had read in years that actually had any trace of "True Fucking Grit."

————

A car horn honks somewhere out in the street, wrenching me from my reverie.

Our living room, I suddenly realize, has returned to the Ice Age. That's when I remember that the thermostat is set to automatically drop into economically arctic temperatures during the nighttime hours when we're all cozy and warm in bed. Only I'm not in bed, am I? And whether it was out of negligence or spite (one suspects the latter), Jane has failed to give me any extra blankets. I'm freezing my ass off under the single, threadbare afghan we keep on the couch.

"Shoot!"

All of the extra bedding is kept in the closet in our bedroom. To hobble in there and get a blanket would probably wake Jane, magnify my indignity, and make me look even more weak and pathetic than I already do. Not an option.

I try to make myself smaller, curling up like some tiny forest creature. Would that I had a long, furry tail! But it's no use. I'm shivering like crazy. I'll be dead by morning.

I assess the situation with the reasoning of a coolheaded trapper lost in the frozen Yukon. I tell myself this is just a little test in survivalism. If I had two sticks, I might rub them together to build a fire out of the coffee table.

What would Richard Banal do?

Granted, Dick would never find himself in such an embarrassingly domestic fix. But if he were to advise me – his most devoted disciple – I suspect he might suggest something unreasonably manly to compensate for my current dearth of masculine chutzpah. I thumb through the Banal wisdoms and aphorisms I keep handy in my head until I find something that might pertain to the situation.

When a man is faced with hardship, he should not cower in its shadow, but embrace it like a friend. Because, fella, that adversity is a gift sent to shape you into a hero.

With those emboldening words resounding in my soul, I throw back the afghan. I balance on my good foot and then hop to the kitchen. I rummage in the drawer next to the sink until I find a plastic bag and a rubber band. I slip the bag over my bandaged foot like an ill-fitting condom, and then carefully slide the rubber band up above my ankle to make it watertight. Next, I hop over to the glass doors.

Peeling off my t-shirt and boxers, I toss them to the floor. After a deep breath, I slide open the door and hop onto the balcony, wearing nothing but the plastic bag.

It's like diving into a glacial tarn. My skin tightens. My scrotum slams up into my throat. My breath comes out in panicky little gasps that I'm unable to control.

"Man up, Kirby!" I pant. "Grow a pair!"

I clench my fists against the cold, and then work my way to the edge of the balcony, weaving through the deck furniture until I am standing at the rail.

The city is laid out before me. The rain-doused buildings. The glistening streets. I become highly attuned to its details. Halos of light glow dimly atop lamp poles. Dull neon signs flicker in distant shop windows. A barber pole slowly twirls like a giant peppermint stick; I hear its electrical motor grinding. I hear rats scratching in alleyway dumpsters. I hear clouds bumping overhead.

The windows in the other apartment buildings are dark. They look like the blank screens of a thousand down-powered televisions. No doubt people are sleeping behind those glass squares and rectangles. They are all tucked into their beds, lost to their angst-ridden nightmares.

But not me.

Not tonight.

I am separate from those quotidian dramas of soul-numbing humdrummery. I have joined the exclusive brotherhood of the aloof. By extracting myself from that soap opera, I have become superior.

The icy rain washes over me. It drives down on the top of my head and runs over my face. I am both joined with the torrent and removed from it at the same time. I close my eyes in meditation. In my mind, I am carried away from the detritus of my daily life – all the tedious domestic bullshit – until I am standing on a beach looking out at green waves and blue sky. The sand is hot under the sole of my foot; the tropical breeze and sunshine cause my well-tanned skin to glisten with sweat.

ESCAPE FROM OBLIVIA

I breathe in – "Om."
I breathe out.
From somewhere drifts the birdlike laughter of females.
I grin a manly grin.

22

ALTHOUGH I've evidently been going nowhere for years, I feel I've traveled too far to ever turn back now.

I'm not entirely sure what I mean by this. It's just a vague notion I have of being on some sort of secret journey. Maybe that's a bit too histrionic. Possibly, it's more commonplace and boring than that. But when Jane cavalierly suggests I should just go back to my technical writing, I am seized with a tremor in my guts. No. There's no way I can do that. That's not who I am anymore. I'd die. I've reached the point of no return. Fuck reality! Adventure calls. It's forward for me, or nothing. The problem is, when fully awake, and not lost to some fantasy, I'm having trouble discerning which bearing, of all the possible points on the compass, is truly forward. It's like treading water in the midst of an ocean – every direction looks the same.

So, I take a few days to sort it out.

Stumbling around town on crutches would be demoralizing, so I just hole up at home. Besides, I require an objectivity that those blue and green-eyed sirens at the library would not allow.

We have a closet-sized room off the side of our apartment

that I've set up as a writing nook – a table and chair, an antiquated computer, a few reference books – but I've not used it in months. The door creaks on its hinges, revealing a chamber that strongly resembles a crypt. I step through the darkness and part the blinds, allowing melancholy light to ooze in through the tiny window. Cobwebs dangle in the corners. Everything lies under a patina of gothic dust. The room smells of damp mummies.

The computer grinds and shakes as it boots up, a process similar to starting an old jalopy. I half expect it to backfire and belch a puff of black smoke.

My brain, sadly, is grinding, too. I don't know if it's writer's block per se, or if I just need an oil change and a tune up. At any rate, it's not running right. My thoughts are muddled and clanking in my head. My metaphors are mixed – not like the elaborate, elegant conceits of the metaphysical poets, but more like a blender full of turds.

"Okay, Kirby. This is it – your moment of truth – the fulcrum point upon which your heroic destiny teeters."

I hunch at the computer like a medieval organist, fingers curled above the dusty keyboard, staring into the luminous void of the screen.

A long moment passes.

Then another.

Demon Doubt slithers in the dark corners of my cell.

But then, from the hinterlands of my psyche, I hear my muse's gentle voice.

"Ecstatic," she whispers, "paroxysms."

My body fills with tropical warmth, and the next thing I know, I am typing madly.

Phrases begin to drop in like mortar shells.

Lists unfurl like semaphore flags.

The rattling of my fingers over the keys sounds like the fire of machine guns.

Intelligent thoughts are brought down like heavily strafed Zeros.

I just let it happen, no judgment, no checks on this spontaneous skirmish of inspiration. I simply trust that something is going on, some subliminally logical sorting process that I don't immediately comprehend. It's as if I'm in a trance, being made to act by some invisible, mind-bending ray.

After about an hour, the fracas subsides.

When I finally stop typing, I am panting; I feel like I've been in a dogfight.

But there's no time to catch my breath. I need to sort through what I've written while it's still fresh, search for the rhymes and reasons hidden behind the smoking words and between the smoldering lines.

A plan forms in my mind's eye.

"Yes!"

I will begin my magnificent book in medias res, using that jump-right-into-the-action approach used in all the best men's adventure stories. I'll start it right smack in the middle of the scene where Banal finds himself crashing into the Pacific. In many ways, it will be like letting him write his own story. I'll simply allow him to speak through me. I will be Dick, and Dick will be me. A synergy of fictional genius will occur. A reciprocity of literary adroitness.

"Ha-ha!" I laugh. "A ha-ha-ha-ha!"

———

At some point, Ava comes into my room wearing her tutu and tiara. The blue light glows atop her head like an evening star.

The day has passed.

"Hi, Daddy. We're home." She steps over and rests her hand on my shoulder. "What are you doing?"

"Hey, darlin'. I'm working."

Ava squints at the computer screen and nods. "Are you coming out for supper?"

"Mmm." I shake my head and pat her fingers. "Not right now. I'm kind of in the middle of something."

"Okay. I'll tell Mom."

She leaves the room, closing the door behind her.

The truth is, I'm just being cagey. In my own sneaky way, I am being manipulative and cunning, using the tactic of a quarrelsome teenager snubbing his mother with the silent treatment. I can't help myself. When Jane is in close proximity, I feel pissed. I blame her for something. She's at the root of my problem. Or at least she's my most readily available scapegoat. I'm almost clever enough to understand my own psychology about this. But not quite. So the best approach I can come up with is to hide in my room and pretend I'm too busy being a literary genius to ever stop for something so trivial as nourishment and conversation.

I keep at task, but I hear Ava and Jane out there – making supper, watching cartoons, chortling like birds. It's annoying as hell.

Jane is obviously playing her own little game. She doesn't even bother to bring me a plate of food. And she doesn't allow Ava to do so either. I suspect she's hoping to drive me out of my bunker through systematic starvation.

Of course, if pressed Jane would no doubt deny this.

"Why, Will," she might say innocently. "I thought you were too busy to eat. After all, I hear Tolstoy once skipped meals for seven whole years."

Hrumph!

After a while, the outer rooms grow quiet. The girls have gone to bed. I am left alone with the drone of my computer, my growling stomach, and, of course, the ever-present rain.

"She'll see," I mutter. "I'll show her."

Yes. I *do* hear the stupidity in my reaction. It sounds like the throwaway line out of an old B-movie. But I can't help myself.

"She'll find out who wears the pants around here."

This makes me cringe.

Ugh!

Sometimes it sucks being me.

23

A week passes, my foot more or less heals, and the momentous day has finally arrived – Friday.

By sundown, I predict, my life will be markedly different. I will have become knowledgeable, savvy, enlightened beyond compare. The solutions to holy riddles will have been disclosed to me for safekeeping. I will smuggle them back to my desk in the bulletproof briefcase of my brain where I will take them out as secret codes to be deciphered and laced into the most brilliant literary work I will ever produce. The world will be grateful to me for my contribution.

Jane will finally respect me.

Ava will adore me.

Men will look to me as an icon.

Pretty French girls will utter my name in their sleep.

And although I will remain outwardly humble on the face of my triumph, I will inwardly feel that my astonishing success has garnered me the sweetest revenge a man can ever know.

To this end, I call up an Uber, slide into the back seat, and give the driver directions to the home of Hadley Allsworth.

We speed away from the trendy, high-rise sector of the city where I live with my wife and daughter to a neighborhood across the river. The brief journey comes with the profound sense of traveling back in time. This is the vestige of that former suburban utopia Americans inhabited in the middle of the last century. It feels like a forgotten movie set. Oaks and sycamores have existed here long enough to become enormous, gnarled, and majestic. Their iron-gray branches arch protectively over the streets like the interlocking girders of abandoned bus stations. The sidewalks are of the variety upon which kids once played hopscotch and darted back and forth on roller skates. I half expect to see Beaver Cleaver and his pals playing Cops and Robbers.

Except for a few modern cars parked in driveways, there are no contemporary trappings.

The houses are of that other era. Some are decorated with strings of Christmas lights that droop from the eaves like glimmering beads. A mechanical Santa stands in the rain behind a white picket fence waving spasmodically to passersby. One suspects he's been performing this robotic rite every holiday season since Eisenhower was in the White House. His mitten is missing a thumb; his suit is no longer bright red, but the faded pink of a plastic, sun-bleached flamingo.

"Here we are."

The driver parks his Wayback Machine at the curb in front of a bungalow.

I peer out through the rain-streaked glass.

After confirming the house number, I climb out of the back seat. The car swishes away as I limp up the walk and onto the porch until I find myself facing the front door. A wave of apprehension washes over me. I'm nervous as a boy on his first date. I take a breath, squeeze a fist, and press the doorbell.

A muffled *dong* resonates from inside. Followed by a pause. The patter of rain on the porch roof. And then the door swings open to reveal a lady in pale yellow pants and a black cardigan. She smiles.

"Ah, Mr. Kirby, I presume."

"Yes." I smile back. "Ms. Allsworth?"

"Please call me Hadley."

"Well, hello, Hadley. I'm Will."

She squeezes my hand affectionately. "So nice to meet you, Will. Please come in where it's warm."

The very daughter of Richard Henry Banal takes my dripping coat and hangs it on a hook behind the door. "Such a wet winter," she says. "I wonder if we'll ever get some sunshine and blue sky." She leads me into her house.

My first impression is of a woman who has aged but has not grown old. She is thin, erect, and well maintained. Her home, too, gives off the same feeling of tidiness. It lacks that clutter one associates with elderly people who have clung to the mementos of their long dusty lives. No bric-a-brac. No pointless bobbles. Just a spare, tastefully furnished sitting room with a few select paintings and a wall of books.

"I've made coffee," she tells me, "but I would gladly brew you a cup of tea if you prefer."

"Coffee's perfect."

She asks me to please sit in a padded armchair before a low table upon which stands an enamel coffeepot and a pair of teal blue cups. A legal-size, manila envelope rests on the table as well. She takes the seat across from me and pours.

"I'll let you doctor it to your taste." She scoots a bowl of sugar cubes and a pitcher of cream to my side of the table.

I dribble a bit of cream into my coffee and wait while she pours for herself.

A gas flame dances in the fireplace beside us and I can feel its warmth on the side of my face. It's very comforting.

Hadley leans back in her chair and crosses her legs at the knee. She cradles her cup in both hands and lifts it to her lips, blowing softly over the brim.

We both taste our coffee while sizing each other up.

I like her at once. Not just because she looks and speaks like a mature Faye Dunaway – she was doubtless what men would have thought of as *quite a looker* in her younger years – but because she radiates such a mix of confidence and kindness.

"Are you married, Will? I see you're not wearing a wedding band."

"Oh." I regard my naked ring finger. "My wife and I hocked our rings years ago to buy groceries." I shrug. "We were pretty broke in those days. I guess it never occurred to me to buy us new ones."

"That's what I'd call a very understanding woman. And you're still married to her?"

"Yes."

"Children?"

"A daughter. Ava."

She catches me looking at her hands and holds up her ringless fingers. "Divorced," she says. "Over before it began. My one and only foray into that world. I was the whim for him that quickly went awry. I think he finally ended up going back to his former wife."

"Should I say I'm sorry?"

She shakes her head and laughs. "Absolutely not! Ancient history. And *no* regrets."

"You kept his name?"

"Yes. But regained my freedom. I had no desire to go back to being Miss Banal. That tag had begun to seem more like a condition to outrun rather than embrace. If I hadn't married Mr. Allsworth, I might have changed my name anyway."

"Banal is definitely an ironic name, but one your father was certainly able to overcome."

Hadley arches an eyebrow and smiles wryly. "I suppose so," she says. "If only by hiding behind his nom de plume."

"Dick Zag."

"Yes. Which reminds me – I quite liked your novel."

"Well, thank you."

I am secretly pleased that the mention of Zag has caused her to think of *Western Wind*.

"It's a very amusing book, very layered, and I dare say that our meeting today depended upon my giving it a good grade."

"Oh? How's that?"

"Our friend, Roxanne." Hadley laughs. "That girl is a sly one. There's more to her than meets the eye. She obviously adores you. She sings your praises every time we meet. But she's very protective of you besides. She understood that you didn't want just anyone knowing about your project, so she worked a cunning test for me to see if I was worthy. She recommended your novel without ever telling me what you were up to. She was working on a sort of secret liaison." Hadley laughs again and sips her coffee. "Only after I told her that I had enjoyed *Western Wind* did Roxanne let me in on her little scheme to have us meet."

"Lucky for me."

She lifts her palm and gestures to the room.

"So, you see, Will, this is the home where I grew up. My mother left it to me. I was living abroad when she passed away, and the place sat unoccupied for a number of years. Well, the first thing I did when I finally moved back in was to go through and clean house. So much junk! Old photos, mouse-nibbled books, and all other manner of clutter my mother had used as an anchor to hold herself in place. No doubt you would be horrified if you could only see all the treasures I tossed out. They might have served you very well in your research. And yet, I saw little worth in any of it."

She gazes into her cup.

"But when I came across my father's notebooks, something gave me pause. They struck me as so poignant. He had obviously worked very hard on them over the years, pouring his secrets into those pages. I just couldn't make myself throw them out. I decided I should at least donate them to the City Central. I figured someone might find worth in them, or if not, at least someone else could take responsibility for relinquishing them to the rubbish heap."

"Well, I'm glad no one did that."

"Yes. But after I learned about your project it occurred to me that those notebooks – those artifacts – came without any road map. They're just mysterious jetsam, tossed off ramblings from my father's overactive mind."

"They're very informative. I've learned a lot from them."

"I'm sure you think you have, Will."

She smiles at me, wistfully, it seems. I don't know exactly how to respond to this, so I feign professionalism by taking out the pad and pen I have brought along for jotting down notes. I hold them up for her inspection. "Do you mind?"

She shakes her head. "Of course not."

"I'm certainly eager to learn as much about your father as you can tell me. And I appreciate you taking the time."

"Not at all. And don't think I'm being entirely selfless by doing this. I suppose I'm hoping it will be as cathartic for me as it proves useful for you."

She sips more coffee and ponders a moment while I wait for her to gather her thoughts. "So," she finally says. "How much do you *really* know about my father?"

"Well, I read a few of his novels and magazine pieces when I was a boy. Even after all these years, his stories stand out in my memory as very thrilling and different. They were important to me when I was a kid. I understood they weren't high literature, but they fed my imagination in a way other books didn't, transporting me to other worlds. I'd say they were what made me first realize I wanted a writer's life for myself. And they've come back over the years to haunt my dreams. In fact, it was while searching for an old Dick Zag novel at the library that I discovered your father's notebooks." I feel myself blush. "It was an incredibly exciting find for me. It felt like destiny. Here were the very journals of my greatest hero!"

Hadley dips her head thoughtfully, without comment.

"But it wasn't until I started studying his notebooks that I really began to understand what a truly amazing man your father was. He had to have lived the most exciting life ever. I mean, my gosh! The adventures he had!"

Hadley stops me and leans forward to take up the manila envelope from the table. She reaches inside and sorts through its contents, drawing out a photograph. She hands it to me. "Have a look at this."

It's a Kodachrome snapshot taken in front of the very house we're sitting in at the moment, but as it might have looked sixty or so odd years ago. It is sunny in the photo; the trees are leafed out in full foliage and the grass is tall and in need of mowing. On the walkway is a young girl holding the hand of a man standing beside her.

"My mother snapped that photo when I was about seven or eight."

The girl in the picture is wearing pink pedal pushers and a summer blouse. Her blond hair is in two braids dangling from either side of her head. She is pretty, smiling happily, and missing a front tooth."

"That's you?" I ask stupidly.

"Yes."

"Very cute."

And then, even more stupidly, I ask, "Who's the man?"

Hadley takes a sip from her coffee and licks her lips. "That, Will, is your hero – Richard Henry Banal."

———

When Alfred Hitchcock made his movie *Vertigo*, he needed an ingenious way to show his audience the subjective state of dizzy confusion being suffered by his main character. To achieve this, the great director invented a camera trick known as the Zolly. In this special effect, the camera is zoomed in while simultaneously being dollied out. The result is a sort of sucking sensation in the viewer's eyes and brain – a vicarious sensation of vertigo.

A Zolly is as close as I can come to describing what I am feeling as Hadley Allsworth's words penetrate the protective casing of my intelligence. The photo in my hand zooms up at me while simultaneously falling away. This is accompanied by a buzzing noise between my ears, as if electrical wires are frying and melting apart.

"I take it that's not how you imagined him."

Hadley's voice sounds hollow and far away, as if echoing from the back of a cave.

I slowly shake my head, being careful not to let it topple from my shoulders and roll across the floor.

The man holding the little girl's hand in the photo is squat and shaped like a bowling pin, or possibly a penguin. He is hatless, and the sun is glinting off his balding pate. He is knock-kneed and pigeon-toed. He is wearing glasses with lenses thick as the bottoms of soda bottles. The look on his face is not that of a cocksure Marine Corp pilot, and not that of a virile ladies' man, but, rather, that of an insecure, roly-poly little boy.

I pry my gaze from the photo, look at my hostess, and stammer, "But he's... He's a..."

She smiles reassuringly. "I think the word you're probably looking for is *milquetoast*."

I feel myself nodding as a rush of nausea makes me shudder.

"And yet," she says, "I didn't think of him that way at all when I was little. To me my father was a great man. He was a writer, after all, just like the great Hemingway. What could be better than that?"

I hold up the photograph. "But this must have been taken after he flew combat in the war. And after he had done most of his traveling."

"The truth is, Will, my father was never a pilot. I don't believe he ever once went up in a plane. And apart from a trip to the seashore that he took with his parents when he was a boy, he never once set foot outside of this town."

The part of me that has always worshipped Richard Banal like a god does not immediately accept any of this. Ha-ha, I think. Heh-heh. Dick sure had them fooled. Even his own daughter didn't know about his secret life! But when I look at the photo again and see the tubby schlemiel with the uneasy look on his face, my delusions begin to fall away. That's no mere disguise he's wearing. No superhero is hiding beneath that banal facade. There's no way a man like that could ever use karate to throttle his enemies.

"More coffee?" asks Hadley.

I must have nodded yes, because she pours some more into my cup.

"You see, Will, my father's adventures were all in his head. That's where he escaped to in order to overcome his embarrassment.

Remember, in his day, all the young men of any worth had fought in the war. He had wanted very badly to be a part of that great patriotic effort right from the beginning with Pearl Harbor. He had a heroic heart, but in every other way my father proved to be Four-F – that humiliating classification of men not fit for service. He was flat-footed, all but blind, and in no way built of the heroic stuff of a soldier. And besides that, frankly, there were the mental problems."

I don't even want to hear about this, but... "Mental problems?"

"Yes." Hadley peers into her cup and swirls it. "My father suffered from schizophrenia. It was a mild case to begin with, barely detectable when he was young. It hadn't yet overwhelmed him when he met my mother. She told me once that he had just seemed to have a very vivid and boyish imagination. In fact, in large part, that was what had attracted her to him. He was hardly a ladies' man. I'm sure my mother was the only girl he had ever known. But for all of his physical flaws, my mother found him quite clever, and very sweet."

I just stare at her.

"To his credit, he turned his defect to his advantage. He simply became those other personalities rattling in his head and eventually funneled them into adventure novels. And of course, at the head of it all, like some great administrator pulling the strings, was his alter ego – Dick Zag."

"Dick," I hear myself whimper, "Zag."

"Yes, Will. I'm afraid it was his persona Mr. Zag who actually wrote the notebooks you've been reading. Although I would be remiss to say he was so separate from my father. Zag was the man my father most desperately wanted to be."

I study, again, the photo of Hadley and her father. I cannot help but think of my own daughter as an infant sleeping peacefully across the room as I worked on *Western Wind*.

"After I was born, my father became more and more withdrawn from reality. He retreated to his attic. My mother told me she didn't really know how to react at first. It scared her. But then he started producing his novels. Desperate for a way to support the family, my mother decided to try to get them published. Her plan worked. She managed his career, staying hidden in the background, assuming the role of his editor and secretary, without anyone ever knowing the truth of his condition. In ways, my parents were co-writers. You see, my mother had to clean up his writing and rework it, almost to the point of translating it, to make it acceptable and readable for the men's mass market. I think she lent it an insider's element of femininity that made it unusual and popular among male readers. But in the end, it was essentially my father's imagination that paid for our living. Indeed, it was successful enough that it eventually even paid for me to go away to college."

I don't speak for a minute.

And neither does Hadley.

She seems to understand that I need a moment to let this all sink in.

"Did your mother ever try to get help for him?"

Hadley sighs. "No." She watches the flame in the fireplace. "And I'll be honest, Will, my mother and I came to feel a bit guilty about the whole arrangement. We were obviously taking advantage of my father's illness. I don't think it occurred to us at the time, but we were keeping him as a sort of prisoner."

I nod, trying to understand, but Hadley obviously sees the confusion on my face.

"Do you happen to know that old novelty song," she asks, "about the crazy man who believed he was a chicken?"

Even more puzzled, I shake my head.

"Well, you see, Will, his family knew the man was crazy to think he was a chicken, and they all felt terribly worried about him, but no one ever tried to intervene because, as the song goes, they needed the eggs."

I just stare at her.

Hadley shrugs. "As long as my father was happy escaping into his fantasy world, and being Dick Zag, we saw no reason to interrupt him, because, as it were, we needed the eggs – his stories and novels."

"Oh."

Hadley smiles and shakes her head. "Sorry. This is the part of our meeting where I satisfy the catharsis I warned you about earlier. My therapy. My true confessions. I've been mulling them inconclusively for many years. I'm sure my poor mother went to her grave without ever getting such an opportunity to air her own sins against my father."

I nod.

"Their relationship was a very complicated one. And yet, I think, in their own peculiar way, my parents very passionately loved each other." She holds up a palm. "In many ways, they were both very weird. My mother indulged my father's eccentricity by role-playing. It was as if she became one of his heroines. They would call each other by other names sometimes, speaking with accents and made-up languages, pretending, winking at one another like children involved in some X-rated game of make believe." She laughs. "Of course, as a little girl, I could only venture to guess what those peculiar voices and moans might mean behind the closed doors of my parents' bedroom."

"So, how did he die?"

Hadley shakes her head. "I'm afraid I have no idea." She refreshes her coffee. "One day, after I had moved away from home and was living in Europe, my mother went up to his writing room to take him some lunch, as was their routine. But when she opened the door, he wasn't there. She called for him but got no answer. Then she saw that the window was open. As it was winter, and cold, she thought this peculiar. Well, in short, after searching all over for him, my mother finally concluded that he had essentially fled the scene. He had finally made his great escape, as it were, through this only available portal."

It is difficult for me to go from being stunned to being even more stunned, but that is what I do. "Oh."

"My mother searched for him all over the neighborhood, calling for him, the way one might call out the name of a runaway house cat. When this brought no success, she notified the police." Hadley frowns. "But it seems my father was more sly and elusive than we might have suspected. They never found him."

I gaze again at the photo, and at the chubby man staring back at me, staring, it seems, into my very soul. It is all but impossible to imagine him crawling out a window with any grace and daring.

"My fear," continues Hadley, "is that he joined the leagues of those mentally ill people you see wandering around the streets, stammering and filthy and sleeping under bridges. My unreasonable hope, on the other hand, is that he found what he was after, that he actually got to where he was striving and lived his truest life."

"Oblivia," I mutter.

"Yes," says Hadley. "You obviously know of that fabled island of Mr. Zag's fondest desiring."

"Sure."

"But there's something else you probably don't know."

I wait, as the saying goes, for yet another shoe to drop.

"I told you that my parents' relationship was a complicated one."

"Yes."

"I believe my father became both resentful of, and grateful to, my mother. She was the friction in his fiction – the power he fled while simultaneously running towards."

"I don't understand."

"There was a push and pull between them. A tension. No doubt all marriages suffer it to some extent. I know mine certainly did. The only difference is that I didn't try to balance out that tension. I simply left, moved on. Sometimes, I think, that's the best course of action." She ponders this a moment. "Yes. I'm sure that's true. But my father, by nature of his condition, was more conflicted. He struggled with what to do. He realized his dependence on my mother, and I think he also realized that we depended on him. Only after I had successfully completed college and was on my own, and only after my mother was financially secure, did my father finally make his escape."

Hadley takes another swallow of coffee, and then stares at me over her cup. For the first time, I notice the color of her eyes; they are vividly blue, like Kodachrome summer sky as seen through open windows.

"My mother's name was Olivia."

"Olivia." I repeat the name, saying it slowly, as if trying to remember a dream. "Olivia."

That's when the other shoe drops.

I must have a shocked expression on my face, because Hadley nods to me, as if confirming my revelation.

"Yes," she says. "It's no coincidence that it's a variation on Oblivia, that make-believe world to which he simultaneously fled to and yet longed to escape. I think in many ways my father considered them one in the same thing... realm... state of being... or whatever one might want to call it. It's hard to know the workings of a delusional mind."

We sit in silence for a moment.

And then Hadley puts down her cup. "Mm," she says. "Would you like to see the scene of the crime?"

"What?"

She stands. "His writing room."

Not really, is my first thought. I feel as if I'm being asked to identify the body of a brutally murdered loved one. I know I should say yes, but I don't want to.

I manage a weak smile. "Okay."

She leads me down the hallway to a narrow set of stairs ascending into a dark void. I follow her up through a door and into an attic room.

It is small. It has a low ceiling, only a few inches higher than my head. A table is pushed against one wall, and a typewriter sits mutely on its top. There are a handful books on a shelf, and a lamp over the table, but otherwise the room is empty.

"It wasn't my intention to make this into some sort of shrine," says Hadley, "but I suppose that's what it's become."

I swallow, and gaze around.

"Well," she says. "Why don't I leave you here for a while so you can think?"

"Sure. Thanks."

She leaves the room, closing the door behind her.

I listen to her heels clopping softly down the stairs.

After swallowing once more, I take a few timid steps into the room. My pulse is racing. I run my fingers over the table, and then touch the keys of the typewriter – a manual Smith Corona.

Everything is covered under a patina of gothic dust.

The room smells, disconcertingly, of damp mummies.

Except for the sound of rain outside, the room is otherwise silent. Unnervingly so. A silence that needs to be broken. Some voice needs to be heard here. Some sound, any sound but of that relentless rain.

I step to the window. It had to be just barely big enough for him to squeeze through. It looks out onto a sloped section of roof covered in black cinder shingles. Rainwater runs down the slope and drops off the edge into the backyard. I place my fingertips on the cold surface of the glass. No doubt he did the same thing a thousand times, looking out.

The wet branches of leafless trees.

The gleaming wet roof of the house next door.

That lead-gray sky.

"Richard, my man." I sigh and shake my head. "How did we ever get here?"

24

ROBOT Santa waves goodbye to me through the rain as I ride away from this twilight zone of yesteryear Americana. The disorienting sensation of time travel returns. It's like being born. Or maybe like being sucked into a black hole and de-born. I'm not exactly sure. I feel myself hurling away from my own childhood, through adolescence, passing through my young manhood, and then onward... onward. I pray this Uber time machine doesn't overshoot my stop and launch me into the deepest galaxy of my old age. Today that seems like a very real danger.

Hadley Allsworth is moving on, too. She told me so as we parted. She gave me a farewell hug and wished me good luck with my project.

"You may call if you need me to answer any questions," she said, "but I doubt our paths will cross again."

Her catharsis is complete.

One can linger in the past, she told me, knocking around with ghosts, or one can move forward into new undertakings.

"I've always been a forward person," she said. "This time here was just a little detour – a swerve back into my bygone life just long enough for me to realize I've outgrown it."

She'll be selling her childhood home after the first of the year and leaving town, volunteering for an organization based in Papeete that is working to rid the world of the Great Pacific Garbage Patch.

"You'll have to forgive my sexist views, but I believe it's a woman's duty to clean up the mess made by all the men throughout history who have worked so hard to destroy our planet," she told me. "Your Ava will be entering a brave new world, and I feel an obligation as her fellow female to do what I can to make it a pleasant place for her to live."

Hadley gave me the manila envelope. She offered me her father's typewriter too, but in a moment of rare sanity, I recognized it for what it was – an anchor I don't need – and declined her gift.

Now I'm staring at the packet in my hands. Besides the seven notebooks in City Central Library, this bulging, yellow time capsule holds the last remaining clues to the life/lives of Richard/Dick/Banal/Zag.

I can't help myself; the suspense is too unbearable for me to wait until I get home. Hadley told me that they were just a few last things she found hiding in her mother's drawer, but I need to know, is there something here – anything at all – that could save my project?

I peer out the window. The car is midway on a bridge, passing back over the wide river toward downtown. A dozen or so yachts are tied up at some docks along the shore. Cold gray rain is falling into the swirling gray water. And then I empty the envelope onto my lap, sorting through and inspecting the items one at a time.

The snapshot of Hadley and her father is on top. I hold it up and study it in the failing light. The zolly feeling has passed, but I do experience a stab of pathos as all the visual elements go to work on my frayed emotions – Richard's dopey expression – that smile on the young Hadley's face as she so adoringly, innocently, holds her father's hand within the parameters of their all but fictional Kodachrome world. The photo strikes me simultaneously as the sweetest thing I have ever seen, and the most heartbreaking.

Next are some random publishing notes and scribbled ideas about book promotion. There are lists of male characters – Mitch Jones, Buzz Langley, Jack Blick – and then another list of female characters – Rhondonna, Chantari, Indira. I guess women only need first names. I find a few love notes exchanged between Richard and Olivia. I recognize his handwriting and assume the more feminine return notes were written by Olivia. They are kinky and weird to the point of disturbing. One detects a hint of insanity. Each note is addressed to, and signed with, names other than Richard and Olivia. Role playing.

I continue to sort through the pile until I come to a piece of folded paper the likes of which I recognize. I rub it between my fingers. I know that texture intimately. I hold it up and sniff it. I know that archival scent of deteriorating paper. It makes my heart drop in my chest. The page is lined. Its edge is ragged, apparently torn from a spiral notebook.

It is with dreadful anticipation that I unfold the paper and study it.

Oh.

It is a drawing.

In pencil.

Artless and crude.

It's the kind of sketch one might find scribbled into a notebook by a bored teenage boy daydreaming in chemistry class, or the kind drawn by a middle-aged schizophrenic searching for escape from one of his less-than-heroic personalities. The line between these two characters – the horny adolescent and the unbalanced old man – is disquietingly thin.

The border of the drawing is covered in clouds and stars and rocket ships. The word Oblivia is printed at the top of the page. In the center of the page is the depiction of a square window – Richard's portal. But the thing that makes it disturbing is what the artist has doodled within the parameters of the window. It is unsophisticated, but there is no denying what it's meant to be.

A vagina.

Perhaps the gloomiest vagina in the whole galaxy.

I sigh.

At the bottom of the page is the number 69.

25

*T*HE *Nutcracker* is blaring on the stereo when I come into the apartment. Ava is kneeling in front of the glass doors, sorting through a box of Christmas ornaments. A tangled constellation of white lights twinkles on the floor beside her. Our annually exhumed fake Christmas tree is leaning on its stand. A few of its plastic, green branches jut from one side of its thin aluminum stalk, while the other side remains bare – Oh, Tannenbaum caught mid erection.

Ava looks over at me and brightens – the innocent face of a joyful pixie.

"Daddy!"

She skips across the room in beat to the music and throws her arms around me.

"Oh, honey." I hold out my arms. "I'm all wet."

"I don't care." She squeezes me around the waist. "I'm glad you're home."

She is wearing her tiara with the blue star shining on top of her head.

God, she feels good!

"Where have you been?" she asks. "We were supposed to decorate the tree."

"Oh, well…"

She hands me an ornament – an old one from Jane's childhood, dragged through the holidays for untold generations. I examine it carefully in my fingers. It is a grenade-sized bulb of fragile red glass frosted with asbestos snowflakes.

"This one's my favorite," says Ava.

I nod. "Where's Mom?"

"In the bedroom packing for our trip."

A rush of panic. It occurs to me that I still don't know the details of this mysterious *trip*. By now, no doubt, I should.

Ava grabs my sleeve and pulls me toward the living room. "Come help me put the branches on."

"Okay, Ava. Just a minute."

As she dances back to the tree, I lay the Christmas bulb on the counter and hang up my coat. The manila envelope is folded in half and stuffed deep into the coat's internal pocket. I'll sort through the twisted wreckage of my hopes and dreams later.

When I turn back to the apartment, Jane is charging out of the bedroom, carrying what appears to be a large and battered piece of paper.

"Mom, Daddy's home! Now we can trim the tree!"

I wave uneasily to Jane from the entryway. Jane glances sideways at Ava, and then abruptly stops. "Dammit, Ava! I told you, you're going to run the batteries dead in that thing if you don't turn it off! How impressive is it going to be if no one can see you dancing in the dark?"

Ava's joy melts. She reaches up and takes down the tiara, cutting the power to the blue star while self-consciously standing with it in both hands against her lap. Her voice becomes a quiet fizzle that I can just barely hear over the ballet music swelling from the speakers beside her. "I'm sorry."

Jane shakes her head irritably, and then resumes marching my direction.

Instinct tells me to keep the kitchen island between us. "Hi,

Jane," I say, and offer a weak smile. "What's going on?"

She doesn't answer. Instead, she brandishes the piece of paper like a weapon, and hisses, "What the hell is this?"

I regard the wrinkled document presented to me like an indictment. Its corners are ragged, apparently from being violently ripped from its staples, and it appears to be a bit wrinkled from the rain. The silhouette cowboy looks more trail weary than I remember him from when Roxanne first showed me the poster at the library. His faithful horse is more sway-backed, verging on downright lame and destined for the glue factory.

"Well, it..." I stammer. "It's a surprise."

"A surprise?"

"Yes. I was going to tell you about it this evening. I thought it might be a fun surprise." I shrug and blink. "I thought we could all go together, as a sort of celebration, so you and Ava could see me read and... you know, in front of a few people who actually like me."

Jane grits her teeth. She slaps the poster on the island and positions it so that it's upright before me, and then she stabs her finger at the line announcing the date. "That's tomorrow night!"

"Yeah," I say. "I know."

Jane grabs her face in her hands. "God, Will!"

"What?"

Jane's eyes begin to glisten. "When are you going to wake up from this dream you're in?" She shakes her head, hopelessly. "Don't you *ever* hear what I tell you?"

I don't know the correct answer for this. It might be a trick question. I think I hear her, yes, but maybe not. Besides following an entirely different logic from mine, sometimes she and Ava seem to be speaking a different language as well. It's possible I'm missing important information coming in on another frequency.

I just stand there with Tchaikovsky throbbing in the background, waiting for my enlightenment.

Jane stares at me, exasperated. An angry tear rolls down the side of her nose. She speaks loudly and slowly, as if to a child with a hearing impairment. "Tomorrow night is Ava's dance performance. We're going on the train and staying in a hotel." She sniffs and wipes her cheek. "Remember? We've been planning it for two months!"

I feel confused, cornered, losing hold of my nerves and sanity. I take a breath and try to calm myself. "Oh." I gulp. There is a sinking sensation in my gut. The room is slowly spinning, zollying in and out. "Well..." I focus on the refrigerator, squinting helplessly at the tiny magnets we use to hold notes and grocery lists to the door. "I wish we would have put it on the calendar or something."

Jane doesn't immediately respond. Instead, she trembles. She flushes red. Then, before my very eyes, the woman transforms from a haggard, world-weary wife and working mother into a rabid, man-eating psychopath.

"Ha!" she screams. "It wouldn't fucking matter, Will! I could spray paint it on the wall and you wouldn't even notice it! You're too lost in your own little world to ever see anything that might be important to this family!"

"Hey, that's not..." I begin but have nowhere to go with it.

Jane is shaking all over, clenching her fists. "What the hell happened to you, Will?" She points at me over the island. "Where's that clever, sweet guy I married? Where did you go?" She holds up her hands, half curling her fingers so they look like talons. "You've become such a dumbass pitiful excuse for a man!"

Whoa!

That does it.

I can take a lot of abuse, but when Jane says that... The whole world hits the brakes. The load is too great for it to bear. With a sound of screeching tires, planet Earth abruptly stops turning on its axis. I sense, very profoundly, that I am now faced with a choice – I can either cower beneath Jane's fury, as is my habit, or I can choose another more manly course of action.

I don't know if it's the strain from my depressing, delusion-shattering afternoon at Hadley Allsworth's, or the many years' buildup of playing the humiliating role of Mr. Mom, but something in me snaps.

I lose it.

I explode.

"Well maybe I'd be able to think straight if you weren't always busting my balls!"

Jane glares at me, shaking her head in disgust, but I don't give a damn. It's too late to change course now. This beast has leapt from his cage!

"Do you have any idea what it's like living with a bitch like you? You're strangling me! You never let me breathe!"

"For God's sake, Will, I give you all the freedom in the world! And how do you use it? I come home every day and you're either watching some idiot show on YouTube, or asleep on the couch. How much more freedom do you need? It's already like you're on some sort of permanent vacation!"

"I work hard!"

"Prove it! Show me one single thing you've done in the last seven years."

I clench my fists. I look past Jane at the rain lashing like a hurricane against the glass door, keeping frenetic time with Tchaikovsky. Ava is kneeling by the tree. The Christmas lights are blinking spastically, as if shorting out. The terrified look on my daughter's face is painful to see, but I don't know how to stop what I'm doing. It's as if I'm fighting for my life.

"Show me one single thing you've done!" Jane taunts. "Just one!"

Of course, I don't have anything to show her. I'm not some friggin' carpenter, or blacksmith. All my recent products are of the intangible variety. The last chance I held for redemption was in tomorrow night's reading, and now Jane has managed to torpedo that hope as well. There is no way out for me. I just stand there, rattled and writhing.

Tchaikovsky has reached a crescendo. In an instant of lucidity that usually only comes to a man at the brink of his death, I understand very clearly what I am hearing – "Battle with the Mouse King" – that point in the ballet where the heroic nutcracker drives his sword into that evil rodent's heart. But before I am slain, I do the only desperate thing I can think of.

"Aaaaah!" I snarl and grab the Christmas bulb from the counter. I direct my fury into that stupid little orb, and then I fling it at the wall.

It explodes with a muted pop, sending glittery red shrapnel tinkling over the kitchen floor.

I meet the man-eater's eyes. She has them fixed on me, and they are filled with loathing.

"I don't need this!" I growl. "None of it!"

And then I turn on my heel, grab my coat, and stomp out of the apartment, slamming the door behind me.

BAM!

26

 .

I clomp blindly through the downpour, dry as a pissed-off desert nomad. I radiate such a force field of otherworldly rage that even the onslaughting rain can't penetrate to my existential plane of being. The shower parts before me and then turns to vapor in my wake. I inhabit the spaces between the raindrops – that arid wasteland between being and nothingness, between the transmuting cells of that pussy-whipped mouse I so recently was and this free-ranging brute I have become.

Only after I've covered about two-dozen blocks do I slowly begin to meld with this tangible otherworld unto which I've been beamed.

First, I feel a painful twinge as my heel strikes terra firma.

Next, my lungs materialize with the heavy huff of my breath.

Then the dank ghoul of my mortality re-inhabits my skin until, at last, I realize I am here, alive, traveling solo, and suddenly sopping wet. "Damn!"

When I take my bearings, I find I am at the edge of Riverfront Park. I wipe the rain from my face and look back at the monolithic buildings looming behind me out of the noirish mists. It's as if I've stepped into an expressionist painting.

I am at a loss for what to do next, and which way to turn. I have become a character in a story desperately seeking a plot. I am like an escapee from a zoo or an asylum who doesn't quite know how to react to this newly gained freedom. How does one stalk and lurk? I try to remember. How does one roam and prowl?

My shoes and socks are squishing.

Rainwater runs down my neck.

Step one, I decide, is to seek shelter from the elements.

A nearby bike path winds into the darkness and I jog along it until I am under a bridge. I lean on the railing and catch my breath, gazing out. The river is deadly dark and slurping around the cement pilings with the doleful musicality of a dirge. Intermittent traffic passes overhead, strangely distant. The whole realm of humanity seems to be on the other side of the world right now. It's as if I've been dropped into a remote wilderness. I savor this...

But then my phone dings.

"Geez!"

Is there no getting away from these things?

I dig it out of my pocket. The screen glows eerily in the dark as the message appears. It's not from Jane; it's from Roxanne.

Hey, cowboy. Getting worried. Haven't seen you all week. You will be reading for us tomorrow night, yes?

I consider this. I turn over the possibilities – the slim chance that I might be able to repair the damage I've done to my family. I suppose I could still bail out on my reading and surprise them by showing up to Ava's performance. A scenario plays in my mind where I give the girls each a bouquet of flowers and we all kiss and make up and return to our life together as America's ideal happy family. It's like a heartwarming finale to some prime-time television show. The tiniest wave of nostalgic warmth passes through me as I imagine the feeling of Ava's arms thrown around me in a hug. It's certainly tempting...

But no – that's way too Hallmark for a real man like me, way too *It's a Wonderful Life*. Besides, my battle with Jane is too fresh for such a saccharine and deferential reunion. I don't care if she is probably right and morally superior. I newly despise her.

"There's no way I'm going back to her sly and condescending man control!"

Another part of me thinks, why not just abandon all of your old ways and blaze a new trail? Leave everything behind – family, writing, this rain-drenched hell town – and move into a whole new life and identity. Maybe I could become a bush pilot, or the skipper of a fishing boat, and just leave banality in the past. Maybe I could even change my name to something catchy like Buzz Langley or Jack Blick.

"Shoot, Kirby, why not just be the man you've always wanted to be?"

I don't need a hero to emulate; I don't need a new name; I just need to let loose the hero that's chained inside of me.

But maybe I'm being foolish. It might be too hasty a move to burn *all* of my bridges at once. After all, Hadley assured me that Roxanne adores me. Maybe I've been mistaken about her. Maybe that bibliobimbo is my people, my only friend and truest ally. There's possibly more to her than meets the eye. Maybe Roxanne is offering me the opportunity I've been longing for – a portal unto which I can launch the rocket of my dreams into glorious orbit.

Of course, none of this is completely formulated in my mind. It's all just a barrage of sparks and thought bubbles. It's like my head is a cement mixer full of tumbling concepts and inbred similes. I sense this. The endorphins and adrenaline coursing through my system right now have me in such a fight-or-flight state of heightened anxiety that it's impossible to think rationally. Still, some impulsive intelligence in me decides to follow my instincts. I hold up my phone, position my thumbs, and observe myself pecking out a reply to Roxanne.

Fear not, gorgeous. Your loyal cowpoke won't let you down.

Before I have time to reconsider, the message is off and away with a whoosh. To punctuate the gesture with an irrevocable finality, I haul back and fling the phone as far as I can out into the river... plunk.

I bob my head once, as if in affirmation of this spontaneous and daring decision. There! Now I've cut my lifeline to that other reality. I'll either sink or swim by my own hand, by golly!

My phone tumbles down through the current, pulsing and sputtering past drowsy carp, down and down into the silent murk.

A tremor passes down my spine.

Traffic rumbles overhead like thunder.

And then a rough voice calls out to me from the shadows, causing me to nearly piss my pants.

"The bull is loose in the playpen."

When I whirl around, no one is there. I peer into the darkness. Was it just a voice in my head? Is my mind playing tricks?

But then a shape appears, a figure. I lean forward and squint, trying to understand what I'm seeing. I take two cautious steps forward.

"I said," repeats the shadow, "the bull is loose in the playpen."

It becomes humanoid – a man.

He coughs.

My eyes adapt just enough to discern his shape amidst the clutter. A shopping cart is parked next to the wall, piled high with garbage, and there's a box of something that looks like bottles, or maybe plastic milk jugs. The man is stirring between these, rising out of the dirt like a hologram.

"What?"

"I said, the bull is loose in the playpen." He coughs again and waits. Then – "Come on, man! Get with the story. Now you tell me your part."

"My part?"

"Of the code, man. Tell me your part of the secret code."

"Oh."

I'm stumped. I understand that he's probably just some crazy homeless guy, and yet I feel like it's very important for me to answer him correctly. It's as if he's a gatekeeper, and I need him to let me pass to the world of fantastic possibilities awaiting me on the other side.

He waits.

I stammer.

Then it comes to me – "The bull is in the playpen and... the sky is blue!"

A moment passes, until he says, "Right on, man. You're clear."

I find myself oddly relieved, and oddly pleased.

He struggles to his feet and asks, "Can you spare a dollar?"

"A dollar?"

"Yeah, man. Do you have a dollar I can borrow? I need to buy my lady friend a Christmas present and I left my money in my other pants."

"Oh, I, uh, sure."

He staggers my way while I pull a dollar out of my wallet. It occurs to me that he could very well murder me now, take everything I have on me, and dump my carcass in the river. Should I trust him? I ready myself to battle him hand-to-hand if I need to, and then I give him the dollar bill.

"Thanks, man." He stuffs it down the front of his pants, grinning in the near darkness. He peers to one side, then the other, before he leans forward and whispers, "Or should I say, thanks, Ivan?"

"Huh?"

"Relax, man." He chuckles. "Don't worry about it. I won't blow your cover."

"My cover?"

"Yeah, man. You don't have to play dumb with me. I know who you really are. Ivan the Pinko." He's whispering again. "Double agent, am I right?"

He's obviously off his wobble, and yet I play along. "Oh, yeah. I guess so. Sure."

"I knew it." He smiles so big his teeth gleam. "I love your work, man. You're a friggin' unsung American hero. It's an honor to meet you, man." He holds out his hand. "Agent Johnny Quest, at your service."

We shake hands.

"Quest?"

"Yeah, man."

The light under the bridge is just strong enough for me to see the character's general details. He's my height, and maybe my age.

He has long whiskers, long tangled hair, and is wearing a blanket like a robe. He could be Socrates or Christ, or maybe just an out of work stagehand for the Grateful Dead. It's hard to decide which. He is shirtless and shoeless and wearing baggy pants. He smells very strongly of sweat and urine.

He sways before me, beaming.

It's irrational, but all at once I feel myself filled with envy for this guy. His primitive lifestyle. His ability to work in deep cover and live a wild existence in the very heart of such a tame and modernized world. It's like looking into a magic mirror, one that reflects a way that I too could be living if I weren't so damn civilized. I wonder if I could follow him around for a while, learn his tricks and survival skills. I see us scrounging happily together in dumpsters. I imagine him showing me how to catch rats for food.

Of course, he's a total nut job. But then, so what? How many of the people I pass on the sidewalk are just wavering on the edge of a fantasy? The only difference between him and them is that they're just barely hanging on while this guy here dared to venture one step left of center.

"Do you have the packet, man?"

"What?"

"The packet. I thought that's why you showed up here at the drop."

I'm disappointed that I don't have the packet he wants. Without it, I fear, this make-believe will have to end. Too bad. I was enjoying it. I was merging with his fiction. But then I remember...

"Hey! Yeah, Johnny! Hang on."

I reach into the pocket of my trench coat and pull out Hadley's manila envelope. I hold it in both hands. Suddenly, I am overwhelmed with grief as I think of Richard, of his life, and of my own skewered innocence. It feels like God has died. Or worse – that He proved to be nothing more than a man. The envelope goes blurry before my eyes.

I realize I am weeping.

After a minute, the homeless guy reaches over and takes hold of the envelope, but I can't release my grip.

"Hey," he assures me. "Don't worry, man. Everything's going to be all right."

I think of young Hadley's smile in the Kodachrome photo; I think of her father's timid and boyish mien. At last, I remember myself as a stupid young kid diving into novels and comics in my tree fort and believing that someday I'd live a heroic life of glorious adventure.

"Don't worry, man. You can count on me. The mission is secure."

I sniffle and finally relinquish the packet.

With a bit of effort, he stuffs the envelope down the front of his pants, adjusting himself and squaring his shoulders before me. He places his hand on my arm and gives it a fraternal squeeze. "You're a good man, Ivan. Don't let anybody tell you different."

I sniffle and nod and wipe my nose on my cuff.

"Well." He scrubs his palms together. "Duty calls." He lets the blanket drop to the ground at his feet. He slaps my back, steps around me to the edge of the bike path, climbs over the railing, and wades into the edge of the river. "Don't worry, man." He does a couple arm swings to loosen his shoulders and calls back over the noise of the current surging against his shins. "I'll get this to the Head Office, toute suite."

He steps forward and sinks into the black swirling water – an action hero rejoining with the stream-of-consciousness from which he was born.

Traffic rumbles overhead.

The river blurps and burbles.

Rainwater pours off the bridge in a veil.

"Shit!" Did I just watch a man drown?

That's when I remember – there's no reason to worry.

He's Johnny Quest.

27

NO dreams pester my sleep.
At least, I don't recall any.

It's as if I've been floating through the dark and silent pages of a firmly closed book.

And yet, when I wake, I can't be certain that I've surfaced in the real world.

So much about the setting – its mise en scène – seems surreal.

Looming to my one side is a wrecked and abandoned interplanetary rover – or possibly a rusting metal shopping cart. On my other side is a crate full of scuba tanks – or possibly plastic milk jugs. I am shivering under a mastodon pelt – or possibly a polyester bedspread that is ripped and ragged and reeks of burnt garbage and stale pee. The air feels post-apocalyptic.

I hold still for a moment, trying to get myself grounded, fearful of upsetting some fragile balance, until I hear voices over the sound of the rain. I squirm and rise to an elbow.

A man and a woman are walking on the bike path by the river beneath me. They are wearing pressed suits and each is carrying an open umbrella. Hers is sky blue. His is black. They appear to be office professionals. He is carrying a briefcase. And yet, the man's long, root beer-colored beard and imperial mustache seem incongruous. He's like Paul Bunyan incognito. A closet lumbersexual. I'll bet he has a big blue ox tattooed across one of his butt cheeks.

They haven't noticed me; she is listening intently to what the man is saying.

"Howdy, folks." My voice is raspy with waking. "Working on a Saturday then, are we?"

They all but leap sideways and look askance to where I'm wriggling in the dirt like a maggot. The woman huddles close to the man and clutches his arm.

I grin. "Gotta keep that Gross National Product rolling along, now don't we?"

They are awkward, suspicious, until the man answers glibly, gallantly, for the benefit of his lady, "It's a bull market, friend. Buy low, sell high."

They both break into laughter at my expense, and then, sharing his big shiny umbrella, they hurry from under the bridge toward a glass office building rising out of the fog on the waterfront.

"Smart ass," I mutter. "I'll bet she thinks you're pretty cool."

And then I yell after them, "Hey, sweetheart, you ought to ask your friend Paul there to show you his friggin' tattoo!"

I watch the river for a minute, listening to the traffic passing up above. Gosh, my head aches.

Some fighter jets drop from the gray sky. They fall out of formation, metamorphose into pigeons, and, with their wings snapping, swoop up to perch in the girders.

The birds shake the raindrops from their feathers and shit and preen.

They rumble and coo.

28

THE apartment is Outer Space cold. Icy puffs of breath rise before my face. I hang my soiled coat by the door and hug myself in my arms.

"Ava?"

My utterance implodes under the enormous black hole vacuum force of the room's gravity.

I don't bother calling for Jane. It's already the middle of the afternoon. They have obviously left on their little trip.

I scan the perimeter, assessing the situation. It feels like I've stepped into a diorama. There is an intangibly feminine quality about the setting. Delicate, cutout paper snowflakes are taped to the glass doors. Our Christmas tree is fully decorated with a lady's touch. Bulbs and garlands dangle merrily from its plastic branches. A string of darkened lights is looped round and round its girlish girth. A dark star is perched on the tree's tippy top.

So, I realize, this is a snapshot of their girl-world life without me in it. Admittedly, I'm a bit disappointed that it looks so perfect. It's as if they've already moved on, as if some messy and unruly pet has finally been sent to the pound, or perhaps even put down.

But wait a second. No. I'm not completely forgotten. I spy it hanging on the refrigerator. They've left me a message.

Will,

I'm writing this on the off chance that you're not as stupid as you're acting. And because I have no other way of communicating with you since you never answer your damn phone!

From my point of view, you're being a dick. Any way I look at it, that's what I see. But maybe I'm missing something. Honestly, I just don't understand what's come over you lately. You're like a different person. Maybe you need help. We can do that if necessary. We can find a professional to help you sort yourself out. At any rate, you and I need to talk first. We need to get on the same page with some things. I'll save the details of that for when, and if, it actually happens.

For now, I guess you just get to enjoy a little vacation without us. Ava and I will be gone all weekend. Consider this a reprieve from fatherhood and marriage, a little test to see how you like life without us. You have my blessing. Just forget me for a while. Maybe I'll do the same with you. That might be just what we both need. Honestly, it sounds kind of nice. Consider yourself free as a bird.

There's obviously a lot more to say, but we're in a rush.

Just remember, Will — Ava loves you. That's a respnsibility you won't ever outrun. I guess I love you too.

I'm just getting tired of your bullshit.

Jane

I reread the note twice more, studying it for some hint of tenderness hidden between the lines. I can't find any. The words seem deliberately chosen to be mocking and spiteful and coming from a place that is holier-than-thou.

"Hrmph!" I mutter. "Professional help, my dumb ass!"

I crumple the note in my fist, drop it to the floor, and kick it across the room.

I stand there for a while, at a loss, listening to the chill silence.

I momentarily flounder.

Finally, I go take a shower and get ready for my reading.

29

M Y Uber pulls to the curb in front of the library.
The building is aglow and rising monumentally into the
chimerical clouds scudding over the city. People with umbrellas
are climbing the stone steps and pressing through the front doors.
Apprehension convulses through me as I am reminded of an old
Autochrome photo I once saw of the unsinkable Titanic taken
shortly before it sank.

"Huh," says my driver. He cranes around for a better view. "Must
be something pretty special going on here tonight."

My mouth is dry as talc. I can but grunt in response.

I get out of the car and stand in the rain, preparing myself
to merge with the herd of people filing like cattle into a barn. I
don't understand why there are so many of them. I feel awkward,
dematerialized, doubtful. I am pondering the idea of sneaking off
and hiding under a bridge when a shadow comes up beside me and
takes my hand.

As I turn, I am relieved to find – "Oh!" – it's Martine.

A twist of damp hair dangles over her left eye; her lip ring glints when she speaks.

"Tu es en retard," she whispers. "Come with me."

Martine squeezes my hand and extracts me from the crowd, leading me around the dark side of the building to a secret door hidden like a rabbit hole behind some dripping shrubs. Her fingers are warm and damp. My hand feels happy in hers. Although honestly, the moment feels less like a friendly rendezvous than it does an abduction. The urgency in her actions suggests she could just as soon be leading me by gunpoint.

Martine punches a code into the lock and swings open the door, dragging me down a flight of stairs into a long hallway.

Our hasty steps echo against the bare walls; fluorescent lights buzz and flicker overhead. The air smells faintly of old documents.

At the end of the corridor, we come to a service elevator. Martine presses the button, eliciting a clank and hum from the building's mechanical innards. We both watch for the light above the door, holding hands, not speaking, waiting for the lift to descend.

Water drips from my trench coat.

Martine impatiently taps her toe.

The doors slide open and we enter. Only now does Martine let go of me. She presses another button and leans against the wall, grasping the rail on either side behind her back.

The doors close.

I don't know. I suppose it could just be the elevator rising, but as I regard the stunning young woman before me, I feel I am experiencing my first ever zolly of the soul. Her effect on me is both visceral and mystical. I am transported to the very brink of an all-encompassing swoon.

Martine is dressed in a black, short-sleeved turtleneck, black tights, licorice-black boots, and a burgundy miniskirt. Raindrops sparkle in her dark hair. Her arms are wet. She resembles a chic and stylish exclamation point, shamelessly declaring herself to the world.

"Je suis ici!" she seems to proclaim. "I exist!"

I'm not so sure the same could be said of me. I feel more like a question mark. Am I truly here? Is this really happening? I feel made-up, false, like a fictional apparition being yanked willy-nilly through some fanciful storyline.

"I really dig your lip ring."

No doubt this is not an appropriate line for a middle-aged, married man and father to say to a sexy French girl, but the words just sort of tumble out of my mouth. Something separate from me has overtaken me, indeed, is working me by remote control.

"You look very pretty."

Martine gives me an affable smirk that says, we both know I look way better than just *pretty*.

"Are you excited?" she asks.

"Yes." I feel the tops of my ears turning red. "I am."

She smirks again and laughs. *"Alors!"* She tucks her hair behind her ear. "I mean about your reading."

"Oh."

Before I can formulate a clever response, the floor of the elevator presses beneath our feet and settles. The doors slide open. Martine reaches over and takes my hand, leading me out.

We move quickly through a storeroom, down another short hallway, around a corner, and finally through a door upon which is painted the word Auditorium. Martine drags me into the wings. A din of voices drifts from beyond a tall curtain. I catch a sidelong glimpse of the stage, and of the podium placed like a dinghy in the center of its immensity.

Martine peers around, searching for someone, and then she pulls me forcefully to where a trio of stagehands is taking instructions from their boss. Martine lets go of my hand and deposits me before said boss.

"Voila!"

The boss – Roxanne – turns.

A smile spreads across Roxanne's face and she shakes her head in relief. "Holy cow, Will! You certainly have a flare for drama." She strides forward, wraps her arms around me, and gives me one of those big, bosom-smashing hugs of the variety I am coming to associate with thoughts of Stromboli.

"Sorry," I mutter. "I didn't mean to be difficult."

Roxanne, too, is drop-dead gorgeous, hotter, as the saying goes, than a two-dollar pistol. She is a pale compliment to Martine's dark and enchanting mien. It's as if these girls' after-hours under-beings have wiggled free of their demure, diurnal, librarian disguises. They each exude a feral femininity.

Roxanne helps me out of my coat and thanks Martine for delivering me.

"Pas de probleme."

Next, Roxanne has Martine and me step over to the curtain. She parts it a crack so we can peek out at the auditorium.

I gulp.

To tell the truth, *Western Wind* only sold modestly well, and yet it appears everyone who ever bought a copy of my novel is here this evening. The place is packed.

"Whoa," I say. "I didn't realize I was opening for Stephen King."

"Are you kidding?" Roxanne grins. "They're all here for you." She places her hands on either of my shoulders and looks into my eyes. "You're a rock star, Will, and I'm your agent. I spread the word all over town and online, everywhere I knew your fans were hiding."

Fans, I think, *fans*, trying to recall that word's definition. I've never really thought of myself as someone who ever had any of those. That I might have fans now – that someone out there might actually give a damn about what I do – makes me instantly alarmed, pleased, and slightly seasick.

"Well, cowboy," says Roxanne, "are you ready to do this?"

No way, I think.

"You bet," I say.

Roxanne uses her fingers to press out a wrinkle on the front of my shirt and then her green eyes brighten. "Oh, wait! I almost forgot."

She lopes over to a table and opens a big round box from which she extracts a brown felt cowboy hat. She carries it back, grinning. "Surprise!" She holds up the hat for me to see.

I pretend I'm favorably astonished. "What the heck!"

"A present." Roxanne places the hat on my head, scrunching it down to a point where my ears stick out. "There!" I feel like Dopey.

She steps back and admires my head. She appears very satisfied. "Perfect!" She looks to Martine for confirmation.

Martine nods and grins. "Very nice."

"Gee, Roxanne." (I'd really love to ditch the hat.) "Thanks."

"It's just like Buck's," she says. "And look..." She raises the edge of her skirt to above her knees. Her thin white legs both disappear mid-shin into a pair of red cowboy boots. She turns a boot on its heel, modeling. "They're just like Sally Storm's."

"Wow," I say. "Snazzy."

She laughs. "If you like that, wait until you see my other surprise."

"Oh?"

"Later." She winks playfully. "After the show."

At that moment, one of the stagehands dims the house lights, indicating that the performance is about to begin.

"Okay," says Roxanne. She leans forward and gives me a quick peck on the cheek. "Go out there and show us your stuff." And then she whisks out onto the stage to make her introduction.

My stuff?

Everything is suddenly happening fast.

The audience applauds as Roxanne strides to the podium, adjusts the microphone, and thanks everyone for coming out this evening. She assures them that they're in for a special treat. She thanks her helpers, and then the Head Office in Administration for allowing this event to take place. She tells everyone how she's my biggest fan. At last, she starts singing my praises, prattling off a list of Will Kirby accolades that sound like make-believe. She either knows more about me than I do, or she's messing with the truth.

I shiver and turn to Martine. "Be honest with me." I lean to her and speak softly. "Do I look absolutely ridiculous?"

Martine steps before me and does a quick inspection. She crosses her arms and assesses me top to bottom, spending a little extra time considering the general region of my noggin. *"Oui,"* she finally says, and reaches up to wipe Roxanne's lipstick from my cheek with her thumb. "But ridiculous in a good way." She smiles. "You look bigger than life. They will love it."

I am somewhat encouraged.

And that's when Martine does something I'm not expecting, something, indeed, verging on the fictional – she steps up close and, placing her palm on my chest, leans in, kissing me directly on the mouth. The thin, metallic edge of her lip ring presses against my own lower lip, causing the whole world, for a short time, to simply dissolve.

I tumble into a black hole.

Becoming one with gravity.

Submitting to a slight paroxysm.

Until, with a faint pop, Martine releases her lips from mine. She steps back, letting her fingertips slide down and away from my chest.

I feel myself bending somewhat forward, as if her suction has pulled me off balance, my lips still held in an attitude of semi-puckered readiness.

"*Bonne chance*," she whispers.

Someone very far away announces my name.

Followed by applause.

Martine hands me a copy of *Western Wind*, turns me around, and shoves me toward the stage.

30

THE applause continues as I stumble out from behind the curtain.

One could almost call it thunderous.

A few of the more enthusiastic members of the audience whistle and whoop like cowboys.

Roxanne, all smiles, meets me beside the podium and gives my arm an affectionate squeeze before abandoning me to the spotlight.

I place my book on the lectern and then grasp the rails in both hands while squinting out into the dimly lit sea of ghostly faces and clapping hands. I tip down the brim of my hat to block the glare.

I've seen film of celebrities in similar positions – Mick Jagger, Bonito Mussolini – but I personally have no precedent for this experience. I don't know how to act. The few readings I've given in the past have done nothing to prepare me. Those were merely small showings held in the shadowy back corners of bookstores, almost all of which were attended by no more than a handful of mute and drowsy bookworms. But this is another gig altogether. I fear I might publicly puke.

And then I become paranoid.

One can't help but suspect this whole evening is nothing more than an elaborate joke. That's just how life has been going for me lately. Perhaps it's nothing more than a prank designed by Jane herself as punishment for my many failures as a helpmate. A premonition flits across the screen of my mind in which I see myself mistakenly feeling loved, even adored, just before a bucket of pig blood dumps down on me from the rafters. My delusions are subsequently dashed. Everyone present is granted a good hearty laugh. Jane's revenge is complete.

I brace myself for the worst, but no blood rains down.

It seems the audience is sincere in its jubilation.

I smile shyly to the crowd and wiggle-wave my fingers. They take this as a signal and the hubbub subsides.

Then they wait.

Shuffling in their seats.

I'm scrambling to remember the procedure here. What am I expected to do next? It's harder than one might think. I adjust the reading light. I fidget. I straighten my cuffs. There is a bottle of water sitting on the edge of the lectern and it occurs to me I should maybe wet my whistle. I unscrew the cap and drink.

And drink

And drink.

I can't stop.

I had no idea I was so thirsty. As the water glugs down my gullet, I am aware of some twittering up in the cheap seats, but it doesn't slow me down. I just keep gulping and gulping until the bottle is drained. I wipe my mouth on my sleeve and, for no sensible reason, toss the empty over my shoulder.

"Dehydrated," I mutter, and let loose a lengthy burp.

The burp booms back to me over the sound system, followed by a wave of laughter and more thunderous clapping. One of the cowboys whoops appreciatively.

The water was apparently faulty; it did nothing to quench my thirst. But I'm feeling real pressure now. It's time to get this show started. I should probably say something clever or thank someone for something or other. No doubt, that's protocol. But I can't think how to do that, so I just cut to the chase and open my book.

Dang!

It doesn't appear to be in English!

The words are printed in Chinese, or possibly Algebra. There's no way I can read them.

But wait. No. Whew! I was just having a brain fart, a dyslexic seizure. I turn the book right side up. There. That's better.

Still, the act of transposing those abstract little glyphs across the conveyor belt of my brain, and then infusing them with the proper cadence and meaning by way of the rusty gizmo in my throat, seems utterly impossible. How, I try to remember, do I do that?

A tension settles over the auditorium; the audience is growing restless.

Flop sweat flows freely under my arms.

In the heightened state of my panic, I smell burning ozone.

Someone quietly boos.

Or maybe moos.

Either way, it doesn't exactly give me courage.

I swallow. My knees tremble uncontrollably. I think I need to pee. And then I lick my lips.

That's when it happens. As my tongue touches my lips. I am granted a sensory recall. A force surges through me and I hyper-zoom back to the moment when Martine's tender mouth was pressed warmly against my own. I feel, again, the thin edge of her lip ring. It serves as the metal post on a battery, or possibly a lightning rod – a conduit through which I accept the transformative transference of a sure and magnificent power.

Atom bombs explode! Nuclear reactors sizzle! Suns burst into fragments!

Shazam!

I am made mighty; I am a mutation of Dick Zag and Will friggin' Kirby – writer, adventurer, love wizard, and all-around man extraordinaire.

With this masculine power flowing through me, I begin, with supreme confidence, to read from the opening pages of *Western Wind*.

———————

A storm was coming.

Buck Wilde could smell it in the air.

He tasted rain on the wind.

The clouds had not yet risen above the mesa, but Buck knew they were there and moving fast his way. He could feel them building.

"Dammit, Lucky." The weary cowboy patted his horse's neck and then stood in his stirrups, peering out at the thousand head of Longhorns milling over the plain. "This ain't good."

The cattle were in a bad spot. A long, steep canyon cut like a scar through the desert on the far side of the herd. It stretched both directions for a dozen miles. If a peal of thunder riled up the dumb beasts, they'd likely stampede in the wrong direction, plummeting over the cliffs into a pile of broken bones and cow shit.

"But we ain't going to let that happen now, are we, boy?" Buck wiped the sweat from his brow and then snugged his hat down on his head. "Not on my watch."

With a gentle kick to his horse's flanks, Buck set off at a gallop to get himself between the cattle and the gorge.

———————

I read through the first scene where all hell breaks loose as the storm sweeps in hard, replete with lightning, driving rain, and cow hysteria. My pacing is impeccable and sure. I sense the audience moving to the edge of its seat as I direct their excitement like a wrangler herding cows. With flare and riveting drama, I continue on to the thrilling turn in the action where Buck, after saving the herd, is trampled while heroically rescuing Fitch – a fellow cowpuncher whose horse has taken a tumble amidst the melee of hooves and horns. This leads to Buck being hurried off for medical attention at a nearby ranch – a big spread run by Sally Storm, a feisty, alluring, straight-shooting sort of gal who, in spite of her better judgment, takes a shine to the wounded cowboy. The ensuing ranch romance – composed, as it is, of two independent spirits – is inevitably fraught with a tempestuous mix of squabbles and passion.

After about an hour, at the end of the chapter where the chemistry between Buck and Sally really begins to smolder, I decide it's time to stop reading. I close my book, tip my hat to the crowd, and say, "Thank you very much."

They applaud.

I wave in appreciation as I swagger from the stage.

Job done.

———

Roxanne and Martine are waiting for me offstage. The big smile on Roxanne's face tells me I done did good.

"That was amazing!" she says and throws her arms around me.

Martine steps close and squeezes my hand.

The applause out in the auditorium does not subside; it grows. I hear a few more cowboy calls, and then the ruckus changes into a chant of *Salt and Whiskey! Salt and Whiskey! Salt and Whiskey!*

Initially, I'm confused. It makes no sense. I turn to Roxanne for an answer.

"They want more," she explains. "They want an encore."

"Oh."

Martine takes my copy of *Western Wind* and flips through the pages until she finds a particular passage. "*Voici,*" she says. "Read this part."

I take the open book and read the first lines to myself. "Oh, okay. Sure. I get it." I take a breath and shamble back out to the lectern.

As I emerge from behind the curtain, the audience ceases its chant and erupts into one more round of enthusiastic bellowing and applause. They expectantly take their seats.

"Well, thank you kindly, folks." I am still in cowboy character; I drawl in western fashion into the microphone. "Much obliged."

Then, again, I read.

31

THE excerpt is an odd one, what has come to be known as the Salt and Whiskey scene. And yet, of all the parts of my novel, it is the one that got the most attention from reviewers. Depending upon the critic, the passage is said to be either "loaded with nuance, tension, and brazen literary genius," or "corrupted by a hack writer's clumsy idea of symbolism." Either way, I don't personally feel like I had much to do with its creation. Of all the episodes in the book, it's the one where I most felt taken over by unseen forces. It came during one of Ava's naptimes, while I was in a trance, on a drizzling afternoon when I was obviously being mind-controlled by aliens using me to write a story about a happy-go-lucky cowboy and his domineering, blood-sucking sweetheart.

The scene follows the chapter where Buck Wilde, driven crazy by the constraints of a domestic relationship, has run off to a whorehouse with his fellow cowpokes. Sally is left at home on her ranch to seethe. To appease her own anger and frustration over Buck's wayward shenanigans, she calls for her workhands to bring forth a bull that has been goring steers and generally causing mischief with the herd. The unruly brute is led in by a ring through his nose. After a heroic tussle, he is finally hobbled and forced into a tight stall that serves as a sort of taurine straitjacket.

Normally, such a renegade would be summarily executed. After all, once a bull has gone rogue, disrupting the harmony of polite bovine society, there's not much else one can do with him. But Sally is feeling extra vindictive this day. She wants to set an example. A bullet to the brain is too good for this son of a bitch. As a dust devil swirls forebodingly across the desert behind her, the cowgirl speaks soothingly to the beast.

"Poor fella," she coos, and strokes his neck through the rails. "You just can't be happy with your lot, can you?"

The bull's flesh quivers beneath her fingertips; he senses the mockery in her tone.

"Well," she says, "maybe ol' Sally can ease your suffering."

She draws the bowie knife from the scabbard on her hip and lays it flat against the bull's throat.

"The secret," she explains, "is not to remove the object of desire, but to remove the object doing the desiring."

With that bit of philosophy, she squats and reaches through the rails, grabs hold of him down low, and with one deft flick of her blade, separates the bull from his oysters.

The bull – suddenly a eunuch – watches in stunned, cross-eyed pain as Sally strides back to the ranch house, her bloody knife in one hand, his former love components dangling from her other.

The scene ends with Sally humming happily at her cook stove while frying up her little treat in a skillet full of salt and whiskey.

32

AFTER the reading comes a reception in the lobby. Hors d'oeuvres are available, along with a choice of wine, beer, mineral water, or, thematically, Red Bull energy drinks. Roxanne escorts me through the crowd and delivers me to a padded armchair against the wall.

"Here's your throne," she says, "in case you get tired of standing." She hands me a cold can of beer produced at a local craft brewery. It has a silhouette cowboy on the label and is called, aptly enough, Cowboy Beer. Roxanne explains that she's worked out a deal with the brewery as promotion for my career. "We're advertising it on your fan page," she says, "and they're peddling your book on theirs. Which reminds me, we should get a photo of you enjoying a can of their beer for PR." Then she tells me she needs to go chat with a producer who is interested in optioning the movie rights for *Western Wind*. "I'll stay within whistling distance, if you need me." In parting, Roxanne kisses me on the mouth, as if it's the most natural thing in the world, before hurrying off to her business appointment.

I watch her walk away. I drop into the chair, tip back my hat, and, with the slouch of a ranch hand relaxing after a long day of riding fence, take a big swig of my beer.

It's weird.

Something has changed.

Ever since I stomped out and slammed the door on Ol' What's Her Name.

Or maybe since I delivered the packet to Agent Johnny Quest.

But at some point, apparently while I was in a suspended state of hypersleep, the story of my life has been revised. The elements of my world have been rearranged. I am no longer on a trajectory to Loserville. I'm no longer a zero with a capital Z. Instead, I've passed through some sort of magic portal, or possibly a sequence of portals. What's more, I am no longer striving. Instead, amazingly, I have evidently arrived at my long-sought success. I gaze out at the room. It's as if I'm holding court. My many admirers mill and murmur and glance bashfully in my direction, trying to muster enough courage to approach me.

Finally, a bold young couple steps forward.

"Hello," says the girl.

"Howdy."

I feel like I might have seen her somewhere before, maybe pulling shots of espresso behind the counter at Chez Pearl. The scrawny guy with her has affected the image of Shaggy from the cartoon *Scooby-Doo*. His hair is disheveled to the perfect degree of indifference, and an apathetic patch of whiskers is sprouting from his chin. His most significant accouterments are a ring through his nasal septum and a faded green t-shirt that says PLASTIC SUCKS.

"We totally love your book," says the girl. "It's, like, so the way it is."

"Well, I appreciate you saying so." I go into my default mode of gracious and humble.

"It's, like, people are cows." She shrugs self-consciously. "Or, like, cows are like people."

Her boyfriend bobs his scruffy head. "Totally."

"Well," I chuckle wisely. "People can be all kinds of animals, but good eye. You're right about that in the novel. You caught the metaphor."

This pleases her to no end. She feels smart for having figured it out. Honestly, the first time I saw that symbolism myself was when it was pointed out in a review. It was a bit of a shock to realize I was so good at employing literary devices without even knowing it. Of course, there were plenty of critics who thought it was a ham-handed effort. But screw 'em! As long as my many young fans are happy.

The couple stares at me, as if expecting me to do a trick, or maybe scratch them behind the ears. I take a hit from my beer and just stare back at them, sucking at my teeth.

The guy points his thumb at his girlfriend and says, "Daphne here's a bona fide Kirby Girl."

"Oh?" I have no idea what he means.

The girl blushes and punches her sidekick in the arm.

He laughs. "Well, you are!" He tugs at her sweater. "Show him."

She squirms in response.

"Come on, Daph, show him." He turns to me. "You want to see, don't you?"

I shrug. "Not if she doesn't want to." Although, I am sort of curious what the hell he's talking about.

After some reluctance, the girl finally gives in. She glances around the room to make sure no one is watching. Plenty of people are, but it actually makes no difference. She steps sideways to me and, with a bit of coy bravado, instructs her boyfriend to pull up the side of her sweater.

A flock of tiny birds is tattooed above her hip. Their blue and red wings contrast vividly against her pale skin. It's very striking, but I'm confused as to how this makes her a "Kirby Girl," or even what that means.

"Higher," says the girl. She bends sideways, awkwardly presenting her upper flank for my viewing.

Her boyfriend hikes up her sweater to as far as her bra strap, until I am able to see what all the fuss is about. Tattooed over her ribs is some sort of palm-sized hieroglyph.

"There!" says the guy.

I lean forward and halfway rise from my chair, squinting, cocking my head, trying to comprehend what I'm looking at. It appears to be a letter, maybe in Cyrillic, but something about it is not quite right. Then I get it.

"Oh!"

It's not one letter, but two joined together. It's a W married to a K, in the fashion of a brand, the kind cowboys burn into the hides of their animals as a mark of ownership.

"Pretty dank, huh?" The boyfriend is very proud. "She got the idea off your website." He lets the girl's sweater fall back into place and then turns to me while pointing at his own nose. "And I got the ring." He tips back his head so that I get a good look up his nostrils. His metal ring dangles against his top lip like a tiny doorknocker.

"Wow," I say. "Nice."

After that, it's as if a gate has been flung open. I am subjected to a string of fans showing me their brands and nasal irons. I have never been accosted by so many flanks and nostrils. It's overwhelming. Depending upon whether I'm being presented with feminine torsos or masculine snouts, I am jerked between the extremes of titillation and repulsion.

One girl is dressed in a black, floor-length gown. Her face is powdered white, her lips are painted deep purple, and her heavily mascaraed eyelashes flap like the wings of bats. With a sly smile, she informs me that her own tattoo is in a "cloistered zone" that would cause a scandal if shown in public. Her voice is the rustle of velvet bed sheets. She then gives me a slip of paper upon which is printed a phone number and the name, Gothina. "If you'd like to inspect it sometime," she says, "give me a call." She shoots me a come-hither wink and slips back into the room like a sensual wisp of smoke.

A hand grasps my shoulder.

It's Roxanne.

"Having fun?"

"Sure. You bet."

She takes my empty and hands me a fresh Cowboy Beer.

"But, hey," I say, "what's with all these brands and nose rings?"

"Oh, that's your gimmick. Do you like it? It's a way I invented for your fans to be part of their favorite author's fictional world and process."

"Hmm."

Honestly, I don't know how I feel about this. It seems a little extreme. Something about it smacks of a cult. The Reverend Jim Jones and his Kool-Aid party come to mind. Or Charlie Manson and his brainwashed family. Something about it seems marginally politically incorrect. I swallow some beer and turn the idea over in my head. Well, I decide, I guess it doesn't have to be a bad thing. Maybe it's just cool, a sort of fan base fun and games. True, I'm less taken with the guys and their nose rings, but yeah, I could get used to having such a devoted following. And let's be honest, pushing all social propriety aside, what red-blooded American man wouldn't thrill to have hundreds of women walking down the street with his personal stamp hidden under their clothes?

I look up at Roxanne. "Do you have one too?"

She feigns offense. "Why, Will Kirby, I declare! I'm your number one fan." She bends to my ear and asks in a whisper, "Do you honestly think I'd get inked with the same mark as this common bunch of heifers?"

"No. I guess not."

"Damn straight." She takes my beer and, in purest Sally Storm style, guzzles half the can, wiping her mouth on the back of her wrist when she's finished. "This ranch gal's got something special in store for her favorite cowpoke."

"Oh?" I swallow. "What's that?"

She hands back my beer and grins. "You'll see, cowboy. Later. After the coyotes all go to bed."

33

EVENTUALLY, the gathering dwindles. Like aimless livestock, my adoring fans all wander out beneath the EXIT signs to meld into the various corners of the night. The janitorial crew sweeps up the mess and disappears. Roxanne and Martine patrol the library for stragglers, turning off lights, after which the three of us don our coats in the darkened foyer.

We step outside.

Roxanne locks the door behind us.

"Well," she says cheerfully, "that surpassed expectations."

The steps are wet and gleaming. Raindrops fall like gnats through the illuminated air beneath the lampposts. A single dark sedan swishes by in the street. Roxanne opens a big black umbrella and hands it to me. She and Martine each take an arm on my either side as I center the umbrella over our heads. It's a little awkward with my hat in the way, but I manage to make it work.

"Where shall we go to celebrate?" asks Roxanne.

They discuss options while I wait. I hadn't considered what might come after the reading. Well, no, that's not entirely true – a man entertains certain fantasies. But I hadn't truly considered the chill void waiting for me if I should choose to return to my former place of residence. And I had also failed to fully consider the reality of traveling solo. Sure, we're all ultimately alone in the end. That whole *no man is an island* idea is just a load of wishful bunk. Let's not kid ourselves on that point. No fella worth his existential backbone could ever convince himself otherwise. Life is arguably just one fleeting, lonesome ride. Still, it's an unexpected relief to realize that this night is young and the party's just getting started.

An objective is decided upon.

A heading is chosen.

We set off.

———————

As we travel along, a peculiar sensation begins to overcome me.

Gradually, somewhat surgically, like the skin of a rat being peeled from its carcass...

I don't know. Maybe I'm only suffering from too many cans of Cowboy Beer. But as we stroll arm in arm in arm, I start to feel my self disconnecting from myself. Next, I begin to dangle slightly overhead, observing the top of our umbrella from the vantage of a surveillance camera. The girls are reviewing the evening's highlights, and I'm answering their questions, even throwing in the offhand witty remark, but our voices are remote. Our footfalls clop distantly on the wet cement. It's like watching a crane shot transition scene in an old Bogart movie.

My companions are escorting me to a subliminal part of the city where I've never been.

Leading me into ink-black byways.

Transporting me unto an alternative point of view.

Rerouting my plot line through a maze of pie-in-the-sky meta-reality.

Until we reach our destination.

A pulsing red sign pierces the night like a neon wound.

HOOT'S

Both Os in the word HOOT'S encircle an enormous yellow iris, complete with a pupil, creating the omniscient eyes of a nocturnal bird of prey.

The giant bird's gaze follows us as we pass beneath the sign and push through the establishment's front door.

Yet another portal.

———————

The bar is a shelter from the cold. It is cave-like. Claustrophobic. Dim. Peopled with the odors of spilt liquor, overflowing ashtrays, lascivious longing, and budget perfume. Honestly, it's pretty dodgy and run down, the charmless underbelly of a bygone era – a lonely-hearts watering hole – a gin joint full of ill-advised trysts – a veritable scrapyard of broken dreams and readjusted outlooks on life.

Jazz moans drowsily from the jukebox.

One wonders how some entrepreneurial hipster hasn't snatched up this place and sanitized it to suit contemporary sensibilities. It seems to be a refuge for endangered species – rheumy-eyed rummies and frazzled floozies – a little corner of wilderness where such beasts can still be spotted in their natural environment. A dozen of these damaged denizens cower in the shadowy corners and at the far end of the bar. They regard us suspiciously over their drinks.

"What do you think?" asks Roxanne.

I look around the room. It feels like we're sort of out of place, like tourists, or foreigners.

I shrug. "Good."

Martine agrees.

We hang our wet coats and umbrella by the door and then sidle to the bar. The girls pull up stools on either side of me.

The bartender, who appears to have been yanked straight from the pages of Mickey Spillane, wanders indifferently to where we're waiting.

"Hey, Roxy. What'll you have?"

"Hi, Big Joe. Shots and chasers times three." Roxanne seems to be our tour director. She knows the fauna and speaks the language.

"You come here often?" I ask her.

"From time to time. Whenever I need to do research for my novel, or let my Ms. Hyde stretch her legs."

Big Joe brings our drinks and sets them up on the counter. Before turning away, he scrutinizes me, my cowboy hat, and the two luscious dolls at my sides. He shakes his head; Big Joe's seen it all.

Roxanne holds up her shot glass and Martine and I follow suit.

"To the stuff of fiction!"

We clink our glasses together.

As I throw back my shot, I notice a dusty stuffed owl perched above the bar. The joint's mascot perhaps? Maybe Ol' Hoot herself. A decorative string of tinsel is tangled in the owl's talons. I set my empty on the bar and run my tongue around my teeth. Whiskey fire burns in my throat as I study the filthy fowl glaring down at me through her marble eyeballs. It's a cut-rate stuff job, to say the least, as if done by a mortician who dabbled in taxidermy on the side. The feathers are sticking out at odd angles and the mummified bird's posture is stiff and unnatural. And yet, there's a hint of animation lingering there. Some spasm of a beaten predator's dying spirit. Some paltry remnant of a humiliated hunter's fading arrogance.

I wink at the bird and tip my hat with a grin. I couldn't say exactly why. I guess I'm feeling pretty smug.

Then I lean back and wrap my arms around both girls, bringing them in close. They don't resist. They laugh. They press against me willingly, their soft feminine curves contouring nicely around my hard edges.

This is how it begins, I think. Although at this point in the evening, I'm still cautious enough not to predict what that *it* might turn out to be.

34

MORE whiskey. More beer.

Our little soirée continues.

I don't normally drink this much. Or do I? I can't recall.

At any rate, I normally drink this much tonight. I feel all loose and glad and extemporaneous.

Roxanne starts telling dumb writer jokes. After an eye-roller about a rattlesnake with a typewriter, she asks, "What happens to a novelist when he doesn't get his coffee in the morning?"

Martine and I frown at each other and shrug.

"He goes into a comma."

We all laugh and sag against one another like sloppy barflies. It's fun.

Big Joe brings another round, wipes the bar with a rag, and carries off our empties.

Somebody at one of the far tables makes a loud, inarticulate remark. It might be directed at us; it might not.

We drink.

Roxanne takes hold of my left hand and turns it over. She

examines it closely. She strokes my lifeline and then my empty ring finger. "You ever think about getting hitched, cowboy?"

I stare at her until I realize that outside of our encounters at the library, and apart from what she's conjured in her imagination, this girl knows next to nothing about my life. I turn to Martine and recognize that the same is true of her.

I'm a blank page.

It's astoundingly liberating, as if waking up to find oneself released after a long incarceration. The faintest quiver of guilt creeps up my neck, but the alcohol clouds my ability to understand just why, and then it all melts away anyway, leaving me charged with a sort of boozy, languid verve.

"I'm not the marrying type, sweetheart." I finally answer her with a grin. "I prefer to stay free as a bird."

We toast, "To *free as a bird!*"

Again, someone in the hinter regions makes a comment, louder this time, and definitely directed at me and my companions. I turn and squint toward the three masculine shapes hunkering in the gloom like inebriated wolves. Their faces are obscured behind a haze of cigarette smoke, but their postures suggest that they're scowling. Maybe they had a bad day. I hold up my glass in their direction and nod with a smile. No reason to be unfriendly.

Roxanne nearly falls off her stool and I catch her by the elbow.

"My hero," she giggles, and then tips back my hat and drops her face into mine, giving me a whiskey-flavored smack on the lips. "I gotta go make a call," she says, "and see a man about a horse." She taps my nose with her fingertip and staggers away toward a payphone hanging on the distant wall.

Martine and I are left alone at the bar.

"She's funny," says Martine.

"Yeah. *Elle est drôle.*"

"*Oui.*" She smiles. "*Drôle.*"

I laugh. "I'm afraid that's about all the French I know."

Martine tilts her lovely head, tucks a strand of hair behind her ear, and exudes the most delicious, sweet lemon pheromone one could possibly imagine. "*Alors,*" she says. "I will be your tutor."

The blood coursing through my mortal being begins to percolate.

We gaze at one another.

And then she kisses me.

Working her mouth on mine like a tool.

Our tongues frolic like lizards.

Until Martine disengages.

The whole exchange lasts forever and is over all too quickly.

"Lesson one." She sips her drink. "How we make kiss in France."

I rub my fingers over my lips and swallow my heart back down to its proper slot in my ribcage. "How'd I do? Could I ever become fluent?"

Martine squeezes my thigh. "We will practice more."

It's all a bit campy, a bit over the top. I sense this, but somehow it feels fitting and agreeable. Something about the setting makes it okay to play the game. We could be acting out a scene from a cheesy novel. I could be Mike Hammer or Sam Spade. I just need to trade in my cowboy hat for a felt fedora.

Martine and I continue with our tête-à-tête. Non-sequiturs segue one into the next by way of the random. The words don't much matter, just the sensation of speaking, of swapping thought and breath. We chat about whiskey, the Eiffel Tower, Simone de Beauvoir, different breeds of cows...

I'm starting to feel like it's time for another kissing lesson when someone comes up behind me and tips my hat forward over my eyes.

I adjust my lid and turn. Of course, I'm expecting Roxanne to be coming back from the powder room and being playful, so I'm a little surprised to find myself confronted by three fellows standing shoulder to shoulder. The wolves. I've read enough pulp novels to know I should have seen this coming. Still, it feels laughably formulaic.

I try to keep it sociable. "Well howdy, boys. What can I do you for?"

No smiles, just sneers. The alpha male in the middle looks as though someone pissed in his beer, or maybe his momma smacked him around when he was a tyke. Either way, the result was a surly disposition.

"My buddies and I were just getting worried it might be past your bedtime, grandpa. Maybe you should leave the little girls alone and hobble back to the old folks' home before you miss your medication."

He's wittier than he looks.

"Well," I chuckle. "They let me out to play now and then, as long as I don't get into too much mischief. Besides," I continue, "it might surprise you to know I'm younger than I look. I just got this rugged appearance from my fabulous life of adventure."

He isn't amused.

And neither, apparently, are his lackeys.

They all three stand there like stone-faced clichés. The leader shows me his teeth and snarls. "Seriously, you dried up old fuck, you're disgusting. You need to leave these girls alone."

I glance at Martine who is looking sideways at the wolf. I'm a little drunk, but I sense pieces moving into place – Big Joe stands poised with his hands under the bar; the other customers lean forward in their seats; even the jukebox is cued to a manic, foreshadowing saxophone solo.

"The party's over, gramps. Take that dumb-shit hat off your head and scram." Wolf boy points over his shoulder at the door with his thumb. "Get your wrinkled ass outta here."

Now he's just being mean.

I'm taken off guard. His threatening snarl has me stumped. I can't think of a clever comeback.

Theoretically, according to the genre of the moment, we should all start throwing punches now, and, accordingly, after a few broken chairs and close calls, I, the outnumbered underdog, should rally and come out the victorious hero. But I'm not so sure.

Where, exactly, is the line between this moment's fact and its fiction?

I suspect I might still be a portal or two away from fully fusing with this wonder world's rules of engagement.

That's worrisome.

I waver; I overthink it.

Which only emboldens the wolves.

Alpha male tenses, preparing to knock my block off.

But in the instant before he does, a feminine fist jabs through the air and knuckle punches him squarely in his Adam's apple. In the next beat, I catch a flash of one licorice-black boot hammering solidly into the stomach of the wolf on the right, immediately followed by another boot pounding up between the final wolf's legs. The entire montage lasts, at most, two seconds.

They never saw it coming.

The three hoodlums have dropped to their knees before me, eyes crossed, tongues lolling. One is clutching his throat, another his belly, and the last one his crotch.

When I turn to Martine, she is tucking her hair behind each of her ears with her middle fingers. She smiles furtively, and then tosses back the last of her drink, licking a drop of whiskey from her lip ring.

"Here you go, Joe." It's Roxanne. She slaps a crisp Franklin on the bar.

Big Joe tips his chin. "See ya next time, Roxy."

And that's it; it's all over quick.

I'm sort of sorry that I missed an opportunity to play the hero and show the girls my finely tuned fighting skills, but maybe sometime I'll get another chance. At least I'm still standing and in one piece.

Roxanne takes me by the arm and leads me around the writhing pile of thugs.

Martine meets us at the door, and we grab our coats and umbrella and leave.

35

OUTSIDE, the raindrops have turned to snowflakes. They tumble and twirl out of the darkness into the neon glow of the HOOT'S sign. It's as if we've stepped into a freshly shaken snow globe.

I can't help myself. "Oh ho!" The effect of the liquor, the adrenaline, the girls – it all serves to make me giddy. I press my hat down tight on my head, spread my arms, and tip my face skyward, catching snowflakes on my tongue. I feel like a kid let out of school.

Roxanne laughs and tugs at my sleeve. "Come on, Will!"

A horse and carriage are parked at the curb. A coachman in a long coat and top hat is perched up in the driver's seat, holding the reins. His oil-black horse is steaming in his traces. The horse stamps a hoof and shakes the frost from his mane.

"What's all this?"

"It's part of your surprise, cowboy. Come on!"

Roxanne drags me over and opens the door so that she and I can climb into the passenger compartment. Martine gives the driver directions and then joins us inside the cab. Once we're settled,

Roxanne taps her umbrella against the ceiling to signal that we're ready. The driver whistles to his horse and the coach jerks forward.

The compartment is steamy and warm. The seats are corduroy and there's a quilt to throw over our laps. The little windows are misted over and the girls each rub at the glass with their cuffs so we can peer out. We snuggle close together as we rock and sway in rhythm to the muffled hoof beats clattering soft as clouds over the snowy asphalt. We could be flying. Buildings and Christmas lights all pass by in an impressionistic blur as we're carried to yet another locus of this ever-revolving world.

———

We are delivered to Riverfront Park where we pile out of the carriage. The flakes have stopped falling, but the ground, the paths – everything – is covered in snow. It weighs in the branches of the trees. It crunches under our heels.

The driver and his horse don't hang around. Apparently, other passengers in other realms are waiting to be transported. With a whistle and a slap of the reins, they fly off in a trot back toward the city.

Except for us, the park is empty. We've dropped into some unpeopled schism in civilization's continuum. The only sounds are of distant traffic passing over a high bridge, and the barely audible flush and surge of the river.

"*Allons*," says Martine. She leads Roxanne and me to a ramp descending to the water. "Be careful," she warns. "It is very slick."

A network of docks is floating at the bottom of the ramp. Small lamps are mounted to the pilings, dully illuminating the twenty or so yachts moored in their slips. Most of these behemoths appear to have been put to bed for the winter, but one modestly sized sailboat on the end has light glowing from its porthole windows. Martine leads us to this boat.

"*Voila!*"

Martine explains that the sloop belongs to a friend who is an eco-terrorist working to fight the deforestation of the Amazon. I can't tell if she's joking.

She instructs us to wait on the dock and then, after removing her boots and socks, hops aboard in her bare feet. She switches on a lantern and hangs it from the boom over the cockpit. After fetching a broom from the cabin, Martine sweeps the snow off the seats. Then we join her. Roxanne laughs and pushes at the snow with her hands while I work along the deck. I methodically shove clumps of snow over the sides and they plunk into the black water along the hull.

Once the rear of the boat is cleared of snow, Martine brings out blankets and dry cushions for us to sit on. Roxanne and I huddle under one of the blankets. The air is frosty. Roxanne blows a sparkling plume of breath through the beam of the lantern and laughs.

"Oh," she says. "That reminds me."

After digging into her coat pocket, Roxanne brings out a small tin box. She holds it on her palm, pausing for drama before opening it up. "Ta-da!"

Martine and I lean forward to see as Roxanne reaches in with a thumb and finger to draw out a fat paper joint.

"*Oh la la!*" says Martine. "It is weed?"

"*Oui,* my sexy French friend. Happy grass." Roxanne tucks the fatty between her lips and lights it with a Zippo. She holds the smoke in her chest for a while, and then blows it through the beam of light. "What do you say, kids? Care for a little reefer madness?"

We smoke dope.

Admittedly, I'm not versed in the practice, but Roxanne is very helpful. She sucks down a big drag and then places her open mouth over mine, forcing the smoke down into my lungs. It is acrid on my tongue and delicious. Roxanne then provides the same service for Martine. I hold the smoke inside for as long as I can while watching the two beauties join together at the mouth.

Soon the stuff goes to work on my brain; everything becomes vivid.

"Here." Roxanne opens the blanket, gesturing for Martine to

rest her bare feet on our knees.

Martine stretches her legs across so that Roxanne and I can each take a foot.

"Oh, my god!" squeals Roxanne. "They're like ice!"

I hold Martine's left foot under the blanket in both of my hands. It is a precious object. I close my eyes, gently pressing warmth into her arch, her toes. I have never felt more devout.

When I open my eyes, Martine is studying me, grinning. She tips back her head, purses her lips, and empties herself of smoke. "Now we will go for a ride?"

"Oh yes, Martine!" Roxanne claps her hands. "Take us on an adventure!"

———

Martine asks me to untie the boat as she works to fire up a small, battery-powered motor mounted to the transom. I loosen the lines from their dock cleats and expertly wind them into coils before tossing them onto the deck. My every move is a deliberate, calculated act of precision. The cannabis in my corpuscles requires this of me. And the whiskey and beer concoction still sloshing in my muscles.

Once the motor hums to life, I shove the boat from the dock and nimbly step back aboard.

Martine sits at the tiller. She steers us out toward the open water, operating the throttle with a foot pedal. There is some current, but the motor has just enough power to overcome it.

We motor upstream slowly, keeping to the middle of the river, passing under suspension bridges, past the ocean-going freighters settled up to their draft lines along the wharfs. The snow-rimed city is mirrored on the surface of the water, projecting a sort of subliminal counterpart to its more factual self. The lights reflect in a distorted, rainbow pastiche of buildings and towers, a plasticized version of human habitation. This is our liquid path. We travel over it toward those distant headwaters of the river lying somewhere in yonder invisible mountains. We slip into the great beyond, deep into the heart of darkness wherefrom flows this wellspring. We crawl slowly as evolution toward the very source of our fabulated existence.

I don't know exactly what I'm saying. The peyote-like potion inside of me has made me verbose and poetic. I only know for certain that tonight my friends and I are the sole voyagers on this stream of amplified consciousness. Reality has been altered. Or even replaced. Ours is a unique vantage from which to view Truth, a privileged and fluid state of being detached from the pedestrian predictability stranded on the shores. The difference between that domain and ours is as big and full of possibility as is all the cosmos, as big as the disparity between Kansas and Oz.

Abruptly, as if to further elaborate this division, the moon breaks out from behind the clouds.

"Oooo!"

It floats in the heavens like the over-watching eye of an administrator in that great head office in the sky.

Martine kills the motor, and we drift, bathed in lunar light.

Everything is luminous.

We lift our faces to the moon, as entranced and reverent as disciples at the birth of religion.

And then, from far away, we hear the mournful serenade of coyotes. First just one – a clear-throated soloist – but soon joined by others. They are all around.

Ubiquitous.

A chorus of primitive angels.

"Oh." Roxanne says the word dreamily. "That reminds me, cowboy." She smiles in the moonlight and takes me by the hand. "It's time for the rest of your surprise."

36

BELOWDECKS is warm as a womb and lit by a small lamp providing just enough light for me to see the layout of the cabin. The ceiling is low. A galley and a dining nook are tucked across from a sofa built into the opposite wall. The room is separated by a narrow aisle running lengthwise down its middle.

A portrait of the environmental activist Greta Thunberg is hanging below the lamp alongside a rifle mounted on hooks. The incongruity represented by the juxtaposition of these two objects – their differences in philosophy and psychic relativity – melds within the overall oddness of this night and its meta-fictional venue.

Again, I couldn't say just what the hell I mean by this assessment. I am simultaneously me, and not me – both hyper-aware, and completely oblivious. I am split down the middle, at once abstracted and concretized. I am no expert on the variable objects of this world and their arrangement; I am but an object myself.

As we peel off our coats and slip out of our shoes, I lean forward to examine the rifle – a classic Mannlicher of the make used by Hemingway to bring down water buffalo.

"Whoa, Martine." I run my finger along the gun's barrel. "Just what kind of eco-terrorism is your friend involved in?"

"She is a sniper," says Martine. "She shoots the men who cut the trees."

She is perfectly serious.

"Desperate times call for desperate measures," says Roxanne. She shimmies out of her skirt and deftly flips it to the side with a foot. "It's time for a sea change, time for we gals to take charge and turn the tide." Next, Roxanne steps before me, grabs two fists full of my shirt, and rips outward. A spray of buttons rattles over the floor. She laughs like a little girl opening presents on Christmas morning. She yanks my shirt free of my arms and tosses it over her shoulder. "O brave new world!"

The moment has the obliquely fitting weirdness of a dream – a dream that may well be mine and is even decorated with my own psyche's absurd symbolic flotsam, but one for which I'm fairly confident I can't be held accountable. I am merely caught up in some undercurrent, some flow of the moment. Surely, I am not so much the guide here as I am the opiated passenger.

Roxanne pulls me through another portal into the boat's fore-berth.

Martine follows and closes the door behind us.

A dozen round portholes are spaced along the top of the wall. Shafts of moonlight shine through each little window, giving the compartment the ambiance of a space capsule. The girls glide through the beams of milk-blue light, crawling over the v-shaped bed, cooing in some primordial language, removing one another's clothes while petting and kissing. They are a living cubist sculpture of legs and breasts and arms all tangled and writhing in an amorous paroxysm of feminine ecstasy.

I watch like an intoxicated voyeur, swaying, until they turn to me. They work me out of my pants as if extricating a rhyme from its sonnet.

It is impossible to say just what I mean. The experience is inexplicable. It's as if I've entered into the prologue of a psychosomatic novelette – a story that was conceived in the heroic heart of that long ago character I used to be, languished a bit too long in that pitiful way I have recently been, and is now speeding toward the third person I could quite possibly become.

My clothes fall from me like chains.

I float free as a bird, wearing nothing but my cowboy hat. The girls stimulate me further.

Until, at last, Roxanne positions herself on her hands and knees. She backs toward me.

"Can you see it?"

I don't understand what she's asking. I gaze down at her pale derriere rising toward me like Venus. The rest of her body is lost in shadows. "Um."

Martine assists by placing her hands on Roxanne's waist and moving her into the light.

"*Voila!*"

Now I can see Roxanne's tattoo. It originates at her tailbone and winds in an s-shaped curve over the small of her back.

"What do you think of that, cowboy?" Roxanne waggles her hips. "Do you like it?"

I am trying to comprehend what I'm seeing. I reach down and trace the course of the image with my finger. I think at first it might be a serpent, or possibly a rose on a vine, but then...

"Ah!"

It becomes clear.

It is a tail.

Indeed, the upturned tail of a receptive heifer.

It flicks and twitches over her skin in the moonlight.

"I got that one special for my favorite cowpoke." Roxanne wiggles and presses against my Sputnik in invitation to partake. "Surprise!"

I have drifted far away from reality now, but not so far that I don't still recognize this instant for what it is – my suspenseful moment of truth.

A force has built inside of me. Gravity? Testosterone? Narration?

It's as if I'm being manipulated by something I can't control, as if I have no choice now but to make a dramatic choice.

I hover over Roxanne's backside, drifting between the worlds of today and tomorrow and yesterday, keenly aware that I am orbiting perilously close to a point of no return.

Hesitation grips me.

And a slight fear.

And yet, I see that there is no drama in a return to the banality of my daily life. That way is cold and gray and anticlimactic. There is no satisfying resolution to be found there. But, likewise, I sense the danger – the utter destruction – of moving forward into this black hole of the soul. Still, I cannot dally in this limbo for one more second. This crisis calls for a total, unalterable action.

I hear a voice in my head.

"Man up, buddy," he says, "and grow some friggin' balls!"

I take a deep breath.

I peer into the oblivion of that yonder *mise en abyme*.

I grasp Roxanne by the hips.

And then, with a whoop and hardy high-ho, I launch myself into the inciting incident awaiting me on the other side of this irrevocable portal.

37

WILL Kirby awoke to a melody of lapping water and snoring dames.

Nice sounds.

Pleasant.

The stuff of a man's fondest daydreams.

But those happy little noises weren't what had yanked Will out of la-la land. No. It was that other sound that had snapped him back to consciousness like a cold slap in the face – that barely audible growl of an airplane.

He held himself still and listened.

Something about that plane sounded wrong. It was only a hunch, maybe just a touch of paranoia, and yet if Will Kirby had learned anything over the many years of his life it was to trust his gut. Doing so had saved his skin more than once. And now, as the drone of that aircraft grew louder, Will decided he didn't care for the sound of it one little bit.

He opened his eyes.

Harsh sunlight burned through the porthole windows and Will

winced at the pain it caused in the back of his eyeballs. He raised himself to an elbow.

The girls were still asleep and strewn over the bed beside him. Martine, the svelte French brunette, lay on her back with Roxanne, the busty redhead, using her friend's thighs for a pillow. Roxanne's arm was thrown over Kirby's waist and a glistening thread of drool was dangling from her full red lips. Both girls were naked as the day they were born.

Will Kirby vaguely recalled the night before, briefly indulged himself in a grin, and then gently lifted Roxanne's arm from his hips and laid it in the rumpled sheets. Hopping silently from the bed, he slipped into his khakis, grabbed his cowboy hat, and left the berth.

———

The plane was still a long ways out but was speeding their direction. Will tipped his hat to block the glare, but it was no good. The pilot had positioned his aircraft directly in line with the sun. That in itself was suspicious. That was a tactic used by sky hunters in wartime.

Will listened more closely to the engine – not American. Not a Hellcat or a Corsair. No, sir. It had an entirely different rhythm, a different timing and horsepower. That's when Will recognized it. How could he not? That threatening mechanical purr had been hardwired into every man's nightmares since the attack on Pearl Harbor.

"A Nakajima Sakae rotary engine," muttered Will. "The kind used to power a Japanese Zero." He squinted toward the plane. "What are you up to, you old bastard?"

The aircraft barreled down out of the sun. It leveled into a direct flight path toward the sailboat.

Will glanced at the wide ocean. It stretched to emptiness in every direction.

"Damn!" He clenched a fist. "We're sitting ducks!"

In the next instant, the pilot opened fire.

———————

Two rows of 20 mm slugs ripped across the belly of the ocean.

Will dove into the boat's cockpit and covered his head with his arms as the bullets strafed across both the bow and the stern. Chunks of teak exploded out of the deck boards; the transom was reduced to kindling.

Will lunged belowdecks, yelling to the girls. "Get up! Get out!"

He didn't wait to see if they responded. Instead, he grabbed the rifle from the wall and leapt back topside.

The plane was clearly visible now as it circled back for another pass through the cloudless blue sky. It was a Jap Zero all right, armed with a belly-mounted torpedo. The emblem of the Rising Sun shined in a bright red circle on the fuselage. This was unbelievable. The war had been over for ages, but there had been rumors of a few of the Emperor's soldiers and pilots who were unwilling to accept the surrender. More honorable to go out in a blaze of glory than to languish into old age as a humiliated loser. Apparently, this pilot was one of those holdouts, and he was hungry to make a kill.

Kirby gritted his teeth in determination. "Not on my watch." He worked the bolt on the 6.5 Mannlicher rifle and drove a cartridge into the chamber. The pilot had the advantage – twin machine guns, a torpedo, and flight. By comparison, Will was armed with barely more than a cork gun. But Will Kirby would be damned if he was going to take this lying down.

The girls tumbled out of the main hatch, naked and scared.

"What's happening?" cried Roxanne.

"*Qu'est-ce que c'est?*" asked Martine.

Will shouted back, "Just keep your heads down!"

The pilot banked his Zero and redirected his course toward the boat. The flyer hadn't bothered to line up with the sun this pass, apparently believing he was swooping in to finish off a defenseless target.

Will Kirby smirked at the pilot's arrogance. "Big mistake, buddy." He threw the rifle to his shoulder. "You obviously don't know who you're dealing with."

Will knew a thing or two about war birds, and Zeros in particular. He knew, for instance, that Japan's aeronautical engineers had been so determined to build a plane maneuverable and able to reach all corners of the Pacific that they had compromised their machine's safety for fuel efficiency. Instead of protecting the Zero's underside with heavy bulletproof armor, they chose instead to keep it light by only covering the structure with paper-thin metal. The fuel tank was as vulnerable as a co-ed in a Marine Corps barracks.

Will Kirby lined up his sights on the approaching plane. He calculated the speed and trajectory and moved his muzzle to just the right degree so that his bullet would pierce the plane's vital organs.

"Steady, Will." He took a deep breath.

The pilot assumed his angle of attack.

Will squinted down the barrel, adjusting his aim to the rocking of the splintered deck beneath his bare feet.

The plane bore down on the crippled sloop. Kirby squeezed off a test round. The Mannlicher barked and punched him in the shoulder. The bullet tore through the left wing, causing no damage. Too far out. Will slammed another cartridge into the chamber and leveled the rifle once again.

As the plane moved into alignment with the boat, the pilot dropped his torpedo.

Will didn't flinch. He held steady, waiting for the Zero to get into closer range. He knew he only had one chance. He had to make this shot count.

Steady, thought Will. Steady as she goes.

Again, the pilot opened fire.

Bullets tore through the boat's hull.

Roxanne screamed.

But Will Kirby held rock solid. He had learned long ago how to be a straight shooter. It didn't matter if it was a charging buffalo, an angry assassin, or, as in this case, a hell-bent fighter pilot. The skill had become automatic, like the reflex of a Puma. Pull that trigger too soon and the bullet would go wide, too late and you'd be dead before you knew what hit you. A man just needed to stay cool, bide his time, and wait for that right moment, that exact instant when the voice inside your head tells you everything is lined up for the strike.

The plane was so close now that Will could see his adversary's face. The pilot was wearing goggles, but Will could still see his eyes – eyes burning with hatred.

Now, whispered the voice.

Will dropped his aim to the plane's belly and squeezed off – BAM!

The Zero burst into a ball of flame. Burning debris rained down over the ocean.

"Yes!" cried Roxanne. She clapped her hands and jumped up and down, her breasts bouncing like a pair of bottlenose dolphins. "Good shot, cowboy!"

She was about to grab hold of her hero and lay on a hug and big sloppy smooch on the lips, but Will held up his hand to stop her.

He growled, "No time to celebrate just yet, sweetheart. We got ourselves another problem." He pointed into the waves.

A hundred feet out, like a barracuda dialing in for the kiss of death, the torpedo was splitting through the water. A hissing stream of bubbles washed in its wake as it plowed their direction.

"We've got to jump!" shouted Will. "And get away from the boat!"

All three passengers dived over the side.

Will Kirby plunged into the sea, the hollowness of underwater replacing the noise above the surface. And yet, he could still hear the torpedo coming – that frantic whine of its propeller driving the payload toward its target. He frog-kicked desperately away from the doomed boat, hoping to God that the girls were doing the same. Timing his swim with the projected impact of the torpedo, he rose to the surface. It would be fatal to be this close to the blast while still under water. The concussion of the explosion would turn his brains to pudding. Of course, the other worry was that shrapnel and scattering wreckage would fatally strike him and finish him off anyway, but that was a chance he'd just have to take.

Will's head and shoulders broke the surface at the exact instant the torpedo's nose-plunger smacked the boat's hull.

BOOM!

A rush of heat and fire swept outward over the waves.

Will quickly dove again, waiting for the debris to settle, and then came back up in the waves. He called out for the girls – "Roxanne! Martine!" He couldn't hear his own voice. The explosion had been so loud that his head was filled with ringing silence. He raised himself as high as he could, searching for the girls. There was nothing left of the sloop but a few flaming scraps.

There was no sign of the girls.

Damn, thought Will. It looked like they hadn't survived the blast.

But then he spied a wet head bobbing in the trough between some rollers. He couldn't yet tell if it was still attached to a body. "Roxanne!" he hollered.

She didn't respond. She was facing away from him.

Will swam to her. "Roxanne!" He grabbed her shoulder and turned her around. She had a small cut on her cheek, and her green eyes were vacuous, as if she were peering into darkness.

"Are you okay!" asked Will.

She stared at him, a dazed expression on her face. She slowly nodded. She spoke, but Will couldn't hear it over the ringing in his ears. Then a voice began to come through on a different frequency. But it wasn't Roxanne's.

"Mayday!" it called. "Mayday!"

The voice grew louder, and more frantic. Will began to recognize it as Martine's.

"*M'aidez!*" she called. "Help me!"

Will turned, gazing frantically in every direction. At last, he caught a glimpse of Martine's arm just as it disappeared beneath the surface.

Will swam quickly to the place he had seen her go down. He dove. The sunlight streamed through the water and he could see Martine bent in half about fifteen feet below him, writhing, struggling with something at her ankle. He stroked down into the aquamarine murk.

As Will drew closer, he saw that Martine was tangled in a line that was being pulled downward by the piece of wreckage it was attached to at the other end. He kicked after her. The pressure built in his head and he released it by pinching his nostrils and blowing outward into his ears.

Martine was clutching madly at the rope tangled around her ankle. Will knew he had to work fast. She had to be running out of breath. He grabbed hold of her foot, quickly assessing the knot. It was only a simple half hitch, but the weight on the line was cinching it tight. A knife would have been handy, but Will didn't have one on him. The wreckage was pulling them down and down into the cold grip of the Pacific.

He grappled with the rope, clawing and pulling.

The pressure grew worse as they sank deeper, squeezing them like a slowly tightening vice.

Will tried to pry his fingers between the rope and Martine's ankle. His lungs began to scream with their want of air. We'll go to the bottom together, thought Will, before I'll ever give you up.

His fingers worked under the rope, loosening it just enough for him to get hold of the coil in both of his hands. He gripped it tight and, with one last desperate effort, he pulled outward with all of his strength.

Martine's foot slipped out of the loop and she immediately shot toward the surface. Will dropped the rope and kicked as hard as he could after her.

They burst above the waves, both of them gasping, coughing and puking up seawater. They gulped in deep breaths of delicious oxygen.

Roxanne joined them. "My God! I thought you were goners."

Once her breath had slowed, Martine looked squarely at Will, her blue eyes filled with gratitude. "*Merci.*"

Will answered her with a nod and a smile.

The three of them bobbed in the waves.

"All right," said Will. "Next problem."

It was a big one – they were in the middle of the Pacific, without lifejackets, and with no clear idea of which direction to the nearest landfall. This ocean was huge. The odds of another boat coming by and rescuing them were laughably slim.

Will had been in plenty of bad situations in his life, but this one ranked right up there with the worst. If the sharks didn't get them, exhaustion eventually would. They were as good as dead. But Will Kirby wasn't a man to give up without a fight. For the girls' sake, he had to show strength, he had to make it look like he had everything under control, even if he didn't.

While Martine and Roxanne came to grips with their predicament, Will surveyed the horizon in every direction, searching, searching for anything that might be a sign of hope.

Water and sky. Water and sky. That's all there was anywhere he looked. A hopeless blue. But just as he had scanned a full 360°, Will spotted something that piqued his interest. There, very far away, and small on the horizon, was the faintest puff of a cloud. Of course, Will couldn't be sure, but there was a chance that that cumulous wisp was forming over a hot and humid piece of land. It was worth a shot.

He looked to the girls who were waiting patiently, treading water. He noticed his cowboy hat floating in the waves right behind them. He didn't exactly understand why, but the hat made him feel a little better. It gave him courage. He swam to the hat, grabbing it up and placing it on Roxanne's head. She was the one with the fairest skin, the one most in danger from the brutal sun. "Well," he joked, "Now I'm sorry I kept you girls up so late last night." Will grinned. "I'd have let you rest if I'd known what kind of a day it was going to be."

They laughed bravely in response.

"Let's go," he said. "Slow and steady." Will took his bearings one more time. "With any luck, we'll all be playing humpy-humpy again by nightfall."

They set off, swimming toward the cloud.

38

HOURS passed.
The morning crept into the afternoon.

The cloud built, faded, and then disappeared altogether before magically forming again. It was like a beacon, but one Will wasn't sure he could trust. And yet, what was their choice? Pathetic as it was, that tropical puff of steam was their only hope. It taunted them, pulling them forward, even as it never seemed to be getting any closer.

Will worried about the girls. Of course, they had the advantage over a man in an endurance swim like this one. Nature had provided them with a subcutaneous layer that, besides making them shapely in all the right places, helped keep them afloat. Hell, Roxanne's boobs alone were as good as an inflatable Mae West. Will's own lean and muscled body had to work like hell to stay above water. But fatigue was the real danger. And dehydration. Eventually, even the most buoyant and fit body would just give out and go tits up in the sun.

As they swam, Will began to feel an odd sensation. He couldn't quite place it. He couldn't be sure, but it seemed like something was below them, something big and alive and keeping pace with their slow crawl across the ocean. A whale maybe? A submarine? No, neither one of those. Will sensed it cruising in the deepest darkness. It unsettled him in the way a little kid is unsettled by a fear of monsters hiding under his bed.

Get a grip, Kirby, he thought to himself. The sun must be cooking your wits.

But as the day wore on, Will became sure that he was right. Something was down there all right. It wasn't a friendly presence, but neither did it seem like an immediate threat. He glanced at the girls, their faces flushed with weariness and effort. Neither one indicated that they suspected anything.

Well, thought Will, at least it's scaring away the sharks.

Whatever it was, it would either protect them, or eat them for lunch. There wasn't much Will could do about it one way or another. They just had to keep swimming.

———

The trio spoke rarely, saving their strength. The waves grew bigger and became increasingly more irritating to manage, slapping their faces and stinging their eyes. Occasionally, Will would offer the girls a bit of encouragement, even tossing out a joke to lighten the mood, but otherwise they were silent. Will's throat felt caked with salt. His tongue was swollen and dry. The situation was looking pretty grim.

———

The sun traveled across the sky and eventually sank into the western horizon. The first stars began blinking on in the twilight rising out of the east like a great dark wing.

Through sunburned eyes, Will squinted into the stars, trying to pick out constellations as they emerged from the darkness. Without the sun, the heat source had been eliminated and their guiding cloud evaporated and disappeared for the night. Will now needed to use the stars to triangulate his and the girls' position so they could maintain their heading.

He found the constellation known as the Southern Cross. Although it was a struggle to work out even the simplest equation in his weary brain, Will projected an imaginary line from y to a at the foot of the Cross 4 ½ times its length. That point in the sky marked the celestial South Pole. Their cloud had been in the southwest, so now they just needed to hold that point obliquely to their left and keep moving. With any luck, if they survived the night, their cloud would form again in the morning. Or better yet, they would happen across some land before dawn.

Will didn't let himself entertain that last idea with too much enthusiasm. He knew it was about as realistic as stumbling across an ice-cold bottle of beer in the middle of the Sahara. In spite of his determination to survive, he couldn't help it – his mind had started drifting toward peaceful thoughts of death.

He fought them off.

———

At some point, their bodies switched over to autopilot, stroking mechanically through the waves, sluggish as zombies. They edged from one side of reality into another. Their thirst was incredible, their lassitude growing.

———

Will didn't know where it had come from. He hadn't noticed it at first. But now a fat full moon glided through space above them like an all-seeing eye. Its brilliance washed out the stars, but that didn't matter anymore. Their forward progress had all but stopped. Their strength was spent. Their arms and legs felt made of lead. The three of them drifted close, rising and dipping in the monotonous waves, joining together for one final powwow.

Dammit, thought Will. So, this is how it ends.

He gazed at Roxanne and Martine. Their weak smiles indicated that they were thinking the same thing. Even now, they were damn good-looking in the moonlight. Savvy. Tough. And gorgeous. Some of the best gals Will had ever known. He would have liked for their little vacation to last a while longer. A few more laughs and tumbles in bed would have been real nice. Pity it was all over so soon.

Will thought for a moment. He thought of the presence he had felt cruising in the shadows. Maybe that had only been Death all along – Mortality – and he had been kidding himself to think he could ever outrun it.

As he saw it now, they were down to just two choices. One – they could tread water until their bodies went into convulsions, struggling against the inevitable panic of drowning. Or two – they could use the last of their strength to dive deep and suck their lungs full of seawater. True, the second option was more immediately terrifying than the first, and would take some serious determination to pull off successfully, but it was the quicker alternative, shortening the time they would suffer. Either way, the end result would be the same.

"Well..." His voice was barely more than a croak.

But Will Kirby didn't need to say anything more. Both Martine and Roxanne knew clearly what thoughts were going through his head.

They all dipped and bobbed in the waves, facing each other.

Finally, Roxanne reached out and took both Will and Martine by a hand. She laced her fingers in theirs and gently squeezed. Will understood it was her way of saying goodbye.

Roxanne let go and stroked back from them.

She treaded water. She rose and sank with the waves, mustering the courage she needed to perform her last act on earth.

Will could hardly stand to watch, but to turn away would be a betrayal of their friendship. He needed to give Roxanne the support she deserved right up to the very end.

Roxanne took in a breath. Then another. She closed her eyes. She raised herself up at the top of a wave, her beautiful bare torso gleaming in lunar light. She looked like a Roman statue wearing a cowboy hat. And then she sank down, bending forward, going into a dive...

"*Non!*"

Cracked and hoarse, Martine's voice sounded in alarm.

Roxanne stopped herself with a slap against the surface, right at the brink of death's portal. She searched Martine's face for an explanation. The look on her own face was one of annoyance, as if she resented having to pluck up her nerve for suicide all over again.

Martine couldn't speak. She tried to explain, but her throat was too parched. Sounds came out, like the mewing of a cat, but no words. She held up her hand, swallowing... swallowing... trying to make herself understood. Finally, she uttered a single word in French – "*Écoutez!*"

Listen.

Roxanne and Will did as they were told.

And yet, there was nothing to hear but the immense breath of the Pacific – that watery slosh and oceanic heave of the tides.

They cocked their ears.

Nothing. No boat motor. No plane engine. Nothing.

Maybe Martine was merely going punchy with fatigue.

Then the air shifted. The breeze changed direction and carried a small but unmistakable disturbance in the uniformity of sound.

It filled them all with renewed power, refueling their exhausted bodies for one more push of effort.

I'll be damned, thought Kirby.

The distant crash of waves on a beach!

39

THE ocean was swollen with the full moon's gravitational pull. The tide was high and powerful and restless as a female in heat. The big rollers crashed dangerously onto the shore.

Will led the way. He swam toward landfall until he felt himself rising up on a swell. He was hurled forward on the surge. The wave broke with a roar beneath him and he dropped in a rush, tumbling through the surf and rolling onto the beach like a washed-up flounder. His breath was knocked out of him, and the beach worked like a belt sander against his skin, but Will didn't let that slow him down. After a quick gulp of air, he bounced to his feet, ready to help the girls.

Roxanne came through next, cartwheeling in the wash, sprawling like a rag doll onto the sand. She was completely spent, too weak to move by her own strength. Will ran and grabbed her by the wrists, dragging her above the high-water mark before the next wave crept in and hauled her back out to sea. She rolled onto her side, coughing and gagging. She was a little beat up, but otherwise okay.

Will turned back to the shore. Martine had already come through the breakers and was on her hands and knees. She staggered to her feet and stood panting and unsteady. The surf washed back in around her thighs. She looked like a newborn goddess plucked fresh from the womb of the sea. Martine stared for a moment into the swirling foam beneath her, studying something. Finally, she reached in and picked out a piece of flotsam. Afterward, she came up the beach and dropped to her knees next to Will and Roxanne.

"*Voila, ton chapeau.*"

She handed the dripping cowboy hat to Will.

Will chuckled, relieved as hell that they were all still alive. "Thanks," he said. "*Merci.*"

Will Kirby couldn't remember the last time he had been so drop-dead tired. And still, he knew they couldn't rest just yet. Their thirst had reached a life-threatening level. They needed to rehydrate fast. But how?

The moon lit up everything plain as day. Will surveyed the scene. The island appeared to be an atoll – maybe four or five miles long, low-lying, its highest point barely ten feet above the mark of high tide. Except for the occasional rainstorm, it was probably without a source for fresh water. Will gazed into the cloudless sky. No rain tonight.

The next option meant work, but as there was no other choice he could think of, Will resigned himself to the task.

"Wait here," he said, and left the girls on the beach.

Wearily, he limped to a grove of palms swaying in the breeze. Coconuts were strewn over the ground, but they would likely be dried out inside, or offering nothing but a gluey laxative that would only weaken them more. He peered up into the branches. After choosing one of the shorter trees, Will shimmied up its trunk and twisted off a pair of the fruit, letting them drop to the ground below with a thump – thump. That job, although difficult enough for a fellow who had just swum halfway across an ocean, was the easy part.

"Damn," said Will. He rubbed his chin, thinking. "I'd give my left gonad for a machete right now."

He squinted toward a small headland down the beach. He nodded to himself, and then picked up the two coconuts, one in each hand, and walked to the spit.

Will knelt in a tide pool and pounded the coconuts against a piece of volcanic rock shaped like a shark fin. The tough spongy casings held tight, but he kept at it until he had exposed the fibrous under-shell. He rummaged in the pool until he found a sharp piece of coral, and then carried everything back to the girls.

The coral cut his palm as he poked it into the coconuts, but Will managed to pierce the wooden casks through the soft spot on their tops. Roxanne took one nut, Martine the other. Both gals threw back their heads and guzzled. Viscous streams of nut milk trickled down their chins.

"Oh, my God!" gasped Roxanne.

They shared the juice, the sweet nectar saturating their tongues, their bodies screaming with appreciation for the liquid sustenance. Although they all could have easily taken more, Will was just too wiped out to get up another tree until he had rested.

He looked at the sky. The stars and the moon. Dawn was still a few hours away.

"Let's get under shelter," he said. "We'll want to be in the shade when the sun comes up."

They all three stumbled to a place in the palm grove and collapsed onto a carpet of fronds scattered over the ground. The girls passed out instantly with fatigue.

Will regarded his companions in the dappled moonlight streaming down through the rustling branches. Their bodies were scratched and bruised, but they were as exquisite as ever. Maybe even more so for having survived their ordeal.

Survival.

Will laughed to himself and considered the word. He wasn't exactly sure what survival meant in this particular situation. After all, they were on a desert island in the middle of the Pacific Ocean. No food, no knife, no gun, no matches, no radio. Nothing. Hell, the girls didn't even have any clothes. What did that mean? How would they manage? Those were the real questions facing them now.

Will shook his head. It was too much to think about at the moment. He needed to recharge his batteries.

The man stretched out his muscular body onto the ground next to the girls, sighed once, and then, with one eye half open, let himself go to sleep.

40

COYOTES.

That's what Will Kirby first thought he was hearing when he woke up.

Yapping coyotes.

But then the surf broke onto the beach and he remembered where he was.

The mid-morning sun streaked through the swishing palms. The sky above was clear except for the faintest wisp of white drifting in the blue. That had been their guiding cloud yesterday, and now it was being reborn this morning with the rising tropical heat.

Will sat up and cupped a hand to his ear. The peculiar sound was still coming through, but now he heard it more clearly. No. Those were definitely not coyotes. They were people. Laughing and cheering.

"What the devil?"

It sounded like nothing but women!

Will struggled to his feet. He arched his back and rubbed his neck. He felt like he had been beaten with a pipe. He had a killing thirst. *And* he was starving.

Martine and Roxanne still lay passed out on the ground, their bodies powdered with fine coral sand. Their chests rose and fell with their breath. After studying them for a moment, Will decided to let them sleep.

He left his hat for Roxanne and carefully stepped over the girls into the hot sunlight. He listened again more closely, trying to understand what those feminine noises meant. His instincts were tingling again. For a second day, Will Kirby had awoken with the gut feeling that something was very wrong.

Well, anyway, he thought, at least the sounds are human. Although, he knew from experience that humans, of all the animals, could be the most inhumane. That savage din coming to him now was definitely of that worrisome, cold-hearted variety. Nobody cheered like that unless it involved blood.

But people meant food and water. Maybe they even meant radios and boats. Sure, there was definitely something pretty chilling about a bunch of women screaming like banshees at a cockfight, but Will decided he needed to go investigate.

———————

His guess was right. The place was lousy with dames.

About thirty of them.

A real variety pack – big and small, whites, blacks, Asians. Although the paler-race girls were so tanned they were hard to distinguish from the others. Most of the girls wore short skirts, some made from animal skins, but no tops. A few wore nothing at all. As the girls cheered and waved their arms, the sun-roasted lobes of their breasts bobbled and swung like ripe fruit.

The group had formed a ragged circle that moved fluidly over a wide plot of sand. In the midst of this makeshift playpen, two men were fighting.

Will crouched behind a palm. The crowd was so engrossed in the action that they hadn't noticed him. He assessed the scene.

This didn't look to be a fun-and-games wrestling match, not just some playground fisticuffs between a couple of ornery schoolboys. Will could see that it was more serious than that. The brawlers' desperation and strain indicated that this was a battle with greater consequences.

This was a fight to the death!

The combatants were shirtless, their torsos glistening with sweat.

One man clearly outweighed the other and appeared to be older. He was a bit padded around the waist and had a bald patch on the back of his head. His rounded, hairy back gave him the look of a mature bull.

His opponent appeared to be a younger version of himself. Wiry, quick, but not nearly as big, as if he still had some growing to do. He could have been the older man's son, but Will thought something about that idea felt off the mark. These men knew each other somehow – that much was sure – but in a way that went to mysterious depths.

The younger fighter pitched forward, leading with a sharp right jab. The bigger man was too slow to react and the knuckles smashed into his nose, causing his head to whip back. Instinctively, the larger man wrapped his arms into the air before him, clutching at his opponent whose forward momentum had thrown him in close. The bigger man wrapped his rival into a bear hug, squeezing, trying to crush the younger man's spine.

"Aurgh!" He roared with the strain.

The big man arched backward, lifting his victim's feet off the ground.

Pain played out on the younger man's face, but he overcame it. He spread both of his arms in the air and pounded his fists together like ballpeen hammers against both sides of his foe's head. Bam! Again and again, clouting the man's ears. Bam! Bam!

Dazed, the big man fell onto his back – oomph!

The weight coming down on top of him, along with the clubbing of his brain, caused him to lose his grip. The younger man sprang to his chest, pummeling him in quick succession across the face. Teeth and blood sprayed from the big man's mouth.

With a desperate surge of strength, the big man tossed his abuser into the air. As the younger man rolled away, his rival scrambled to his feet. But he wasn't looking for a way to overcome his opponent now. Something had snapped in the big man's mind. Will could see his wild panic. That wasn't the look of a hunter; it was the look of prey. Of the two options available between fight and flight, this guy was now frantically searching for an escape.

The girls laughed and cheered. They smelled the man's fear. It excited them.

The big man lunged, breaking out of the circle and lumbering over the sand to where Will was watching from behind his tree. Will saw no reason to hide. He stepped into the open as the frantic man spied him and staggered his way, obviously seeking help.

The whooping women followed.

The man fell twenty feet short of Will. Heaving, he struggled to his knees, desperately reaching out to Will like a drowning man begging to be saved. He peered directly into Will's eyes. Will took in the man's face. The scar under his eye. The blood streaming over his mustache. Will saw his terror. He saw the poor slob's whole vivid life flash before him in an instant. But more than anything, Will saw the face of a man about to meet his maker.

Will was tempted to step in and alter fate, but before he could, the younger man leapt through the crowd and landed on the big man's back like a steer wrestler in a rodeo. With one deft move, he grabbed his opponent by his chin and forehead and twisted.

The sharp crunch of cervical bones rose above the cheers.

The big man's neck bent at a grotesque angle. He dropped to his belly. And then the young man let his victim's head plop to the sand.

The conqueror stood, straddling the defeated and damned, raising his arms into the air like a prizefighter.

The mob of women swarmed him, cheering, covering him with hugs and kisses and pressing his face into the sweetest corners of their naked bodies.

Will watched it all. The grin on the young man's face struck him as that of a boy who had just won all the marbles on the playground.

The crowd had seen Will plainly now, but were too occupied with their celebration to immediately pay him any attention. They had business to attend to.

A buxom gal in a leopard skin mini skirt stepped away from the group, tipped her face to the sky, and hollered, "Mad Olgar!"

This acted as a cue to the others. They parted from the triumphant battler and started loping to the shore. They began to chant – "Olgar! Olgar!"

Soon, all the girls were gathered near the water's edge, their voices raised in chorus, calling out to the waves – "Olgar! Olgar! Olgar!"

"What the blue blazes?" muttered Will. This show was getting weirder by the minute.

Up on the beach, the champion knelt beside the lifeless man and rolled him over onto his back. He grabbed one of his limp arms, pulled the corpse into a slumping seated position, and then struggled to get him over his shoulder. He stood, bounced a couple of times to position the load, and hunched beneath the dead weight draped over his shoulder like a side of beef. He then staggered toward the girls.

Will stayed back, cautiously watching.

Once he had reached the chanting horde, the young man dropped his burden.

A pair of girls rushed in and stripped the body of its trousers. They ceremoniously positioned the corpse with his arms and legs spread wide, feet to the surf. The dead man lay face up in the sun. He could have passed for any other holiday beach goer, drying himself after a refreshing dip, but that he was butt naked, and his head was unnaturally cocked, making his appearance look both obscene and macabre.

"Olgar!" The girls chanted louder and louder. "Olgar! Olgar!"

They all faced out to sea, their arms raised, as if waiting to embrace a friend.

Will squinted out at the waves. He saw nothing that merited this bizarre expectation. Just ocean. And blue sky.

"Olgar!" droned the crowd. "Olgar! Olgar!"

"Huh!?"

Will glimpsed an enormous shadow beneath the water.

He saw a flash.

There came a hanging moment of silence.

A surge of the tide.

And then, like a detonating depth charge, it exploded from the sea.

41

W ILL lurched back.
His reflexes fired in recoil.

"Mother of God!"

Will Kirby had seen some unholy things in his life, but never anything quite so massive and gruesome. It was a creature, but not one naturally of this world. Nothing earthly moved like that, both halting and swift at once, like a live wire whipping out of the sea. It reared up from the waves with a roar, filth and detritus spilling from its writhing, serpentine bulk.

Will could see instantly that it was female, but of a wombless sort, with dugs for breasts and spark plugs for teats – a one-off mutation born from mathematical miscalculations and bomb tests gone horribly wrong. She seemed all teeth and sinew.

The she-bitch was accompanied by an entourage of lesser beings. Twisted and burnt sirens. Their faces were fried, their arms twitching like the tentacles of palsied squid. They hissed in the surf, pirouetting and squealing through the froth.

Upon the great creature's appearance, the women began

to ululate like harpies. They danced frenetically, as if under the influence of dope, or voodoo.

The young man near the corpse shrank back. He cowered for a moment, and then retreated to the palms.

Will didn't know what to expect. He figured that this monster was the presence he had felt when swimming with Roxanne and Martine. She could have easily devoured them then had she wanted. But she hadn't. Will didn't know why not. She was obviously working by a different sort of predatory logic. Still, Will felt it wise to give her a wide berth. He stepped behind a tree to watch.

The beast moved toward the shore, plowing through the spray and slithering onto the sand. She towered over the dead man lying spread eagle beneath her. Globules dripped from her bulk like sizzling fat dribbling from a grilled steak. She roared, sending a vile wind up the beach.

Will cringed at the stink blowing from her toothy maw. He threw his palm to his face, gagging at the sudden stench of radioactive cadavers left out to bloat and rot in the sun. The women all raised their arms to the towering creature. They wailed and pranced in a frenzy.

The creature – the Mad Olgar – acknowledged the women. She nodded her hideous head their direction. Next, she moved to the dead man laid out in offering on the sand. She hovered over the lifeless form, sizing it up the way a diner might size up a tasty entrée. She licked at the thin gristle of her lips. At last, with jaws open, she plunged her face into the dead man's crotch, tearing his male organs out by the roots. She reared back, chomping like a dog chewing taffy.

Out of respect for the poor slob, Will glanced away.

"Sorry, buddy," he muttered. "I guess it's dessert first with this bitch."

The creature moved onto the rest of her meal, the sound of meat and bones champing in her teeth. She threw back her head, gulping, the dead man's offal sliding in a lump down her scaly throat.

Her minions swarmed over the sand beneath her, cackling, lapping up the spray of blood and liver scraps.

When she had finished her lunch, the Olgar reared up, threw

her face to the sky, and belched.

The sound was nothing Will had ever heard in his life. It was like a fury let loose from the very pits of hell.

The Olgar then quickly turned back to the water. With a constriction and a bound, she flung herself seaward, crashing into the waves. Her underlings followed. They all disappeared beneath the surface.

The Olgar's wake washed high onto the beach.

The surf returned to normal.

The green waves rolled in tranquilly beneath the torrid blue sky.

42

IT had all happened fast.

In fact, except for the shallow, blood-spattered crater on the beach, there was no sign that it had ever happened at all.

Will shook his head and whistled lightly over his lips. Whew, he thought, that was one seriously bizarre shitshow!

The pack of women had turned from the sea and scrambled up the shoreline, all of them eager to rejoin their young champion who was waiting in the shade of the palms.

Will spied Roxanne and Martine cowering on the perimeter. They met his gaze over the distance. Their faces were blanched with shock. Will guessed that they had witnessed the whole grisly spectacle with the creature.

He jogged over to them. "Are you okay?"

"What in the world was that?" asked Roxanne. Her voice quavered. "What is this place? Where are we?"

"I don't know, but it's pretty clear we need to watch our backs."

Cheers and laughter drifted on the wind. Will, Roxanne, and Martine all turned to where the women had reunited with the young man beneath the palms. They seemed to be having a party.

"*Alors,*" said Martine. "What is it that we do now?"

Will scratched at the stubble on his jaw. "Well, like it or not, I guess we have to go talk to them. We need food and water. And maybe they have intel that can help us get back to civilization."

Roxanne clutched his arm. "Cowboy, I don't mean to be a candy ass, but that was pretty horrible to watch, the way that animal... that monster..." She trembled. "I'm scared."

Will forced a reassuring smile. He tipped back the hat on Roxanne's head and chucked her lightly under the chin. "Don't worry, gorgeous, your loyal cowpoke won't ever let you down."

He wrapped his arm around Martine.

"I'm not going to let anything happen to my two best gals."

Although in truth, given the information he had gathered so far, Will Kirby's gut told him that it wasn't so much the girls who needed to be worried, but he himself.

———

They approached the revelers guardedly, without knowing what to expect. It was quite a scene. The women were all laughing and feasting on chunks of raw fish and taro root. Some of the girls were sprawled over mats woven from palm fronds, moaning happily, kissing and fondling one another's naked body while doing their best to stretch the term *bosom buddies* to its fullest and most erotic definition.

But it was the young champion who was enjoying this day the most. His trousers had been shucked and tossed to the side. He lay flat on his back with his head resting in the lap of a dark-skinned beauty with breasts parked on her chest like a couple of 1952 Buicks. Two other gals were giggling and taking turns poking their tongues down the young man's throat while a third sat astraddle his waist with her hands on his knees, her eyes half closed, moving her hips rhythmically in that way that could only signify a certain act of nature.

Upon seeing the three outsiders, a pair of girls came over for a formal greeting. They fawned over Roxanne and Martine, stroking them, taking each by the hand and urging them toward the orgy, inviting them to join in the fun.

Roxanne and Martine shot a sidelong glance to Will, halfheartedly resisting, but the draw was too strong for them to overcome. It wasn't the debauchery that lured them in, but the food. They both dropped to their knees before a large leaf serving as a platter heaped with fish fillets and oysters. They stuffed the meat into their mouths, chewing ravenously. A girl handed them each a coconut and they threw these back, guzzling until the nuts were completely empty of juice.

Another pair of girls stepped over to greet Will. They looked Japanese, but Will couldn't be sure. This entire tribe of women had spent so much time out in the sun and wind that they had more or less devolved into a single race, as if they had all returned to the source of their primitive roots as the Wild Women of Wongo, or some such thing. At any rate, they spoke a lingo that might as well have been called Wongoese. Will had picked up a smattering of languages from his travels, but he had never heard anything like this one. It was almost birdsong – a musical, avian argot that seemed to be hatched right from the very environment in which it was being spoken.

"*Ala oo wah*," warbled one of the girls. "*Noo wa Noo wa Noo wa!*"

Will shook his head and shrugged. "Sorry," he said. "I guess I don't speak your tongue."

"*Eelee aboo.*"

Will glanced past the girl to the banquet. He was about as parched as he could get, but somehow his mouth began to water at sight of the food. His stomach growled like a bear. He smiled and lifted his chin to where Roxanne and Martine were gorging themselves on fish. "I'll tell you what," he told the girls, "we'll all talk and get to know each other later." He patted each girl on the arm. "But first, I'm going to have myself a little snack."

He stepped forward, but the girls held onto him. They were both smiling, but they didn't allow him forward.

Will tried to step around them. They hung on his arms.

He laughed. "Now come on, girls, you don't want ol' Will to starve now, do you?"

In answer, one of the girls squared herself before him and, with both hands on his chest, gently pushed him back.

"Huh?"

The other girl lifted her hand and pointed behind him, saying something that sounded like a command. Will assumed they were telling him to leave, although he couldn't figure why.

Another pair of girls stood and joined in, all of them pointing behind him now, and telling him something he couldn't understand. They twittered and cooed like a flock of excited doves. Soon, more of the girls had gathered before him, forming a wall between him and the buffet.

"Okay, okay." He held up his palms and smiled. "I get it. You don't want to share your grub. Fine."

Will didn't want any trouble. He especially didn't want to jeopardize Roxanne and Martine. At least they were getting some lunch. These island dames might be unpredictable and dangerous. After all, hadn't they just fed a dead man to a hideous beast? It was no doubt bad practice to piss them off. Maybe the best course of action would be for him to go hunt for his own food in the tide pools. Will was just about to do that when he heard someone howl like a wolf.

"What the... ?"

He jerked around to see who it was.

43

THE howler stood on the far side of the clearing, feet firmly planted, shoulders squared, holding what looked like a long staff. He was too far away to see with any detail, but Will recognized the fellow's stance – that of one man challenging another.

"Oh, great," sighed Will.

This guy must have been what these Wongo broads had been trying to show him. It didn't take much for Will Kirby to see that he was the one being challenged.

The party hastily disbanded as the merrymakers became more interested in this new drama. The girls piled off their young champion and pulled him to his feet. A baffled grin played over the Casanova's face. It was obvious, given the state of his jack-handle, that the youngster wasn't quite ready to call it a day with the ladies.

A half dozen of the girls led their bewildered champion away through the palms, escorting him to a quieter piece of real estate down the beach – some dappled garden where their eager young bull could further render his services.

The remaining girls moved en masse to greet the new arrival.

Will caught a sideways glimpse of Martine as she skipped past. She flashed him a guilty smile smeared with fish oil but was swept along with the mob. Roxanne's red hair gleamed in the sunlight as she dashed away with the others toward the clearing.

"Well, huh."

It wasn't his habit to be a whiner, but Will would have appreciated a little backup from his friends. Given what the three of them had been through these last couple of days, he thought it curious that Roxanne and Martine could so easily forget him in the face of this newest challenge.

Will spied his hat trampled on the ground. He picked it up, punched it back into shape, and brushed the salt and sand from the brim. He regarded the platter of fish and copra, licking his lips. That's what he most needed to do right now – put on the feedbag and lounge in the shade. He was feeling pretty low in the gas tank. And yet, he didn't figure chow and a siesta were in the cards for him at the moment.

One of the girls ran back from the others and grabbed him by an elbow, laughing and pulling him toward the gathering.

"*Mawa ony ee aye!*" warbled the dollybird. "*Ala oo wah!*"

"Okay, okay."

Will Kirby hung his battered hat on a stob jutting from a tree.

The girl scampered a few steps and signaled for Will to follow. She was a willowy thing, brown from head to toe, with tits like mortar shells and a sweet little caboose in the shape of an inverted heart.

Will shook his head. In spite of himself, he chuckled.

Whatever this place was, Will Kirby sure did appreciate its decorations.

"Okay, darlin'." He stepped forward and took the girl's hand. "Lead the way."

———

The fellow's staff turned out to be an oar. Will studied it as he advanced. That was encouraging. If there was an oar, maybe there was also a boat and all the civilized connections that came with it. He filed that bit of information in the back of his mind and readied himself to deal with the next step in the situation.

The girls gathered in a circle, eager for this encounter between Will and the howler.

Wearing his best big friendly smile, Will approached his challenger. He had a pretty good hunch what the female contingent was expecting from this meeting – an all-out man-battle where they could cheer for a while, watch one gent murder another, and then feed the lop-necked loser to their pet monster. But Will wasn't planning to oblige them. For one thing, he was still pretty beat from his swim. Breaking this guy's neck sounded like it might take more energy than he had in him. And for another reason, Will reckoned it made more sense for any menfolk on this godforsaken outpost to stick together. After all, besides the Olgar and her troupe of disfigured mermaids, who knew what other threats were lurking in the shadows? With these thoughts in mind, Kirby greeted the fellow with all the charm of a diplomat.

"Well howdy, friend. It's sure good to find another man around here." He winked and pointed to the girls with his thumb. "I was beginning to feel a little outnumbered."

If the fellow responded at all, it was only by puffing his bare chest.

Hmm.

Still smiling, Will sized him up.

The guy was young, barely old enough to call himself a man, with a full head of sun-bleached hair sprouting up top like a clump of dry grass. He was built like a brick shithouse, solid, rippling with muscles that looked almost comical in their perfection. Compared to Will, whose own body bore the dents and scars of many battles, the youngster's physique looked as fresh and unblemished as a schoolboy's, implying inexperience. Will noted that as his own advantage if they should come to blows. But the young man's expression was what struck Will the most. It was strangely unsettling. It had been a while since Will Kirby had felt inclined to wear a grin that self-satisfied. The kid's arrogance almost made Will laugh out loud, but he held it down.

"There's another guy up the beach a ways." Will lifted his chin that direction. "But he's too busy entertaining his lady friends to talk right now."

The young buck stood silent and unflinching.

Will started to feel like he was talking to a department store mannequin. The kid never so much as blinked. Then something occurred to Will. It was an odd sensation, wriggling like a worm in the depths of his memory, but Will wondered if it might be true.

"Say, kid. Do I know you?"

The man-boy didn't answer, didn't budge.

"Have we met somewhere before?"

Nothing. No response.

Will scratched his chin and shrugged. He was having a hard time figuring this guy out. Maybe he didn't speak Will's language, and so didn't understand what he was saying. Or maybe he was deaf and dumb. Hell, maybe these wacko dames had cut out the kid's tongue and fed it to the Olgar as an hors d'oeuvre. At any rate, Will couldn't read him. The kid was about as mute as a snapshot.

The girls were getting restless. Apparently, they didn't much care for this friendly waste of time. They were ready for a fight.

Will sensed that things could get out of hand real fast if he didn't hurry and come up with a way to enlist this beefcake as an ally.

One of the girls shoved Will from behind. He stumbled forward. "Hey!" Will half turned, ready to slap her silly.

That's where he made his mistake.

Will knew it even as he did it.

You dumbass! The thought came in a flash. Never turn your back on a potential enemy!

But it was too late. Next thing Will heard was the swish of the oar swinging through the air, followed shortly by the heavy whump of wood smacking against his flank.

"Umpk!"

A rib snapped.

The girls cheered.

Will's feet went out from under him and he slammed to the

ground. Pain shot through his ribcage, but Will knew he couldn't spare one slim second to indulge it. He flung his arm up to protect his head as the oar cracked against his wrist.

Dammit! thought Will. This ain't good. He was down before the fight had even started. He needed to get sharp, and quick.

Before the arrival of a third blow, Will lurched out of the way. The oar blade bludgeoned the sand – Bompk! Will windmilled his legs into the kid's calves, knocking him off his feet. The kid threw his hands back to catch himself and lost his grip on the oar.

Both grapplers scrambled to get position. From a squat, Will launched himself like a linebacker, tackling his opponent around the waist and taking him to the ground, but the kid squirmed out on impact and rolled, tossing Will to the side and kicking his heel full force into his chin.

Sparks flashed before Will's eyes as his head snapped backwards. From far away, as if echoing down a tunnel, Will heard the girls' excited shrieks and laughter.

Will Kirby hopped to his feet mechanically, even as he was on the verge of keeling over in a faint. The kid stood before him, vignetted in darkness, zooming in and out of focus. Will swung a desperate right hook toward the kid's head, but he easily dodged it. Will jabbed once – twice – at the kid's grinning mug, but his punches met with nothing but empty air. Will felt like a rusty old robot shadow boxing.

Come on, Kirby. Get hold of your wits and deal with this punk before he finishes you off. Will knew that even allowing that last idea to take shape in his rattled head was a sign he was feeling beatable. That kind of thinking was fatal. He needed to turn this situation around. He needed to quickly transform himself from prey to hunter.

From nowhere, the kid's fist drove like a ramrod into Will's belly. The wind rushed from his lungs as Will folded in half, wrapping his arms around his middle, quivering like a spanked puppy.

Damn! This was not how Will Kirby had expected his life to end. The indignity of it would never do. And yet, it was looking more likely with each of the kid's landing blows.

Pow! Bam! First a punch to Will's jaw. Then an uppercut to his chin.

The saltpeter taste of blood filled Will's mouth – the flavor of defeat! The blows were solid and sharp. Bam! Bam! One after another. Will felt like he was being shot, like he was taking heavy caliber rounds to his body and skull. He could barely see. Everything moved before him in a vertiginous blur. The kid stepped away from him – a nebulous form with the grin of an arrogant ass – then he leapt forward into the air, leading with both feet.

There was nothing Will could do. His mind told him to jump clear, but his body misfired, as if there was a short in his wiring. The kid's heels drove into Will's chest and sent him somersaulting backwards, sprawling into a heap of twisted limbs and bruised flesh.

The women began screeching like raptors, emitting the unearthly squeals of harpies and owls.

Will lay belly down in the sand, panting. From beneath a half-open eyelid, he watched the kid hovering over him, arms raised in victory as the girls cheered from the sidelines. They were obviously eager to see how their newest champion would finish off his victim.

Will scrambled in his brain, summoning his experience. He lay motionless, playing possum, buying himself some time to think and recharge. He knew he was running out of options. The clock was ticking.

Okay, he decided. It's not the best idea. Not a sure bet. In fact, it's probably the most pitiful, lily-livered trick in the big book of dirty fighting tactics. Will wasn't necessarily proud of himself for coming up with it, but he figured that the alternative was death. If it went that way, so be it, but he sure as hell wasn't going to just give up and let it happen.

As the kid strutted before the girls, Will scrunched himself like a spring. He tensed.

Will waited like a coiled panther.

The kid pranced a few laps around his fallen opponent, a victorious gladiator with a smug toothy grin smeared across his handsome face, taking in the cheers and laughter of his many female fans. Finally, he kneeled nonchalantly at Will's side. But then he glanced once more to the girls.

Big mistake, buddy, thought Will. Right there. You just lost the battle.

With a lightning quick twist, Will thrust his fist toward the kid's face, opening his palm at the end of his reach and letting loose about a half pound of powdery coral sand.

"Augh!" The kid threw his hands to his eyes.

Will bounced to his feet, snatched up the nearby oar, and swung it like a pugil stick against the kid's head, knocking him to the ground. The kid sprawled flat on his back and Will pounced onto his chest, pressing the oar down hard against his throat.

Will had him now. He knew it. The kid was dazed, helpless, his eyes filled with grit and panic. A splash of blood gleamed on his forehead. All Will had to do now was cut off the punk's wind long enough for him to give up the ghost. It was just a matter of seconds.

But then something happened.

Something strange.

Will had been in similar positions before. Hell, he wouldn't have made it this far in life if he hadn't developed a survivalist skill set that could beat out all those other poor schmucks. And he wasn't above ending another man's life if it meant preserving his own. But in all those other encounters, he had never felt anything to match the eerie impression that he was feeling now. It crawled through him like the sudden chill of a fever.

Now, Will Kirby didn't know much about incest. Of all his life's many bawdy adventures, that one had never really been up his alley. But if he didn't know any better, he would have to say it probably felt something like this. As he forced the oar against the young man's Adam's apple, Will felt like he was doing something not quite right, something, in fact, just plain wrong.

Something taboo.

Like French-kissing your own mother.

The kid's face was powdered with sand. His eyes were popping and tearing. His cross-eyed gaze into the nothingness over Will's shoulder indicated that he was getting close to the end.

But Will Kirby couldn't do it; he couldn't finish him off. At the last second, he lifted the oar from the kid's throat.

The kid wheezed, sucking air like a Hoover vacuum cleaner.

The girls' cheers subsided. They couldn't figure out what was going on.

Will sat on the kid's chest a moment longer. Then he stood.

The kid rolled onto his side, clutching his throat, staring up at his conqueror through blinking eyes.

Will loomed over him with the oar poised, trying to think what to do next.

The girls were beginning to understand now that no one was going to die, and they were disappointed. They started booing in their bird language. A pair of them ran off toward the shoreline.

Will jabbed the oar into the kid's chest. "Get up!"

The kid slowly rose to his feet. He was unsteady, beaten. His arrogant grin had been replaced with a look of humility and embarrassment. In spite of himself, Will almost felt sorry for the punk. But not completely.

"Don't even think about trying anything." Will poked him again with the oar, directing him toward the beach. "Now walk!"

A handful of the girls ran ahead to the water's edge while the others followed Will and the kid. They twittered amongst themselves expectantly. Will quickly scanned the group for Roxanne and Martine, but he was too occupied with his prisoner to glance away for long.

Once they neared the water, Will squinted to the south. The shore stretched unbroken for about two miles. A few palms were strewn along the way, interspersed with open stretches of sand and low-lying hummocks sprouting morning glory vines and pig weed. Will didn't see what he was looking for. He turned and studied the beach to the north. It was more or less the same scene, but at the far end of the atoll, Will saw what he was hoping to find.

"All right, kid, here's the deal."

Will was about to lay down some rules to the punk.

But then the Olgar showed up.

44

THE bitch-beast reappeared with her customary bravado, bursting from the waves like a rocket of freakish corruption. Her butt-ugly flunkies danced around her in a green gray roil of contaminated spume.

Will sighed. This day was turning into one long nightmare.

The Olgar snaked through the surf. She slinked over the sand to where Will was prodding his prisoner with the oar.

The local gals started in with their ululations.

The beast's toadies crawled onto the beach, writhing like demonic maggots. A pair of them rushed forward and circled Will and the kid, scrutinizing them through bloodshot eyes. Depraved sneers twitched on their seared and festering lips.

Will didn't figure it would do any good to run. Instead, he chose a completely different strategy – albeit an irrational one. Will Kirby was not typically what other fellows might call a softhearted patsy, but something about this kid made him feel almost fatherly. It was a moot gesture, given the Mad Olgar's size and speed and proven appetite for testosterone-seasoned meat, but it came over Will automatically. Without completely understanding why, he stepped forward, positioning himself between the kid and the beast, boldly holding up his little oar in the laughable pose of a toddler with a toy sword.

The Olgar crept toward him and stopped. She appeared almost amused by Will's defiance. A gravelly sizzle resonated in her throat. Will figured it was what passed for chortling in her corner of Hell. It didn't exactly fill him with confidence. Still, he held up the oar and stood his ground.

"Sorry, lady. No second course today." He tried to look sure of himself. "This youngster's not on the menu."

Will had no idea if the bitch could understand him. And it really didn't matter anyway. If she wanted to go seconds at this lunch counter, she damn well would. There wasn't much he could do to stop her.

The Olgar huffed and dropped her face to a level where she could get a closer look at the pathetic little man who was defying her. Will met her gaze. Her copper-colored eyes struck him as Slavic. They held that same quality that always made Soviet dames so attractive, if not a bit chilling.

But it was the beast's breath that most overwhelmed the senses. It wafted into Will's face through the twin tailpipes of her nostrils – something along the lines of a uranium smog mixed with smoldering garbage, car exhaust, and the gassing off of rotting flesh. Will didn't know how to categorize it. It wasn't a recipe that occurred naturally. It reeked of cataclysm, of doomsday. And it damn near made him retch.

His eyes watered.

His throat spasmed.

But he held himself together.

"If you're still hungry, you and your girlfriends will have to go catch yourselves some fish." Will tipped his head up the beach. "Or maybe you could go have yourself a nice seaweed salad."

The Olgar grinned. Her twisted teeth lined her leathery gums like bowie knives.

Then she glided a bit to one side, stretching her serpentine neck around Will toward the kid. She hovered close to his face.

To his credit, Will noted, the kid didn't flinch. He stood bravely as the beast examined him from top to bottom.

The Olgar saw the smeared blood on the kid's forehead. She parted her lips and poked her tongue dexterously toward the wound. The limphous, cancerous appendage lapped delicately at the clotted gore. It rasped lightly across the abrasion. The kid trembled, but he stood tall.

The Olgar withdrew her tongue, sucking it clean in her mouth. She swallowed and licked her lips. She constricted a bit, until she was hovering again before Will Kirby's face.

Those Slavic eyes.

That dog shit breath.

Then she nodded once, turned, and, with a guttural hiss, flung herself back into the sea.

Her toadies followed.

Will nearly pissed himself with relief.

He felt rung out, completely squeezed dry of his last drop of adrenaline.

The girls leaned forward expectantly, all of them acting a bit surprised at how the drama had unfolded. Will sensed that they were waiting for him to make his next move. He also sensed, if only marginally, that he had somehow won their respect by staring down the Olgar. He was running the show now. At least for the moment.

He blew out a big breath to purge himself of the Olgar's lingering stench. Then, once more, he turned to the kid.

"As I was saying," said Will. "Here's the deal."

45

WILL laid down the rules to the kid. He pointed his oar to a motu islet at the far end of the atoll. It looked to be about the size of a football field, with a considerable stand of palms, and separated from the main ring of the island by a wide channel of shallow blue water.

"That's your new home, buddy. Your own private Alcatraz." Will glared at the youngster and put on his best impersonation of a playground bully. "Leave it, and I swear to God I'll rip out your throat."

The kid responded with a resigned nod. He sadly regarded the girls, apparently regretting the loss of what might have been if he had only won the fight. Then, with his head hung in defeat, he sulked away toward his exile. The kid's muscular physique was still as impressive as ever, but his smug-ass grin was a thing of the past.

Will almost felt sorry for the kid, but then he reminded himself – Criminy, Kirby, that punk nearly killed you!

Will shook his head, wondering when he had gotten to be such a softy. That's when he spied yet another fellow standing in the shade beyond the clearing.

Will squinted, but he couldn't clearly make him out. Hmm. Maybe this island wasn't all dames after all. And maybe this guy could give him the lowdown on getting back to the real world. Will was just about to go find out when...

... he was swarmed by the girls.

———————

To the victor go the spoils, and boy oh boy was Will Kirby ever feeling spoiled now!

Those island babes gave him the royal treatment, pressing against him, cooing, and softly bludgeoning him from all sides with their bare breasts. Hubba-hubba! Will felt like the guest of honor at a dirigible convention.

They led their new champion to the palm grove where he was handed a coconut juice cocktail and was promptly peeled from his khakis. "Well, like I always say," laughed Will, "subtlety is overrated."

A pair of dolls dropped to their knees before him, fondling his joystick, while he lustily guzzled the juice from the coconut.

Will tossed the empty shell over his shoulder and wiped his wrist over his mouth as he let himself be guided to the next activity on the program. A trio of girls was dancing to the music of the waves and swaying palms. One of them was wearing his cowboy hat. Another girl, this one wearing nothing but a smile, stepped forward, turned her back to Will, and dropped to all fours. Yet another pair of beauties urged the V.I.P. onto his knees into position behind her.

"So much for foreplay."

While Will got to know the young beauty, biblically speaking, the other girls brought him a platter of crabmeat and copra. They set it before him on his new friend's back as if it were a TV tray. Will thought this a bit demeaning for the girl, but he told himself it wouldn't be polite to question the native customs. Besides that, she seemed to like it. He chuckled to himself and partook. The whole experience was like a sort of Vegas nightclub show, but of that secret variety a man barely dares to let himself imagine.

Will feasted, philandered, and enjoyed the entertainment.

Somewhere along the line, this nightmare of a day had turned into an all-out epic fantasy.

———

By nightfall Will had done his heroic best to satisfy every girl in his stable. He was a little surprised by his own capacities, given the physical ordeal of his last couple of days. But somehow his batteries never seemed to run low. The island itself acted like a dynamo that he was directly plugged into. His body felt healed and tireless. Apparently, all that sun, wind, and nooky was keeping him vital and loaded and ready for any action thrown his way.

Now the moon was up.

Big and full.

The ocean slopped and glimmered with waves.

Will sat with his back against a tree trunk. Females lay sprawled all around him, sleeping in the dappled wash of moonlight. The scene looked like a crash site for pinup girls. He studied the tangle of bodies, searching for Martine and Roxanne, but they had mixed so seamlessly into the group that Will was unable to distinguish them from the others. Anyway, all the ladies were snoozing now. He thought he should probably just let them rest.

Will quietly got to his feet and searched for his pants. He found them tossed under a bush. He brushed them clean and then located his hat. He put the hat on his head and held out his khakis for examination. They were a bit frayed around the cuffs, and there was a tear in one knee, but they were otherwise sound. It occurred to him that these pants and his hat and the oar might be some of the few items of civilization in this whole far-flung corner of the world.

Civilization. It had become a vague and tedious idea creeping around in the back of his mind – a headache full of rules, complications, and disappointments.

Will gazed around at the moonlit scenery. No. This place wasn't bothered with the tedious notions of the civilized – and this wasn't a place worried about the future. It was a throwback to the past. A simpler time. Pure. A primitive realm where a man could truly be a man among women being women. Tomorrow couldn't reach you here. This was a place where a fellow could live his truest life without always having to apologize.

Civilization. Phooey! Will was beginning to think he might just forget about it for a while and take himself a little vacation. Anyway, what was the rush to get back?

He shook his head. Nothing pressing came to mind.

Will wandered back to his makeshift bed beneath the palms. He sat, rolling up his pants for a pillow. He positioned his oar like a weapon at the ready by his side. Before settling in for the night, Will let himself enjoy one more view of the beautiful nymphos scattered all around him.

"Sweet dreams, ladies."

He licked the salt from his lips and smiled. Then he lay back on the sand, pulling his hat down over his eyes.

"Paradise," he muttered. "I've landed in a friggin' paradise."

46

THE days and nights that followed were packed with more of the same – feasting and fornicating followed by more fornicating and feasting. Some of these antics got pretty creative, consisting of the contortions of two-backed beasts copulating in every pose imaginable. The girls were open to anything, seemingly pulling their circus tricks right out of Barnum and Bailey's Big Handbook of Acrobatic Hijinks. Will was pleasantly surprised by his own stamina and originality, not to mention his flexibility.

Time passed. Although Will couldn't have said just how much. As his little break from civilization stretched on, he sort of lost track. There were no calendars on the island to mark the months or years, no schedules or clocks to follow, no holidays, or even seasons. This was a place where time stood still. Every day was just like the last, each held in a postcard state of perfection.

It never rained. The wispy cloud that formed over the atoll with each sunrise never quite gathered enough steam to turn into an all-out thunderhead. The afternoon breezes always blew the ragged cloud out to sea, leaving behind a steamy blue sky.

The nights were either full of stars or moonlight.

The only variable on the island was its population, as occasionally another man would wash onto the shore in the same way as had Kirby. These fellows were always accompanied by at least one smoking hot dame, but usually two or three. The new girls quickly joined with the island's primitive sisterhood, easily adopting their language and ways as if they had known them all along.

Will came to accept the weirdness of the place. Or more accurately, he had come to accept the island's standard for normal. For example, each time one of these castaway men tumbled out of the surf, a younger man would appear shortly thereafter. It was as if something was being triggered in the lagoon at the center of the atoll, as if this younger fellow was either being born, or maybe resurrected from the depths as soon as the new man set foot on the beach. It had been a surprise the first time it happened, but eventually Will came to expect a smugly grinning punk to step out of the palms every time the newest wash-up and his lady friends crawled from the sea.

Then came the inevitable fight – the one where the younger man summarily clobbered the older one.

After that came the newest champion's celebratory orgy.

Will Kirby had been the odd man out. Although it had taken a dirty trick to pull it off, he was the only older guy to beat out his younger opponent. And so far, he was the only victor who hadn't killed his rival and fed his corpse to the Olgar.

Will didn't have anything against these new guys. He wouldn't even have minded getting to know some of them, and maybe even being pals. Their age differences made that a little awkward, but it made sense to him that they should all get along for their common good.

Once, a beast – some sort of sabertoothed cave bear – had drifted onto the island and raised hell, mauling a couple of girls and generally causing mischief. With Will as their leader, the boys had come together to kill the bloodthirsty nuisance, all of them working as a team to rid the atoll of this dangerous pest. But after the problem was eliminated, everyone went back to how they had been before.

There was a distance among the male islanders, a wary

aloofness. There was an air of schoolyard competition between them that kept them all privately to themselves. Each fellow staked out a little corner of the island, managing his private piece of property, servicing whatever females came calling, while lording over his personal portion of caveman bliss.

The girls wandered in herds from one fellow to the next. These harems were always shifting according to the whims and cravings of the ladies themselves. No gent ever slept alone in this Eden, and never did anyone go bawdily unsatisfied. There were plenty of fish in the sea, so to speak.

In the first days, Will searched for the two gals he had landed with on the beach, but he could never pick them out from the others. All of the women had become more or less the same animal. They were interchangeable playthings, savage and gorgeous and hungry for sex. Hell, anymore, Will couldn't even remember their names.

47

WILL floated on his back in a secluded corner of the lagoon, peering into the blue sky. Lately, he had started sneaking off to get away from the girls. Sure, the endless debauchery had been a real hoot at first, but anymore, he was starting to feel like a guy trapped in a Shanghai whorehouse. None of the girls were ever happy just lolling in the shade and taking it easy. None of them ever wanted to just chat and get to know him. They were insatiable, with only one thing on their minds. Will couldn't so much as pass a gal on the beach without her jumping his bones and demanding a little pornographic maintenance. For crying out loud, his man tool literally ached with overuse! He had started coming to this secret stretch of the lagoon to hide and take a break.

But more than all that today, Will just needed a place where he could do some clearheaded thinking.

Two troubling facts had dawned on him lately. The first was that he realized he couldn't remember a damn thing! At least not anything that had ever happened before washing up on this island. Sure, he knew that there was a world out there, civilized and full of people. He knew about things like buildings and cities and rivers and mountains. He could bring to mind all the details and various objects that made up that other world, but no matter how hard he tried, Will Kirby could not picture himself ever inhabiting another world outside of this atoll. It was as if he had no backstory, as if page one of his epic life had started here.

The second thing that occurred was that he had begun to dream at night. To Will Kirby's admittedly faulty memory, he had never done that before. Reality was always a big enough job for a man like himself. He had no use for make-believe. And he was sure as hell never one to go in for that namby-pamby try-to-figure-out-what-it-means sort of crap. But... Well... These dreams were different.

He stopped swimming and stood in the shallows. A reef shark stalked past, its black-tipped dorsal fin slicing through the water like a blade.

The thing was, Will's dreams had started leaking in around the edges. He shook his head. He didn't quite understand how it was happening, but somewhere along the line he had become some sort of a portal. It was as if there was an exchange going on, one in which reality was swapping out with another world of the fantastic. These dreams projected on the screen of his brain like the coming attractions at a Saturday matinee, inevitably leading to a disturbing case of déjà-vu. It had surprised him when he first realized it, but it hadn't seemed like too big a deal, given the overall strangeness of his recent life anyway. When he found a piece of rubber life raft, and vaguely recalled that he had only just dreamed about being in a life raft that very night before, it hadn't struck him as anything beyond a coincidence. He held up the scrap of boat and read the mother ship's name partially printed on the rubber – *U.S.S. Marital Int...*

Mysterious, to be sure, but inconsequential.

But then the stakes got higher.

It had occurred to him one morning after waking. He disentangled himself from the pile of sleeping lovers and walked down to the shore. It was just a hunch to begin with, but a strong one. The foggy recollection of his previous night's dreams was sinking into the depths of his mind. And yet, he had a sense of something peculiar lingering there – an inconvenient truth.

That morning Will placed a large rock on the beach at the high-water mark. Over the following mornings, he studied it in relation to the comings and goings of the tides. After a while, there could be no doubt. The rock was no longer at the mark of high tide. And not because someone had moved it. The ocean was getting deeper.

The island was sinking!

What's more, Will suspected that *he* was somehow responsible. It was his dreams that were causing it, and there didn't seem to be a damn thing he could do about it. It made him feel guilty as hell. And yet, he had no control over what he dreamed. The dreams themselves were running the show. Hell's bells, it was starting to look like maybe they *were* the show!

Will let his body sink completely beneath the water, wishing for all this trouble to simply wash off of him like a layer of dirt. He blew the air out of his lungs and sat in meditation on the sandy bottom of the lagoon. He thought about drowning, and even wondered if that would save the atoll. If the dreamer were dead, maybe the dreams would die too. He felt responsible for all the islanders, both the gals and the young fellows. He was older than they were. In an odd way, he felt almost fatherly toward them. At any rate, he wanted to protect them all. From himself? Maybe. At least from the consequences of his dreams.

With his lungs about to pop, Will finally stood chest deep in the lagoon. He wiped his face and sucked in some air. He gazed into the water, and at his blurred reflection. It was the closest thing to a mirror he had seen in a while. He had forgotten what he looked like. He studied his haggard mug for a long time, trying to remember who, exactly, he was.

When he finally turned toward the shore, he was surprised to see someone standing in the palms. At first Will was disappointed. Dang! Some horny chicky bird had discovered his hideout.

But then Will realized it wasn't a girl after all. And neither was it one of the younger guys. It was the man Will had first spied on that day he had fought the kid. Will had seen this guy in the distance a couple of times since but had never talked with him. The fellow had turned out to be older, about the same age as Will, although Will had never gotten close enough to be sure. There was something about the fellow that made Will uneasy. He didn't like to admit it to himself, but the guy had an air that was sort of... well, honestly... sort of intimidating. He seemed bigger than life somehow, ineffably heroic. At any rate, the fellow didn't appear to be just another flat-footed sap walking down the street.

Now the man was standing in the shade, examining Will's oar and cowboy hat where he had left them under a tree.

Will considered calling out to him but didn't. He just watched. Will wondered if he had possibly dreamed the fellow into existence, if he had somehow brought him here by way of his dream portal. Then Will shook his head. "Cripes, Kirby! What the blazes is happening to you?"

The guy turned and peered to where he heard Will muttering to himself in the lagoon.

Will hesitated, but then waved.

The other man didn't respond. He just returned the oar and hat to where he had found them, and then moved off into the palms and out of sight.

48

WITH the next dawn, another creature emerged from the ocean.

Everyone was still asleep when it came.

Everyone but Will.

He had just been stirred awake by an icy tremor in his gut. Something was wrong. He could feel it. By the time he had raised himself to a seated position, the thing had already crawled out of the surf.

Will blinked into the distance, trying to understand what he was seeing. The light was poor, but it didn't take much to realize this wasn't just another castaway fellow and his lady friends. And it sure as shit wasn't some sort of friendly sea sprite come to spread flowers and good cheer on the islanders. No. By the way it moved, both furtive and swift, Will could see that it meant trouble.

He hopped to his feet.

A group of the girls had spent the night on the beach about a hundred yards down from the palm grove. Their vulnerable, shadowy forms lay in a collective heap on the dry sand. The creature had obviously caught their scent. It was heading their way.

Will snatched up his oar. He had recently improved it by attaching a spearhead carved from the femur of the slain cave bear. The bone was long and sharpened to a stiletto point, fitting onto the grip end of the oar like the bayonet of a barbarian commando. Will had used it to harpoon a couple of sharks, but now it looked like he'd get to test his weapon against bigger game. From what he could tell, much bigger!

He set off at a sprint.

The beast had already reached the girls.

At first, they were silent as the fiend plunged into their midst. Then they started to wake, and their shrieks rose over the din of the surf. Will couldn't see what sort of creature it was, only that it was massive and moving like a whirlwind into the crowd. It wasted no time. In a flurry, it snatched up four of the girls and galloped away with the speed of a horse. It disappeared around a bend and into some trees.

The remaining girls were cowering and shaken when Will reached them. One appeared to have a broken arm, while another had blood flowing from her mouth and was holding her jaw. Yet another gal lay in a twisted mass, dead. The remaining girls all cooed and trembled with shock. The beast had made short work of their little slumber party.

Will calculated the mayhem. He studied the creature's tracks tearing across the sand. The marks were almost human, but huge.

One of the young fellows camping within earshot had heard the screams and now joined Will at the crime scene. His eyes were big with excitement.

"Go round up the other boys," shouted Will. "We're going to need all the help we can get!"

The young fellow bobbed his head and raced off.

While he waited, Will served as medic to the wounded girls. He set the one gal's broken arm, fashioning a splint from a pair of sticks bound together with vines. He thought about the kid he had banished to the farthest end of the atoll. They could sure use his strength and quickness, but it would take too long to travel there and back, let alone convince him to join their war party. Will's hunch told him they didn't have the time. He knew the beast would return soon, causing untold damage to the island's female population. Their best strategy would be to gather fast and hunt down the brute, doing what they could to take the upper hand.

———————

The sun had fully risen by the time all the young fellows gathered at the grove. Five of them. Will sized up his rough-and-ready posse. They each carried clubs and knives made from branches and bones. Sure, they were eager and willing, but Will couldn't help but feel like he was playing coach to a little league team of snot-nosed misfits. It was one thing for a youngster to beat up a flabby, middle-aged guy who couldn't punch his way out of a church picnic, but this was an entirely different can of worms. This little band of willy-whackers didn't have a clue what they were in for.

And yet, Will wasn't so keen with taking on the beast by himself. He decided to assume the role of a battle-hardened commanding officer. Maybe if he could get his troops fired up with a plan of attack, they might just come out winners. Maybe.

"Okay, men, listen up!"

The boys huddled around Will.

"This son of a bitch is going to be tougher to beat than that slow-witted bear we took out a while back. What we have to do is flank him and keep him confused. As soon as one of us gets the chance, rush in and stick a blade into him." Just saying it made Will feel doubtful, but he didn't let on. "Once he's wounded, we'll all attack." Will met the eyes of each fellow, encouraging them with a nod. "He'll no doubt go ballistic once he's hurt, so stay sharp."

———————

The beast was easy enough to track. Besides the prints in the sand, there were the intermittent splashes of blood and the discarded, mangled bodies of two of the girls. Will checked each for a pulse but got nothing. "God almighty!" The poor gals looked like they had endured a pretty awful end.

The team pressed on, following the trail of blood, until they heard snarls and grunts coming from behind a hedge of taro. Will held up his hand and put a finger to his lips, gesturing for the boys to stay low and quiet. He waved for two of the squad to move off to one side, and for the remaining three lads to slip around the other way. If they could sneak up on the devil without detection, they might get lucky enough to swarm in before he ever knew what hit him. Crouching low, with his spear at the ready, Will signaled for everyone to move in.

Carefully parting the branches, Will scanned the clearing beyond the hedge. One of the girls was lying on the sand, whimpering, apparently dying from her injuries. About thirty feet beyond her, in the edge of some palms, Will saw the beast. Its wide, hairy back was turned his way, but a pair of tree trunks and some branches blocked a clear shot for his spear. Dammit! He decided not to risk it.

And yet, they couldn't wait long. The beast had the remaining girl pinned on the ground. Her head was just visible to the side, the look on her face telling the horrible story of her ordeal. By the way the beast was moving, it was obvious he was performing the most heinous act of evil this side of Hell. Every second they squandered was one more horrifying moment the girl would have to suffer.

Will crept forward, trying to position himself for a clear shot. The other boys stalked noiseless as shadows on either side of the clearing. The group closed in, as yet undetected by their lasciviously preoccupied adversary.

At last, Will found himself in position. He balanced the spear in his grip. With the stance of a Yankee pitcher about to send a fastball right down the strike zone, he raised his weapon, gritted his teeth, and then...

... one of the boys lunged from the sidelines, knife raised overhead, whooping like an Apache brave.

"Damnation!" Will admired the kid's courage, but he sure wished to hell he had kept his yap shut.

The beast whirled and reared to his feet.

For the first time, Will got a good look at what they were dealing with.

Simply put, it was a gorilla, but not one of those mangy lifers serving time at the city zoo. The thing stood ten feet tall at the shoulder, its bull monkey head swiveling up top like a turret on a Nazi tank. Its body had the mass of an oversized oil drum but moved quick as a cat. Its repulsive pink organ jutted between its legs like a Louisville slugger. And yet, the monster's arms were what impressed Will the most – all four of them – muscled and covered in wiry black hair, each one moving independently of the others.

The knife wielding Apache lost his nerve when the beast stood. Will saw it in his faltering steps. The kid visibly wilted when he realized the futility of his assault, but his momentum was too much to arrest, and he stumbled within the beast's reach. The beast batted him with the back of a hand, sending the kid's body hurling through the air to where it wrapped backwards around a palm, snapped at the spine, and slid lifelessly to the ground.

Will launched his spear.

The beast knocked it away.

Two boys attacked from opposite sides. The beast snatched up the girl by the ankles and used her body as a club, swinging it into the chest of an oncoming attacker with the sickening thud of mortal flesh detonating against mortal flesh. With a bound, the huge ape then landed before the other kid and palmed his head, crushing it like an egg.

This offensive was heading south fast.

Now it was down to just Sergeant Kirby and his last two recruits.

Will considered a retreat, but the beast would doubtless chase them down and tear them apart. Their only chance was to rally and pull off a miracle.

Will's spear lay near the bushes. He leapt toward it as the beast moved to grapple with the other boys. Will didn't see how it ended, but he heard the savage noises behind him as he grabbed up his weapon. By the time he turned back to the action, the boys' bodies were already scattered in pieces, their insides and limbs strewn over the sand and hanging in the bushes.

The beast loomed on the far edge of the clearing. It turned slowly, dramatically, as if relishing the fear it was causing in its final victim. But Will wasn't allowing himself to go there. Fear meant certain defeat. He had to stay sharp. He held his spear at the ready, waiting, waiting...

The big monkey grinned, his yellow fangs flashing between his rubbery lips.

Ha, buddy. You obviously don't know who you're dealing with.

The thought was more automatic than appropriate. In this particular situation, the wiser waste of time might have been for Will to pray for a quick and merciful death. But that had never been his way. If this was going to be his final act as a man, Will Kirby was going to make it as glorious as he could. Out of his own sense of pride, he'd fight this monster with everything he had, right to the bitter end.

The beast stood on his hind legs, one hand apathetically scratching his balls, the fingers of the other three hands all squeezing into fists.

Will knew when it was coming. He felt it in the shuddering ground beneath his feet. The giant primate roared, launching himself into the air with his arms spread like wings.

He eclipsed the glare of the sun, dowsing Will in cold shadow.

Everything shifted to slow motion – suspended – as if heightened to some other realm of time.

Will dropped to a knee, planting the oar blade in the sand, directing his spear toward the great simian wrath dropping from out of the sky.

Down came the beast, down and down.

Until the spearhead met the big monkey's chest, piercing the leathery skin, slicing through the layers, ripping through the twenty-pound muscle of his wicked heart, and then emerging with an eruption of flesh from out the devil's back – Shploook!

The beast's weight drove the oar on through his body.

"Umph!" Will slammed against the ground, enveloped in darkness. He lay flattened and stunned, with the wind knocked out of him, nearly passing out beneath two tons of quivering gorilla meat. Gallons of hot blood poured from the beast's wound as if it were an open spigot.

"Jesus," grunted Will. If he wasn't crushed to death, he was going to drown as the beast bled out. He had to get out of there fast. He worked his arm between the beast and the ground, forcing it along the creature's flaccid abdomen. He grabbed a handful of the monkey's hair and pulled with all of his strength, trying to drag his face toward some oxygen. Light cracked into the darkness as he squirmed and writhed through the gushing gore. At last, he slipped his head from under the lifeless bulk. He gasped, sucking as much air as he could into his dangerously compressed lungs. Once his mind had cleared, he wriggled free his arms and shoulders. The rest of the ordeal took a while, but at least he could breathe during the process. The entire self-extraction felt like a bizarre, exhausting birth in which he simultaneously served as both the midwife and the newborn.

Will rolled away from the enormous, twitching corpse, his body sticky with blood and sand. He wiped the muck from his eyes, panting. He wiped his mouth, gagging at the salt metal taste of the beast's ichor on his lips.

When he was finally able, Will stood. The scene looked like ground zero. Body parts were flung in every direction. There was no need to check anyone's pulse at this bombsite. Everyone was dead.

Everyone, miraculously, but him.

Nauseous and dazed, Will studied the lifeless monster before him. He felt like he had been trampled in a stampede. Everything swam before him in a blur. He could barely focus. When he finally did, his gaze fell on the dead ape's head. It was the size of a five-gallon bucket, its ugly face turned to the side.

Will knew that face.

From somewhere.

He was sure of it.

That's when the earth dropped from under him.

As his own eyes met the death-glazed eyes of the mutant gorilla, Will had a sudden and terrible realization –
He had only just dreamed of this monster last night!

49

NOT all of Will's dreams were nightmares.

He tried to encourage himself with that.

They weren't all inhabited by repulsive, sinister monsters and encroaching natural disasters. They weren't all so full of peril.

One night, he abruptly awoke with a fervent sense of hope. It was as if an angel had shaken him. The feeling was both tender and forceful and came from his dreams. It was as reassuring as anything Will could remember. He tried to keep hold of it – a floundering man reaching for a buoy. But it was no good. The details drifted beyond his grasp. The dream slipped away with the tide.

And yet, Will sensed a trace of it lingering in the oddly motionless air. When he opened his eyes and peered up through the branches, he saw no stars.

He saw no moon.

"Clouds," he whispered.

In all the time he had been on the atoll, Will had never seen clouds form at night.

He untangled himself from his sleep mates and rose from his

bed. He stepped over the dozing girls and crept silent as a thief to the beach.

The surf was calm and barely visible, just a ghostly disturbance surging out of the gloom. Will stood beyond the reach of the lapping waves. He didn't really know what he was doing, or why he felt the need to come down here. But this night was so damn strange. For some reason, he decided, it deserved his attention. After all, this might just be one of those fairy-tale moments that coughs up an answer. Will certainly had a lot of questions. And now there was something... well... there was something almost divine about this darkness hanging heavy as velvet over the island. It seemed like something out of a little kid's storybook or poem, the kind where aliens or fairies speak to earthlings. Will squinted out at the ocean. Fathomless. Growing deeper every day. In cahoots with the sky. And full of secrets. There was something decidedly female about it. As a man who liked to keep both feet firmly planted in reality, Will Kirby felt ill equipped to understand the voices murmuring from the depths of that mystery.

Still, he waited, just in case something came in on a frequency and language he might be able to decipher.

The vast Pacific heaved and moaned before him. Next to it, he was pretty damn small. Its indifference began to feel palpable.

Will chuckled and shook his head. His feeling of hope was reverting back to that of the existential truth by which he had always lived his life. "Face it, Kirby. You're in this one alone." He kicked his toes into the sand. "You're free to do whatever you damn well please."

And yet, freedom had never felt so much like a friggin' cage.

He was about to turn and go when a gust kicked up and caused him to pause. First, he heard it blowing through the palms, and then it swept down the shore, buffeting him from behind. Will tipped his face to the sky. He gave the clouds one last skeptical search for answers and was shocked when they actually came.

Only a few at first, but then more. Fine. Cool.

Like tiny kisses on his skin.

"Small rain."

The phrase leapt like a fish from the depths of his mind.

He shuddered.

"Small rain." Something inside of him said it again. "Small rain." And then, spontaneously, mysteriously – "The small rain down doth rain."

The drops fell on his eyes, on his cheeks. Many of them now, until his face was wet. The rain washed over his shoulders and chest.

When Will licked his lips, something clenched inside of him, something visceral, an electrical charge. He had forgotten how sweet water was. He had drunk nothing but coconut juice since landing here, and now he was reminded how utterly pure and delicious good ol' H2O could be. He opened his mouth wide to catch the drops, gratefully accepting this simple gift from heaven. He was convinced he had never tasted anything so pure and nourishing in his life.

And then, as quickly as it began, the rain stopped.

Will was thirsty for more. He licked the rainwater from the back of his hands, but it wasn't the same. It was tainted with salt. A profound nostalgia swept through Will right then, the kind he might have guarded against at other times. But his defenses were down. The rain had worked like a drug to weaken the man within the man. He allowed himself to be opened up to a flood of longing. In the strangeness of this night, Will Kirby suddenly missed things he couldn't even remember.

Shadows moved all around him over the sand.

Invisible specters floated through the air.

The bank of clouds plowed on through the sky, slow and majestic as an ocean liner, until stars began to appear in its wake.

Blinking, Will peered into those stars. They were blurred, as if viewed from underwater. He wiped his eyes and swallowed at the fist-sized lump in his throat. One star stood out from the rest. Barely above the horizon. A Kodachrome pinprick of summer sky leaking into the night. At any rate, this star wasn't like the others. It was extraordinary. Singular. Mini-magnificent.

Will watched the blue star sparkling in the air. He felt big things – the earth moving beneath him, far off galaxies turning above – until the blue star slipped into that slot between the sea and the sky.

Will watched that place for a long time, waiting, but the star was gone for now. And yet, it left behind a little bit of the hope Will had felt from his dream. He held onto that hope. It was about as easy to hold as a handful of rain, but he did his best to hold it.

50

No, not all of Will's dreams were nightmares, but enough of them were to keep him on edge. He had gotten to where he dreaded waking each morning for fear of what new calamity he'd find waiting to ruin his day.

He had started sneaking off to the lagoon more regularly to think it over. Drifting among the rainbow schools of tropical fish, he pondered the many mysteries of his situation.

Asking for advice had never been something he found easy. In Will Kirby's estimation, the mark of a man worth his salt was in how he tackled his troubles solo. And yet, this problem was different from any other he had run up against. This wasn't something a fellow could just outmuscle or outwit. A man couldn't take it out with a well-placed shot from a rifle, or a knuckle punch. This was abstract, like wrestling ghosts. Christ almighty! He had never felt so ill-suited for a challenge.

But who the hell could he turn to for help?

The island girls all spoke a different language from his. Sure, he liked them well enough, and even considered them all to be his friends, if in some sort of perversely paternal way. But as hard as he tried, he just couldn't quite crack the code of their bird-like warbles and cooing. Not to mention their incomprehensible logic. Most days Will felt less like a man in their eyes – less like a heroic guardian – and more like some sort of a pet. Hell, they were more than just a different sex; they were an altogether different species.

That left the other males on the island. Of course, that damn gorilla had thinned them out considerably. All except for the kid Will had banished up the atoll. Will considered what it might be like to consult with the youngster on the subject of dreams gone rogue. He sighed. Nix that. Besides being his mortal enemy, Will reckoned the punk was too wet behind the ears to be of any use. What Will needed was someone with world experience, someone who had been around the block a time or two. He needed someone as battle tested as himself, but smarter.

That was hard to accept, but it was the conclusion Will had finally come to. He needed a friggin' guru, or – he was reluctant to admit it – a shrink. He needed a sort of mechanic, but one who could work on heads and the complicated ideas grinding away inside of them.

Any way Will turned it, that only left him one option. It was a long shot, and a little bit too desperate to make him feel overly confident.

"But," Will decided, "what have you got to lose?"

51

THE fellow's home wasn't too hard to find. The atoll was only so big, after all. Will just had to do a bit of snooping around. The hut was shipshape, modest in size, and held together with skillfully lashed vines and laced palm fronds hanging on a frame of branches and logs. The sturdy dwelling appeared to be made for weathering storms. It was tucked into a stand of palms, with a shady plot out front serving as a sort of well-kept yard. A sign hung over the door. The letters carved into the driftwood plank read – **HEAD OFFICE**.

Will approached the hut warily, hanging back, skulking like a trespasser. He didn't know yet if this guy was the same as all the others who had washed up on the island – defensive, suspicious, and predisposed to snapping an intruder's neck. And he sure as hell didn't want to start off on the wrong foot. He parted the branches and scanned the yard – no sign of the resident. Will was turning over in his head how to proceed when he felt something sharp press into his lower back.

"Stick 'em up, cowboy."

Will fought down the urge to drop, spin, and take the guy out at the knees. You're here to gain an ally, he reminded himself, not make an enemy. And to be honest, Will was a little surprised to find himself in this position to begin with. He had never been one to let an aggressor get the drop on him. Anyone able to sneak past Will Kirby's finely tuned sense of spatial awareness was obviously not someone to be taken lightly. Will slowly raised his hands.

"Make one wrong move and I'll put a bullet through your guts, understand?"

Will bobbed his head.

"So, what's your business, bub?"

Will swallowed, doing his best to sound friendly. It wasn't easy with a gun barrel poked into his kidney. "I don't mean any trouble, neighbor. I just came by to gab."

The fellow didn't immediately answer, apparently deciding if Will was on the up and up.

"I just figured you've been camped out on this island for a while and so I was hoping you might share some intel."

Again, the fellow didn't respond. Will was beginning to think he had made a big mistake in coming here, but then the pressure eased off his lower back.

"You like oysters?" said the man.

"Huh?"

"Oysters, buddy. I asked if you like oysters."

"Uh, sure. Yeah. Oysters are good."

"Well then..." The fellow stepped back. "Here."

When Will turned, the man was standing before him with a basket cradled under one arm. In his other hand he held a stick, what Will had believed was a pistol. The man grinned, tossed the stick to the side, and handed the basket to Will. "Take these in the house." He thrust the basket into Will's hands. "I'll go grab us a couple of drinks."

"Oh. Sure."

Will watched the man shamble off through the bushes and then turned to the hut. He walked slowly across the yard, regarded the sign, and then stooped through the door.

The room was dimly lit and cool as a cave. Two windows on

opposite walls allowed a sultry cross breeze coming in from the sea to act as a kind of primitive swamp cooler. The space was tidy, almost domestic. The floor was spotless, swept sand with a woven mat spread out neatly against one wall for the guy's bed. A plump wad of woven grass lay at the head of the mat for a pillow. A wide, flat stone sat on the floor off to one side, with a smaller stone resting on its top. Other than that, the room was empty and without decoration. Almost.

Will placed the basket near the stones and took off his hat. He stepped slowly to the far wall. The object hanging there pulled at him like a magnet. He felt helpless to its force of attraction. In the elemental world of this atoll, such an artifact seemed like something from another planet. Will leaned forward, examining the miniature icon in the poor light.

It was a photograph, wrinkled and faded, but still vivid enough to elicit the idea of a whole other existence on the far side of the ocean. The subject of the image was a young girl and what appeared to be an adult, but the adult's image hadn't survived the ravages of time and so was reduced to nothing but a humanoid smudge. The girl was holding hands with the smudge, smiling happily on a cement sidewalk in the middle of a lawn washed in sunshine.

Will studied the photo, his pulse inexplicably rushing. He touched the snapshot with a fingertip, lightly tracing the roofline of the house behind the smudge and girl. The grass in the photo was green. The girl's pedal pushers were pink. The sky above was an otherworldly blue.

"You like my little souvenir, huh?"

Will turned to find the man standing inside the doorway holding a pair of coconuts.

"Yeah."

The man stepped across the room and handed one of the nuts to Will. They stood shoulder to shoulder and admired the photo.

"Looks like a nice place, don't it?"

Will nodded. "Where'd it come from?"

The man snorted. "Beats me. Where does anything come from around here?" He shrugged and twirled the fingers of his free hand in the air by his ear. The gesture struck Will as more of a statement than a question. What's more, Will kind of understood just what the guy meant.

They both studied the photo for a moment longer, until the man held out his hand and introduced himself. "The name's Zag," he said. "Dick Zag."

Will grasped the fellow's paw and gave it a firm shake. "Will Kirby."

Zag bobbed his head. "Well, Will, what say we dig into those oysters?"

———

The men sat cross-legged on opposite sides of the rock. While Zag sorted through the shellfish, Will sized him up.

He had been right about the fellow's age – roughly the same as his own, give or take. He wore tattered khakis and a grimy white t-shirt. His build was solid and fit, with ropy muscles slipping and bulging in his arms as he worked. The man's face was weathered and lined, punctuated by a pair of steel blue eyes that looked as if they had turned in a squint toward the horizon no fewer than a million times. All in all, he was a man's man. No nonsense. Tough as nails. With a clear sense of knowing about the kinds of things a man should know. And yet...

At first Will didn't realize what it was. He couldn't quite put his finger on it. He thought maybe it was just the weak light making it hard for him to see. But then it hit him – somewhere inside that skin was someone else knocking around. Not literally, perhaps, but that's how it seemed. It was subtle, barely noticeable, like an over-dubbed movie that was just a little out of sync. Will couldn't tell if it was himself or his host who was off kilter, but as he watched Zag arrange their lunch, the man appeared the slightest bit blurry. Will felt like he was watching him through a camera lens that's not quite in focus.

Zag placed an oyster in the center of the big rock, raised the smaller rock above it, and then brought it down with a crack, sending a blast of seawater squirting in every direction.

"There you go." Zag scooted the resulting mess across the rock toward his guest. "*Bon appétit!*"

Will scooped the pulverized oyster into his palm and plucked out the fragments of shell. The naked gray creature constricted in its death throes.

Zag smashed another oyster for himself. "Ha!" He pinched a thumb and finger into the lump and pulled out a pearl, holding it up for Will to see. "Gotta watch out for these bastards. They're hell on the choppers." He then tossed the pearl out a window.

Both men stuffed the food into their mouths. They sat chomping like Neanderthals while regarding one another over the slime-smeared rock. The meat was seasoned with salt and sand, giving it the texture and taste of fish-flavored chewing gum rolled in grit.

Zag swallowed, made a face, and then sighed. "Well, it's not grilled cheese, but I guess it'll do."

Will gulped down the meat. "Grilled cheese?"

"Yeah. You know. It's a kind of sandwich."

Will nodded. He had eaten nothing but fish and taro for so long that the very idea of a grilled cheese sandwich made him a completely different kind of hungry.

"I think about grilled cheese sometimes. The way it smells." Zag frowned. "You can't get chow like that around here." He shook his head and smacked his lips. He shrugged and raised his coconut. "Cheers!"

Will touched his shell to Zag's and then both men threw back their drinks, washing the raw oyster taste down with a sweet gulp of juice.

Zag worked systematically through the pile of bivalves, smashing one after another, like he was cracking nuts. They ate the oysters, grunting occasionally, not really saying much.

Finally, with both men stuffed, the feast ended.

Zag wiped his hands on his thighs and picked his teeth with a thumbnail. He worked his tongue around in the corners of his mouth. "So, buddy, I don't claim to be an expert on this place. There's mysterious shit happens here that I just plain don't get. You probably know the kind of stuff I'm talking about."

Will nodded.

Zag plucked a piece of grit from the tip of his tongue and flicked it to the side. "But anyhow, I'll gladly share the skinny on what I've learned. What do you want to know?"

Will picked up his empty hat and stared into it. He had had a list of questions about a mile long, but now the idea of muttering them to a fellow man felt lame-ass embarrassing. They were all concerned with the kind of things men don't talk about. Sissy stuff. Dreams. Feelings. Fears. That whole bare-your-soul routine felt about as uncomfortable as standing butt naked before another fellow and asking him to assess your hardware. Even on this island, where nothing was taboo, it was understood deeply among real men – that kind of thing just wasn't done. And yet, Will didn't want to let this opportunity get away. He decided to start with something basic.

"The dames," he said.

"Yeah. What about 'em?"

"They don't pester you?"

Zag laughed. "Not anymore. They got tired of me. And to tell the truth, I got pretty tired of them too. It was fun as hell at first. Every schoolboy's big dream come true, but..." He smirked and shook his head. "Be careful what you wish for. I got to feeling like a kid being force-fed ice cream." He looked at Will. "Know what I mean? I don't care if I never get another lick of ice cream as long as I live."

Will understood.

"I don't know. It's hard to admit, but maybe I've outgrown my taste for that kind of thing. I sort of lost interest in that whole business. After a while it dawned on me that I wasn't so much hungry for the humpy-humpy itself, I was just hungry for my old hunger for it. You follow? Two different things."

It was a sideways sort of logic, but Will thought he understood just what Zag was getting at.

"Around here, it's smarter for a fellow to just keep to himself." He met Will's gaze. "And safer too. You never know when that bunch of sex kittens is going to knock you in the head and feed you to their favorite bitch from the sea."

"But don't you ever get...?"

Zag raised an eyebrow, waiting for Will to finish his sentence.

Will couldn't find the word.

"You mean, don't I ever get *lonesome*?"

"Yeah."

"Hell yes! But the only thing to make a guy even more lonesome is night after night rolling with a pile of gals who only want you for the ride you can give 'em. That stuff's for young bucks who are cross-eyed horny and playing the field." He laughed. "I guess that makes me an old fart put out to pasture, but I don't care. I have the moon and stars to keep me company. Shoot, it might even sound like a line – like one of those wisdom nuggets you get from greeting cards and crappy books – but, bub, I'm here to tell you, those damn clichés are born out of the truth. At least in my experience. For all of a fellow's he-man camo, we're just one big fat banal cliché underneath. So be it. There's nothing I can do about it at this point. And honestly, I no longer give a rat's ass."

"Have you ever tried to escape?"

"The island?"

Will shrugged. "Yeah. And everything else."

"Buddy, trying to escape is how we got stuck here in the first place. There is no escape! Things follow and hunt you – demons, beasts – until you turn and face them down like a man. And not like some overblown bullshit idea of a man either, but something quieter and less showy, something that isn't all about flexing your muscles. A fellow's got to use the same cunning and smarts that caused the problem in the first place. Only you got to turn them around on the problem. You follow?"

Will wasn't entirely sure that he did.

"But then," continued Zag, "maybe that's just my take on it. I suppose every bozo's got his own version, his own idea of what makes a happy ending. Every poor sucker you meet walking down the street's got to decide for himself what's worth fighting for, and what it means to be the hero of his own little fantasy. Anyway, pardner..." Zag grinned and bobbed his head toward Will. "I guess that right there might just be the friggin' moral of the story."

52

NEXT morning, the island was covered in snow. About three inches of the stuff.

It had fallen just before dawn while everyone was still sleeping.

Will stood gazing out as slop plopped from the palms overhead. Even here, on this island where anomalies were the norm, the sight struck him as deeply wrong. The naked girls were hopping tiptoe through the snow on the beach. They were tossing snowballs and wrestling, laughing and shrieking like gulls. The ocean swelled in the background like an immense maternal being. The sky above was cloudless and full of light. But in spite of the brightness, the whole scene emanated a profound eeriness and gloom, a surreality hinting at both the apocryphal and the apocalyptic.

Dropping to a knee, Will Kirby poked his fingers into the bright white snow. He scooped up a handful and held it close to his face, studying it. The cold on his palm stirred something in his blood. Something ancient. Something elemental. A primitive recollection that trembled in the very center of his cells.

And yet, the reality of the tropical heat was too much. By mid-morning, the snow had completely melted away.

The girls resumed their daily routines.

Will snuck off to the lagoon.

Outside of the lingering puffs of steam rising off the wet sand, there was no sign that the meteorological mishap had ever occurred.

———————

A few mornings after that, the beach.was littered with trash.

It was as if the atoll were a ship that had strayed off course through a great flow of garbage.

The girls did not dance or laugh at the sight of the mess. They did not jump for joy as they had with the snow. Instead, they traipsed quietly through the refuse, warily nudging plastic bottles with their toes, bending to examine drinking straws, scraps of tennis shoes, and withered jellyfish, while wrapping themselves in their arms as if trying to stave off a chill.

Will stood at the edge of high tide, tapping his lips with his fingers while he watched the girls wander along the litter-strewn shore. The scene was so damn unsettling!

Besides the garbage, the waterline was higher than ever. Incrementally – with a torturous indifference and pace – the island was being consumed by the rising sea. Will didn't know if the girls were aware of it, or if they were even conscious of the inevitable conclusion toward which they all were descending, but something in their collective demeanor suggested that they understood.

Will rubbed his face in his hands. "Dammit!"

When he peered the other direction down the beach, his gaze fell on something moving. He walked toward it.

There, amidst the trash, was a green sea turtle lying on its back. One of its flippers was frantically clawing backwards at the sand as the creature struggled to turn itself upright. But the other flippers were bound against its body by a tangle of derelict fishing net. The more the turtle wrestled to free himself, the more hopelessly he became entrapped.

Will knelt beside the turtle. He turned it over, gently resting it on the sand, and began working at the snarl of nylon lines. "Hold on, buddy. Calm down."

The turtle held still, apparently exhausted from his fruitless thrashing.

It took a while – the net had been bound tight around the turtle – but finally Will was able to work the creature free from its bonds.

The turtle rested on the sand beside Will.

Will was taken with how beautiful it was – a true work of art born of Mother Nature. Its bowl-shaped shell was covered in an intricate mosaic of plates highlighted with flecks of red and yellow and orange. Will found himself amazed that anything could be so stunning. The turtle's eye reflected the sky and Will caught sight of his own image bulging on the glassy orb. He didn't understand why, but he felt moved to rest his hand on the turtle's back; he felt the need to reassure the beast at his side.

"It's going to be all right, pal. Somehow we'll figure it out." Will nodded. "We just have to keep going. We have to find a way to fix things up."

Will Kirby didn't really know what he was saying; he didn't know what he meant. The words were being spoken by something deep inside of him. But he sensed a certainty in them. He felt a truth touching him internally like a small hand squeezing his heart.

Will and the turtle sat together for a while beneath the tropical sun.

Finally, once he had recharged his batteries, the turtle crawled toward the water. Propelling himself with his flippers, he awkwardly pulled his bulk forward through the trash, parting the refuse of soda cans and grocery bags, until he slipped into the edge of the sea.

Will stood and watched for the creature to surface, but it never did. He pondered the turtle's life, imagining his existence in the silent vastness beneath the waves. At last, he turned and regarded the beach on which he stood.

The trash went as far as he could see in both directions. He bent and plucked up a lime-green bowl from the flotsam at his feet. He turned it over in his hands, studying it like an artifact.

He read the brand name stamped on the bowl's plastic underside.

The single word resonated like a threat, like an alien battle cry against an innocent and defenseless world.

"Tupperware!"

53

WILL Kirby had never visited the motu islet at the end of the atoll – the one to which he had exiled the kid. There was an understanding between the young man and Will, an unspoken agreement that kept the punk from violating his parole. Ever since that day Will had won the fight, the kid had always stayed put on his remote island prison.

But now Will lingered in the shade, watching across the water toward the kid's solitary outpost. The strait had deepened with the rising sea, and the expanse could no longer simply be waded at low tide. Will squinted across the distance. He thought he caught a glimpse of a shadow moving among the trees, but he couldn't be sure.

He scratched his jaw, thinking it over.

As with most things he had done lately, something besides common sense was driving Will forward. He didn't necessarily understand what he was doing, but he felt compelled by a force that was separate from him, as if he were being manipulated by someone pushing him around like a game piece. Someone smarter than him.

Or maybe someone who was him, but not him, at the same time. It was confusing as hell and making him feel like a friggin' schizo. But the urge was mysterious and strong and wouldn't leave him alone, so Will didn't reckon it made any sense to fight it. Instead, he stepped into the hot sunshine, splashed out into the water, and with spear in hand and his cowboy hat pressed down snugly onto his head, he sank into the chop and began a slow and steady sidestroke across the channel.

He came out onto the motu's narrow beach and stood dripping, getting his bearings and catching his breath. He had accomplished the first part of his mission – breaching the compound – and now he was considering whether or not to turn right around and swim on back to the atoll. But then he noticed the trash strewn along the waterline – the plastic water bottles and milk jugs. He remembered the turtle. Something about the sight of it made Will realize he needed to just bite the bullet and go through with his plan. He crouched and stalked toward the interior of the island, his spear at the ready, hunting for the kid.

The palms were tall and evenly spaced, their tops bending to the wind coming in off the open ocean. The place looked almost manicured, more like the grounds of an estate than a patch of South Seas wilderness. As far as pokies went, this one felt pretty deluxe, if a little lonesome.

Eventually, Will came across tracks in the sand, proof that the inmate was still in residence. He studied the marks. For no good reason, Will placed his own foot carefully into one of the prints.

"Huh," he mumbled. "Perfect fit."

He was pondering this coincidence when he felt the thump of footsteps rushing up behind him.

Instinctively, Will dropped to a knee and ducked.

The attacker's body just grazed Will's back as it sailed over him and rolled across the ground.

"Umph!"

Will leapt to his feet.

It was the kid, all right, scrambling in the sand and wheeling to a wrestler's stance.

Will understood that all bets were off here. The same code of honor that had kept the captive on this island was rendered completely null when the warden dared enter the prison. This was the kid's domain, his own private plot of real estate. He made the rules here. He had every right to rip apart any trespassers. And, as Will could see in the young buck's eyes, that's exactly what he had in mind.

The kid's threatening frown triggered something automatic in Will. He couldn't have helped it if he had wanted to. With a self-preserving reflex, Will raised his spear to a fighting stance.

Snatching up a nearby coconut, the kid hurled it at Will's head. In the split second it took for Will to dodge the projectile, the kid sprang. Will reacted by sidestepping and swinging the spear shaft so that it smacked hard against the kid's hip as he tumbled past.

The kid was like a rabid beast, tipped off balance by his overpowering desire to exact revenge on the bastard who had ruined his life. Will understood this. He knew he had to use the kid's blind rage to his own advantage.

But then Will had a thought. It came to him as a voice in his head. Stick with the plan, it whispered. Remember why you're here.

While the kid gathered himself for another attack, Will stood upright. He squared his shoulders. And then he lowered his weapon.

"Look, buddy, I didn't come out here to fight."

The kid narrowed his gaze, gritting his teeth.

Will sighed. He knew the kid had no reason to trust him. It took all of Will's mettle, or maybe all of his stupidity, but he tossed the spear to the ground between them.

The kid eyed him suspiciously.

"I'm not looking for trouble." Will took off his hat and tossed it to the ground toward the spear. He tried to smile. He held up his hands like a surrendering soldier. "Truce?"

The kid moved fast.

In a blur, he leapt forward, snatched up the spear, and held it at Will's throat.

Shit!

Will gulped, his Adam's apple sliding up, then down, barely an inch before the quavering spearhead.

Will Kirby realized he had just made his final mistake. He couldn't help but imagine what it was going to feel like to have the sharpened femur of a bear thrust up through his throat and into his brain. Not exactly the happy ending he had hoped for.

The kid leaned forward, glaring.

As a last-ditch effort, Will decided he might as well try to keep himself alive for a few more minutes. He might as well get some things off his chest. He licked his lips.

"Look, kid, I'm sorry about sending you out here by yourself. That was wrong. I shouldn't have done that."

The kid didn't budge.

"I really have nothing against you. Hell," Will chuckled awkwardly, "I even kind of admire you. I was just following my gut. I was just being a dumbass."

The kid held his spear poised at Will's jugular.

Will drew a big breath through his nose.

"It's a weird life we're living these days. Confusing as hell. A fellow makes his mistakes. A man tries to be free, but sometimes he doesn't think it through straight. He doesn't see what's most important. He doesn't see the whole story."

Will met the kid's gaze.

"This is your little world," said Will," not mine. I got no business trying to run the show here. Hell, I got no business even being here."

For the first time, Will noticed the kid softening. He saw him let down his guard. Just a little. Will Kirby knew that now was his chance. If he was going to throttle the kid, this was the time to do it. Will briefly reviewed the sequence of his moves for taking the kid out – throw your left arm up and grab the spear shaft – catch the kid in the jaw with a right hook, stunning him – hook his ankle with your foot and knock him to the ground, wrenching the weapon from his grasp as he falls. After that, it will all just be routine to finish him off.

And yet, Will didn't do it. It took all he had in him, but he turned his instincts around and used them to fight down the urge. The kid himself was going to have to decide how this chapter of the story would unfold.

Will braced himself for the worst.

The sound of the surf came to him vivid and clear, like a delicious little taste of sensation before all of his sensation ceased for good.

The tropical breeze blew over his skin.

And then the kid stepped back. He lowered the spear. Not completely, just a few inches. He appeared to be thinking about Will's sad-sack little soliloquy, until, at last, he dipped the spear tip to the ground. He skillfully hooked the cowboy hat under the brim with the spearhead and lifted it out to Will.

"Truce," rasped the kid.

Will took the hat and brushed off the sand. It was pretty battered and bent. He stepped forward and placed the hat on the kid's head, pressing it down so his ears stuck out. Will inspected the kid's new look. He grinned and nodded.

"Perfect fit," said Will. "Just like it was made for you."

54

A storm was coming.

His primal senses told him so.

He could smell it on the air.

Will Kirby didn't know if it would arrive tonight or tomorrow, or if it was still a ways off. He only knew that it was inevitable and there was nowhere on earth to hide. There could be no escape from the reality of the great reckoning tempest gathering like a truth beyond the horizon.

What's more, at this late stage in the narrative, Will wasn't even sure there was a damn thing he could do about it. After all, a man is such a pitiable item sometimes. A laughable, tragic trope. For all of his self-importance, he's ultimately the most ineffective piece of the story. And yet, he knew he had to do something. Through force of will, he had to do what he could to save his own world. If there was any redemption to be had, it could only come through the deliberate union of humility with a manly call to action.

The evening had grown calm, windless, the sea eerily placid.

The sun sank away over the atoll at Will's back, and now he was waiting for the sky before him to darken.

At first, he had company. Two young women sat on either side of him. Will found himself soothed by their presence. They were friends. The three of them waited for a long time, not speaking, just watching the sea and sky.

But then the kid showed up. He stepped from the palms above the beach, carrying his spear and wearing his cowboy hat tipped at a rakish slant on his head. When the girls saw him, they hopped to their feet. The young woman with the red hair placed her hand on Will's shoulder, giving it an affectionate squeeze. The dark-haired girl bent close and kissed him on the cheek.

"*Bonne chance*," she whispered. "*Et bon voyage.*"

And then they wandered off laughing with the young man.

As it should be, thought Will.

The twilight gently gave way to darkness.

The ocean herself became the epitome of silence – the sleeping mother.

Then the stars began to blink on like Christmas lights. Will took that as his cue.

First, he peeled off his khakis and stood naked as a child on the sand.

He rolled his head on his shoulders and swung his arms, nervously shaking out his fingers.

Then he waded to his waist in the water.

He drew a deep breath.

He fixed his course.

At last, like some wannabe hero, he sank into the sea and began his long journey to the blue star.

Thank you for reading! We ask you to please share your honest thoughts and opinion of ESCAPE FROM OBLIVIA with other readers by writing a review at your favorite retailer. For more information visit www.briankindall.com, where you can sign up to his list and get his free ebook, SIDESHOW, entertaining blog posts, and news about new books.

OTHER TITLES BY BRIAN KINDALL:

DELIVERING VIRTUE, adult fiction: Book One of *The Epic of Didier Rain*

Didier Rain is broke, lovesick, and just off a three-day whiskey binge. And yet, The Church of the Restructured Truth has been told in a vision that he's the man to fulfill their Holy Prophecy. He must deliver Virtue – a blue-eyed infant – 1,000 miles along the western pioneer trail to their prophet's stronghold as his child bride to be. Savages, zealots, and wildfire all stand in Rain's way, not to mention a list of Thou-shalt-nots designed to thwart any man's most basic comforts. But there's something holy about the job – something, Rain suspects, that might just turn his sorry life toward a better path.

In Delivering Virtue – Book One of The Epic of Didier Rain – Brian Kindall takes the classic novel of the West and turns it on its head. Grandiloquent humor, pathos, and a cast of absurd and depraved characters all come together in an American Frontier world inspired by myth and legend, creating a surreal and disarmingly poignant adventure reviewers are calling a triumph of American Magical Realism.

FORTUNA AND THE SCAPEGRACE: Book Two of *The Epic of Didier Rain:*

Didier Rain has never been so destitute, forlorn, and in dire need of a bath. As he roams the rain-muddied streets of San Francisco, it appears the angels of good fortune have finally forsaken him.

Hunted by factions that would seek to do him harm, and suffering an acute case of soul pain, the once dandy rogue sees little promise for sunnier days.

But then, miraculously, all the stars of the cosmos move into a seemingly favorable position as a seductive albino soothsayer launches Rain onto the next leg of his life's stormy voyage. Will said voyage carry Rain to the soft bosom of comfort and contentment he so longs for? Is he the Chosen One, singled out by Providence to lead God's people in their new South Seas church? And is Rain truly the newfangled man he believes himself to be? Or, as he fears, are the gods just having a bit of fun with their favorite gullible scalawag?

At turns ribald, horrifying, and hilarious, *Fortuna and the Scapegrace* follows *Delivering Virtue* as book two in Didier Rain's unfolding epic adventure of foibles, hope, and quest for love and redemption.

SIDESHOW: An introduction to Didier Rain of *The Epic of Didier Rain*

The brothel calls, and Velva Velvetonia, the one-legged trollop, awaits. But who can resist the chance to see Poppy the Pinheaded Poet from the Moon? Not Didier Rain, rogue hero and versifier himself, who takes the bait and pays his dollar. And yet, witnessing the mistreatment of a fellow bard is too much for Didier, and a daring rescue plan is hatched. In this dark comedy of the Old West, we introduce our ne'er-do-well Didier Rain - chief player in *The Epic of Didier Rain* novels DELIVERING VIRTUE and FORTUNA AND THE SCAPEGRACE - at his finest as a flawed human being. Rain's madcap acts of bravery as he attempts to liberate Poppy give us some insight into why the gods would later pick him to fulfill the Prophecy of the Chosen One. So sit back and get to know the scalawag behind the legend. Prepare yourself to be amused!

BLUE SKY, middle grade novel:

Blue Sky can climb like an ibex. She was raised in the highest peaks of the Alps by the herd and named for the color of her eyes. They say her father was a fallen alpinist and her mother his beautiful dying dream... and so, as you may guess, she's somewhat magical – strong and sure-footed on the peaks, and natural as an ibex in this harsh environment of wind, rock, and ice. Until the day she rescues a young alpinist from a stormy peak. The boy looks like her, and he tells her of the mysterious world beyond the crags. Sky longs to follow him. Can a girl raised by ibex in the mountains ever join the world of humans? Blue Sky must first fulfill her destiny with the ibex and find the courage to leave everything she's ever known.

A tale of self-reliance about a girl who finds strength in being who she really is and the courage to follow her dreams.

PEARL, middle grade novel:

Pearl can't move. She's never wanted to, until now. Life above the waves beckons to her as she watches the boats moving along the surface of the water above her. Pearl is a statue carved of milk-white stone that has stood on the floor of an ancient sea for a thousand years, but she's waking up, and she wants more. As desire builds within her, it propels her on a journey that takes her to an exotic island grotto, into the midst of a bloody revolution, underground into a rat-infested tomb, and, at last, to a magical mountain paradise. Crazed rebels, wise philosophers, greedy grave robbers, and a few other friendly people and fish accompany her along the way, as she asks the question, "Is desire enough?" She'll have to have faith in the stars. She'll have to muster more courage than she's ever imagined. But perhaps by journey's end, Pearl will believe in herself, experience a miracle, and realize her greatest desire of all.